The characters and events portrayed in this book are fictitious. Any similarity to real persons, living or dead, is coincidental and not intended by the author.

Published by AmazonEncore
P.O. Box 400818
Las Vegas, NV 89140

ISBN-13: 9781612182834
ISBN-10: 1612182836

IN **SEARCH**
OF **LUCY**

. . .

BY LIA FAIRCHILD

This book is dedicated to my best friend for the last twenty-five years, who also happens to be my husband, and to my two beautiful children.

CHAPTER 1

What's the point? Lucy Lang contemplated this again for the hundredth time as she climbed into her faded, light gray Honda Civic. She plopped down in the driver's seat and tossed an empty Starbucks cup onto the floor. *What's the point of even going to work today?* Sixteen months later and she was still a reception- ist at Amy's Nails. *At thirty years old, there definitely should be more to life than this. But what?*

After spending most of her life taking care of other people, she wasn't exactly sure how to take care of herself. In reality, Lucy began her life—if you could call it that—three years ago when her mother took off for the last time. Three years and nothing to show for it but financial debt, professional setbacks, and the monotony of everyday life. Days that started and ended pretty much the same way: alone.

It was late spring, and the weather could not have been more perfect. It was finally starting to warm up, and Lucy hated being cold. She was usually chilly when others were just fine. Even in her own apartment she habitually wore sweatshirts. Long, baggy ones that hung past the knees on her slender five-foot- six frame. While she didn't happen to notice or appreciate this sunny day, she did take note of the clouds—fluffy interspersed clouds that caught her eye because they reminded her of the opening of *The Simpsons.*

Lucy glanced around the floor and passenger seat before snagging a black hair band hidden halfway underneath the seatbelt. She pulled back her wavy brown hair into a ponytail, then put the key in the ignition and turned. After several sluggish grinds, the engine started. At least she got lucky today. A few times a week, she had to pop the hood and spray some mystery gunk into the engine just to get it to start. A wave of panic brushed over her as she realized that the can was almost empty.

As she cruised along, her memory took her back to when she first got that can a few months ago. She had just picked up some groceries and walked back out to her car. After squeezing them in the backseat against a pile of clothes, which were piled on top of a stack of notepads, papers, and drawing pads, she rummaged through one of the bags and pulled out a variety box of donuts. Lucy could never wait until she got home for the something sweet she purchased at the store. She wasn't concerned at all that someone would see her. In fact, she rarely cared what people thought of her, which was one of the reasons she didn't have many friends. There were several casual acquaintances she came in contact with, of course, but there were really only one or two people that she, reluctantly, considered friends.

With a chocolate donut in hand, balanced against the steering wheel, she put the key in the ignition and turned. Just revving. She tried it again. More revving. "C'mon!" She stopped, took a bite of the donut, and glanced around the parking lot. She tried again, pumping the gas frantically as she turned the key. "You piece of shit!" She banged on the dashboard with her free hand. "Crap!" she shouted with an exploding exhale that left her slumped over in her seat.

"That's not gonna do it!" a muffled voice barked from the other side of her window.

Startled, she dropped the donut and snapped her head to the window. She saw a gray-haired, blue-collar-looking man staring at her. "Geez, man, you scared the crap out of me." Lucy motioned with her hand for him to step back so she could open the door. She got out, leaving the door open and looking at him blankly as if to say, "Well?"

"Thought you needed some help," the man said.

"Oh…it won't start," she said, dropping the attitude just a bit.

"Why don't I take a look for you," he offered as he walked around to the front of the car. "Pop the hood." He motioned with a pumping thumbs-up for her to comply.

She got in the driver's seat and reached down to pull the handle. While she was down there, she retrieved the fallen donut and chucked it out the door.

"I got groceries back here," she shouted, leaning out the door.

"Hold your horses, missy," he volleyed back. Without moving from his concentrated stare on the engine, he said, "I think I may know what the problem is."

As she waited, she wondered if he had a family. She thought he was probably the type of dad who teaches you how to change a tire before you go off to college. Or the kind you call when something really exciting happens in your life.

Lucy wouldn't know about that. First of all, nothing exciting ever happened to her. And second, she didn't have a father. Her stepfather, Tom, died when she was twelve, and she never met her real father. Tom had married her mother, Linda, when Lucy was just five years old, and her half sister Katie came along right after Lucy turned six. They actually had a happy little family for about five years before Tom passed of a heart attack.

Tom was one of those flaky, charmer types who was all talk but never came through in the end. The girls loved the charming part, and in the beginning Lucy was too young to notice the flaky part. Towards the end it got to Lucy and her mother. Linda began to drink more than casually when Katie started school. Once it was just the three of them, the situation got much worse and Lucy was forced to take control of the family. Unfortunately, while Lucy struggled to keep her family together, her mother succeeded in pulling it apart.

"Hold on a sec," the man said, jolting Lucy from her thoughts. He briskly walked to an all-white pickup truck about six spaces down the lot. "Let me just get something from my truck."

Waving a hand in the air and not looking very confident he would return with a solution, she gave a halfhearted, "Yeah." She sat and stared at him as he rummaged through a giant gray lockbox in the back of his truck.

What if he wasn't just a nice man trying to help? What if he was a psycho and now he would lure her back to his truck to kidnap her? Who knows what would happen then. What choice did she have anyway? It's not like she had AAA or some capable boyfriend or BFF to call. Who would really miss her anyway if she was snatched away from her meager existence? Maybe it would be a good thing if he was a psycho. She'd often thought about the different ways she could end it all. This, however, was definitely not one of the scenarios.

Quick and painless was more of what she was looking for. And something that didn't take too much effort. Lucy had run through the possibilities in her head more than once. Drug overdose? Pretty tough to get your hands on something that would do the trick. Slit her wrists? Too gross. And she didn't have the guts to do that anyway. What about smoking in bed? Maybe she'd pass out from being drunk. That was believable since she spent many a night overindulging in cheap wine or beer and then falling asleep in front of the TV. Definitely not an option though. She didn't smoke, and the whole apartment building could burn down. Even though she appeared to be a loner, she still cared about people and didn't want to hurt anyone.

Chugging back with a can in one hand, raised up like he was carrying the Olympic torch, the kind man cheered, "Got it."

Usually people who were so positive and cheery annoyed Lucy. But something about this guy was kind of cute. Must be the dad thing. She trusted him and wanted someone like him to take care of her.

"Great," she said. "What is it?"

He waved her over to the front of the car. "Let's try spraying some starter fluid in the carburetor. It used to work great on my wife's old Honda." He shook the can and then gave it three squirts. "Why don't you try to start it up?"

Lucy shrugged. "Okay." She walked around him to the driver's side, hopped in, and turned the key once again. More revving. "Keep going?" she yelled.

"Yeah, try it again," the fatherly type answered back.

She let out a breath and gave it another try. After a few seconds, the engine roared to a start. Lucy revved it up a few more times for good measure, checked that the brake was on, and hopped out. "Thanks."

"No problem." He reached out to her with the can in his hand. "Here, you keep this for next time."

"Thank you." She took the can from him and gave him a closed-mouth smile.

The kind man gave a kind wave and turned to walk away.

"Wait...uh," she said. She ducked inside her car and turned back around instantly holding the open box of donuts. "My name is Lucy." She reached out with the box and smiled, bigger this time.

The man dipped a hand in, grabbed a plain donut, took a bite, and gave her a nod. Then he turned and walked away. He didn't say another word. Not even his name. Lucy stood frozen for a minute, shrugged, and resumed her spot back in the driver's seat.

• • •

Now on the main road headed toward Amy's, Lucy sported a small smirk thinking of that old man on that day. The moment was short-lived as the ring of her cell phone jolted her back to reality. She knew from experience that it was most likely work or a utility company checking on a late bill. She reached for the hands-free button and gave it a tap. "Yeah, it's me," she droned.

"Lucy, Lucy, it's Amy. You get lattes this morning?"

Lucy hated the way Amy said her name. It sounded too much like Ricky Ricardo in *I Love Lucy* even though he was Latin and Amy was Asian. And "Amy" wasn't even her real name. Mickey Chin, the owner, gave all the ladies American-sounding names because he thought it would be better for business and easier for the customers. Amy, Mickey's wife, was really Lan. Suzie's real name was Sunee. Kim was actually named Kim, but that sounded American enough for Mickey.

When Lucy accepted the job from Mickey, she agreed to answer phones until a spot opened up to do nails. Somehow, answering phones grew into making coffee, running errands, and cleaning the stations. Mickey seemed to be in no hurry to move her into a technician spot. Granted, it's not like business was booming, and she hadn't had a day of experience since getting her license. She had the talent, though, and was actually an exceptional artist. She had a love for all things paint, and growing up she had dreamed of being an artist. Like most children, she started out drawing and coloring. Eventually she began to try and re-create her sketches as paintings. She used to paint with her mother, and when Katie was old enough, all three of them would paint together. Those were some of the few good memories Lucy had to look back on.

"Sure, Amy." Lucy tried to sound cordial. "I'll pick them up and be there soon."

"Okay, Lucy, thank—"

Lucy hit the hands-free button, cutting Amy off in mid thanks. "Oops, so sorry," Lucy delighted, doing her best imitation of Amy's voice.

CHAPTER 2

Lucy opened the front door of Amy's Nails holding a tray of coffee in one hand, and a black oversized purse was flung over her other shoulder. The familiar and somewhat pleasant smell of acrylic wafted instantly under her nose. It's a smell that most people find unappealing and most women simply tolerate to feed their vainness. But to Lucy it represented yet another path to a creative outlet as well as the road back to being a financially stable adult. In this economy, and without a college degree, this was about the best she could get. She'd spent some years waitressing, but after seeing what that did to her mother, Lucy didn't have much tolerance for it.

The entry and setup of the salon was very inviting walking in. Although, Lucy felt the front window display was definitely too drab. There were four stations to do nails and six chairs for pedicures, three on each side facing each other with a television hanging from the ceiling in the middle. Pink and black designs were splashed about on the walls, while one wall was covered with every nail color you could possibly think of. There was a black L-shaped vinyl couch in the front for customers to sit on while they waited.

"Oh Lucy, thank you so much," Amy squealed as she rose from behind the counter and scuffled across the floor in her fuzzy pink slippers. She quickly snatched the tray of coffee from Lucy. "You so awesome, girl!" Unlike the other women, who wore sandals to show off their various artistic painting skills, Amy always wore slippers. She was in her early forties, and although she tried to talk and act young, she was very mature and motherly. She often gave Lucy advice and was the only one there who truly seemed to like her.

Amy also was appreciative and recognized Lucy's hard work—when she worked hard, that is. Kim and Suzie didn't seem to respect Lucy, especially Suzie. At times, when they were having conversations in Chinese, Lucy felt as though they were speaking about her. Once in a while one of them would glance up at her and give a disingenuous smile. One time she even noticed Amy giving them a disapproving look and then scolding them in Chinese.

Amy took the coffee over and passed one to Suzie and another to Kim. Of course there was no thank-you to be heard from either of them. Watching Amy carry the tray, Lucy imagined it was a cocktail tray and dreamt of sipping a margarita, rocks, salt, stretched out in the sun.

Suzie, who had shorter-than-shoulder-length hair, had really hairy arms, so she wore long sleeves all the time. Even in the heat of the summer. She was also about eighty pounds overweight, and she liked to balance her cup on her stomach. She promptly got her newly acquired coffee and perched it right into place, then resumed her conversation with Kim and the customer Kim was working on. The woman was a semi-regular who always selected the French acrylics. You couldn't tell from her face, which was pulled freakishly tight, but her hands said that she was probably around mid-sixties.

"It's really getting on my last nerve, Kim," the woman said. She had one hand resting in a bowl of liquid and the other being rubbed by Kim's hands.

"He needs to get a hobby or find some kind of project," Suzie chimed in.

The woman continued speaking, but as she got more riled from her conversation, the hand in the bowl began splashing around. "All this time off and nothing gets done. He spends hours watering the landscaping, and then the rest of the day he goes to Home Depot to exchange some tool or a load of bricks."

Kim sat silently working. This was her usual routine. She didn't like to talk to the customers much. She just let them drone on about work, husbands, or the state of the economy. Eventually, Amy or Suzie would jump in if necessary. Amy scuffled across the room to the woman and rubbed her back. "Mrs. Gordon, you need water? We have bottled water and iced tea in back."

"Water would be nice...thanks."

"Lucy, why don't you bring Mrs. Gordon a water?" Suzie instructed. She had already downed ninety percent of her coffee and was swirling around the last bit.

Already aware the request was coming, Lucy rolled her eyes and walked to the back. She added sarcastically, "You want something too, Suzie? Looks like you already took care of that grande I got you." Lucy grabbed a cold water from a mini fridge in the back and walked back to the station. "Here you go, Mrs. Gordon," she said a little too sweetly.

Amy turned around, smiling her appreciation to Lucy. She understood how hard it was for Lucy to be in this position. She also had some idea of what she had been through in the past. There were bits and pieces of conversations, comments she pieced together. Plus, Amy seemed to have a keen intuition and could really tell things about people.

"Thank you, dear," Mrs. Gordon said.

Kim took the lid off the water so Mrs. Gordon could take a sip and continued to quietly rub the woman's fingernails, pushing on her cuticles. Kim, a shy, slender young woman of twenty-five, had above average looks according to Lucy's scale. Not pretty enough to resent, but cute enough to be drawn to.

Lucy's own looks had been like a woman's diet—up and down like a yo-yo. As a child she was cute as can be—beautiful in fact. People were always telling her mother, "Watch out for the boys when she grows up." Like most kids in junior high, she had an awkward period, which was exacerbated by the anxiety of her home life. Once in high school, and basically taking on the role of mother to her little sister, she began to mature and blossom. She was becoming a woman. But the year just before her half sister Katie left, she felt like a mother being pulled apart from her rebellious daughter. She had no one to turn to, and life took its toll.

Most days Lucy didn't concern herself with her daily appearance either. It was too much work, and after being basically alone for six years, she realized it really didn't make much difference. The only beauty she concerned herself with was when she was drawing or painting. That's when her appreciation for the exquisite really came out. But if you looked closely, you could still see the lovely features that peeked out beneath the apathetic expression on her face.

"Why don't you send him to your son's house to work on that kitchen remodeling you talked about last week," Lucy offered without even looking up from the counter.

Both Kim and Mrs. Gordon looked up in surprise at Lucy's suggestion. Lucy rarely joined into the conversations, and most times it appeared that she wasn't even listening. A smile slowly formed across Mrs. Gordon's face.

"I can't believe I hadn't thought of that. Lucy, that is the best idea! It will help my son, make *me* look good, and get rid of Stephen for a while." Then to Kim she said, "C'mon, Kim, finish me up, I've got some exciting plans to tell Mr. Gordon about."

After Mrs. Gordon left, and sometime later that day, Amy handed Lucy an envelope. It was a tip from Mrs. Gordon. She'd wanted to make sure that Lucy received it, so she handed it directly to Amy instead of including it in with Kim's tip. That was smart thinking on her part.

"Good job, Lucy!" Amy said as Lucy opened the envelope and pulled out a twenty-dollar bill. Lucy beamed at the crisp bill while listening to Amy shuffle away.

• • •

It was seven o'clock on a Friday night and closing time for Amy's Nails. Lucy had begun collecting her things to leave for the day when she noticed Mickey Chin walking up to the door. He usually came after everyone left, and sometimes just before, to pick up the deposit and get Amy. When she did run into him, she always debated on whether or not to ask him about the technician spot. She worried about annoying him, which was not a difficult task. He kept giving her the same excuse about the economy and how the beauty business just isn't what it used to be. The economy—that is what sparked her to think of other ways to make money, ways to use her own skills and talents.

So, last time she spoke to Mickey, it was about the window design at the front entrance. It had been the same since Lucy started, and she knew she could do something fun and more vibrant with it. She had shown him some basic sketch ideas, and he seemed to like them, but since that day Mickey had not said a word about it. From time to time Lucy was able to get other freelance art jobs, but she hadn't had one in a while. By and large they were window or wall displays, and she even did a few wood furniture designs. If Mickey agreed to this, it would give her something to look forward to.

"Good evening, Miss Lucy," he said, walking through the door. He was always very formal in the way he addressed the women. Actually, everything about Mickey was very formal. He always wore suit pants and a nice shirt, and his hair had a little mini wave in the front that looked way too plastered.

"Hello, Mr. Chin," she replied. In the beginning Lucy had addressed him as Mr. Chin to be polite and out of fear of offending him. Since he never corrected her, she hadn't changed it. All the other ladies called him Mickey.

"How are you, Miss Lucy?" he said as he walked past her.

"Fine…uh…?" Lucy answered as her head followed his path.

The opportunity seemed to have been missed. Mickey was already opening the door to the back room. Disappointed, Lucy grabbed her stuff and walked toward the door to leave.

"Oh, Miss Lucy," Mickey's voice came back.

Lucy turned to see him in the doorway where he was standing and holding the door half open. "I almost forgot. I talked to Amy, and she says she *is* tired of looking at this old window display…but I think maybe we should hire a professional. I know we talked about it before, but I'm just not sure yet."

Lucy's expression sagged. She was trying to process the information and figure out what to say when Mickey spoke again.

"Let me talk with Amy and think about it further. Then I'll let you know."

"Well…could I show you some more designs? I've got some really good ideas."

"That will be fine," he answered with a single nod.

"Thanks, Mr. Chin. I'll bring them in next week." Lucy turned to the door to leave.

"One more thing." His voice caught her, and she spun around. "Remember that this would be a project on your time, not during work hours."

"Of course," she said. "I appreciate the opportunity, Mr. Chin." Lucy left frustrated but still hopeful that her designs would win them over. She should have known Mr. Chin would be all business. She wondered if his concern about work hours was one of the reasons he wanted to hire someone else. It was a fair request though, since he would be paying her for her time and work. Or maybe he just didn't trust her with such a responsibility since she wasn't the most reliable employee. Those two slave drivers had probably poisoned his mind against her. At least she had Amy on her side. She would need to come up with some incredible designs that Amy would not be able to resist.

CHAPTER 3

In the car on the way home, Lucy contemplated her dinner options. She originally had only four bucks left in her wallet, and she wasn't getting paid for a few more days. That was typical for her. The second her paycheck was in her hand, it seemed as though every financial obligation she had seemed to automatically suck it right away from her. But now, thanks to Mrs. Gordon, she had twenty-four dollars. She thought about grabbing some tacos on the way home to avoid cooking spaghetti, which was the only thing she had left in her kitchen. Pasta was cheap, and it was truly her favorite, but she didn't feel like cooking tonight, so tacos it was. Another advantage would be avoiding her neighbor Mrs. Allen. She had been asking Lucy for weeks if she could cook her dinner to thank her for finding her cat Peaches. The two ran into each other in the hall the day before, and Mrs. Allen insisted they make a tentative plan.

"How about tomorrow night?" Mrs. Allen had asked hopefully.

"I'll try, Mrs. Allen," Lucy told her with a plastered smile. She often wondered what her smile looked like to other people. It hardly came natural to her, so it always felt forced. "But I may have to stay after work and help...uh, with ordering stuff," she fumbled.

"All right, dear." She put one hand on her hip and pointed at Lucy with her other hand, sending that *you better do what I say* message. "Well you just let me know then…because I won't take *no* for an answer. I'll just keep asking until you agree."

Mary Allen had lived in that apartment for sixteen years. She didn't want to move because her husband had died while they were living there. Lucy, on the other hand, was dying to get out. Next month would mark three years living in a one-bedroom in the Sunset Vista Apartments off East Orange Avenue in Fullerton. She moved in when they lost the house. Upside down on the mortgage and no longer able to make payments, there was a short sale by the bank. Her mother had taken off a year before that, so it was up to Lucy to handle everything. In and out of rehab twice, Lucy tried to think of her mother as a roommate who was away on business. She hadn't heard from her since. It only took a couple of months, and the house that Lucy grew up in was gone.

The apartment building itself was a bit run-down, but unlike her car, Lucy kept her own apartment neat and clean. In terms of decorations, it was simple and understated except for a few of her paintings. She hung a beach scene in her bathroom that she had done after spending the day there walking and thinking. There was another in her room above a blue chair that was of a horse. It was her first painting, and it was just something she drew first from a picture. She had never even ridden a horse before, but she just thought it was beautiful.

The furniture was smart, in shades of burgundy, gold, and black. Once inside, she usually felt comfortable, at ease. Oftentimes when she arrived at her building, she made a beeline straight to her door so she could avoid the more unappealing aspects of her surroundings. At the top of that list would be some of the occupants of the Sunset Vista Apartments.

The manager, Dale, was kind of creepy and spent a lot of time lurking around pretending to be checking something out. He had long, straggly black hair and scary teeth. Whenever Lucy ran into him, he would try to strike up a conversation or ask her if she needed anything. All the questions he asked made her feel uncomfortable. She usually made up some excuse that she had to get to work or run errands. If it really came down to it, she knew she could handle him. He wasn't the type of guy she feared or was intimidated by. Lucy had encountered her fair share of those types growing up.

The apartment also housed a few young couples just starting out and some retired elderly, but the majority of the tenants were thirtysomething men with major financial problems. Many of them were divorced or on unemployment, or both. But the rent was the cheapest in the area, and it was a decently safe place to live, except for that one incident that happened about a year and a half ago. The whole thing was pretty much over by the time Lucy got home, but Dale was all too happy to give her the skinny when he saw her walk up looking confused. Turned out the person they arrested wasn't even a tenant, just some guy who was visiting his girlfriend. They picked him up for a B and E that happened the night before.

Thankfully, all the occupants weren't totally unbearable. Mrs. Allen could be a nuisance at times, but she was old and Lucy had more patience for old people. She always wished she had grandparents in her life. On TV, it always seemed so great and no matter what was going on with your parents, the grandparents were always there for you. Once in a while Mrs. Allen brought over desserts for Lucy and didn't even offer to stay or try to chat Lucy's ear off like some of the other people in the building. Mrs. Allen also had a niece, Anne, who visited often. Lucy and Anne had become close lately and even went out a couple of times.

Anne, twenty-two, went to the JC part-time and worked at the hospital part-time. She planned to enter the nursing program next fall. She was a very peppy girl with a sweet smile. Lucy imagined her as the type of girl who would make the perfect cheerleader, but wasn't popular enough to make the team.

• • •

Finally home with tacos in hand, Lucy felt exhausted as she walked along the sidewalk. The orange glow of the setting sun beamed down on the section of faded grass that lined the pathway to her apartment. The sprinkler on the front corner was still broken, and water was dribbling out onto the cement forming an asymmetrical shape. When she reached the spot just before the outer set of stairs that led to her apartment, she noticed Dale and immediately looked for an escape route. Yes, the sprinkler needed fixing. But was it worth a conversation where she fought to keep from staring at the gold that peeked from behind Dale's two yellow-gray front teeth? Definitely not! Like a truant teen, she turned her back and paused by the door of 4B, Benny Garcia's apartment. From the sounds inside, she could tell he had company, probably Benny's brother and his five-year-old twin boys. They stopped by a few times a month, and sometimes Benny babysat the twins.

When she realized Dale had passed, she began to climb the stairs, and then she heard Benny's door pop open.

"Hey, Lucy," Benny shouted from the doorway.

A tall, dark-haired, green-eyed Latino, Benny was good-looking but could stand to lose a few pounds. You could tell he used to play football or something athletic and had muscles but didn't quite keep up with his workouts, so the muscles had just turned to bulk.

Benny dropped out of college five years ago to pursue stand-up comedy. He had gotten fired from his last two jobs. To most people that would sound irresponsible, but Lucy was in no position to judge given her own occupational history. Usually, his partners in comic crime would go out after their shows, and Benny always had a little trouble getting up the next day for work.

"Tomorrow night is the big one." The twins were causing a ruckus and trying to squeeze through Benny's legs like wild rats trying to get out of a sack. "Knock it off, you two," he boomed as he blocked them with both hands and legs. "Anne said she would come. How about you, Lucita?" he lured.

The nickname, which started a few weeks ago, flattered Lucy. "Maybe…we'll see," she replied as she began to back up the stairs knowing the coast was clear.

"No way, none of this *maybe* crap!" He swished his index finger back and forth like a mini windshield wiper. "I've got extra stage time, and you've only been one time." One of the twins snuck by his side. Benny grabbed him and flung him over his shoulder. "C'mon, girl! What you gonna do? Stay home and paint your toenails?"

Benny had only lived in the building for about six months, but he treated everyone as if he'd known them for years. It was hard for Lucy to evade that, and like everyone else, she tended to get sucked into his personality.

"All right!" she shouted. "But you better make me laugh." Lucy found him funny at times, but she couldn't decide if he really was that hilarious or if it was because he was good-looking, in a sloppy sort of way. Plus, she did like the attention he gave her.

"If you don't laugh, I'll stage dive naked." He swung the boy back and forth simulating flying.

"Please, then I'll really be laughing." She turned and continued up the stairs, waving a hand backward over her head. "See ya."

Benny watched Lucy climb the stairs for a moment, then guided the boy with arms stretched in flight back into the door, kicking it closed with his foot.

At last in her apartment, Lucy grabbed a soda from the fridge and flopped down on the floor between the sofa and the coffee table. This was her standard Friday night: sitting in front of the TV, eating and watching some movie she had seen for the umpteenth time. She thought about the club tomorrow night and whether or not she should really go. She considered coming up with an excuse because she hadn't felt like going out lately. But after giving it some more thought, she figured maybe it would be fun. She had enjoyed Anne's company lately. Sure she was kind of corny and naïve and nosy. But…it was kind of like having a little sister again.

Lucy would spend the day doing laundry and finalizing her sketches for the window proposal for Mr. Chin. Visuals were already floating around in her head, so getting it down on paper would be a cinch. She figured that would put her in a good enough mood to go out. As usual, she would need to have some pre-party libations to help her through the night.

Later that evening, she sat up in bed staring at a page in her sketch pad. A pencil drawing of a young girl, shadowy yet vibrant in the eyes, which drew your focus directly to them. It was obvious that sketch had sparked a memory. Most of Lucy's sketches were of people and things dear to her heart. It was the way she expressed her emotions. Everything just flowed right out of her like a river, from pen or brush to page.

A bottle of red wine was displayed like a cheap vase on the night table next to her bed, sans the wineglass. There was no need for formality, and it was the end of the bottle anyway. The television was on an XM music channel playing the eighties song "Look of Love." Lucy closed the pad and set it down next to the wine bottle. Then she changed the channel to soft hits and turned off the light. Although it was faintly heard, it helped her to fall asleep. There were many nights she lay awake thinking of her mother and sister. Not just when life was happier and Tom was alive, because the bad thoughts always crept in like cancer secretly gnawing at her conscience. The fights, the fear, and the uncertainty were all there, and then she would push those memories back into the darkness. She missed them both even though their leaving left her feeling hurt and betrayed. She missed having someone in her life. Someone she could take care of as she did her sister, and someone who would be there for her. She had no idea how she could ever get that back. It was like a faraway land she longed to visit.

CHAPTER 4

People say if you hear something about yourself enough times, you begin to believe it. Lucy had experienced more than her share of negative criticism and hostility throughout her life. Her mother Linda had gone from a sweet, loving mom to a bitter, cruel woman. And as many victims of abuse blame themselves, Lucy carried her anger, guilt, and sadness around like a bulletproof vest. It kept her safe from being hurt, yet made her stiff and impenetrable. She wondered if there was something more she could have done to help her mother. Maybe if she had been more supportive and less defensive. On the other hand, she wondered how her mother could have done that to her. How could she turn things upside down and then just leave? With no one else to turn to, Lucy did her best to cope and handle the situations that came up. To her that meant protecting Katie, even if it also meant that Lucy would take the brunt of the backlashes from Linda.

Lucy could see now that a turning point came when she was in high school. When she was around sixteen, she was basically taking care of herself and Katie. There were times when Linda didn't even come home at night. She'd leave some cash on the table, tips from her waitressing job she was barely hanging on to. Oftentimes they'd wake up in the morning to her passed out on the couch. On two occasions, Child Protective Services received anonymous calls and a caseworker was sent to the house. Both times Lucy was able to convince them everything was fine, even though Linda wasn't even home for one of the visits. Another ghastly example of the country's economic crisis—overworked social workers.

One particular night when Linda didn't come home until about two in the morning, Lucy awoke to the sound of Linda talking loudly to herself. Lucy realized that she had been looking at the bills that were on the counter. She was swearing about a bill from a hospital they had taken Katie to. Katie had been very sick and wasn't getting better on her own. When she took a turn for the worse, Lucy convinced Linda to take Katie to the hospital, where they ran a few tests. The insurance company was not covering the entire balance and sent the remaining amount to Linda.

Lucy could hear the yelling getting closer and then farther, as if Linda were pacing. "These damn kids! What the hell do they ever do but cost me money." Then there was shuffling around, noises in the kitchen, more yelling, glass breaking. Lucy had become an expert at knowing what each sound meant, especially when Linda was drinking. What worried her this time was that Linda sounded much more agitated than her normal sloppy drunk disposition. She prayed that Linda hadn't been doing more than just drinking. Unfortunately, this wasn't the first time she had been concerned about that.

Lucy had been lying there for about an hour until she was sure Linda was done with her ranting, and then she fell asleep. The next day Lucy got Katie up early, and the girls left for school without even having breakfast. Lucy also arranged for Katie to go home with a friend after school just in case things hadn't blown over at home by the time they got there.

When Linda woke up around one in the afternoon, she wondered where the girls were. She actually thought it was Saturday and not Thursday. She spent the next couple of hours fuming. By the time Lucy walked in around three thirty, Linda had reached her boiling point. She was sitting in a chair just staring at the front door.

"Where the hell have you been?" Linda held without moving a single muscle. Her dishwater-blonde hair was no longer sprinkled with gray, it was drowning in it. Lack of proper health and nutrition exacerbated the cruel changes that age was already executing on Linda's facial features. Instead of looking sophisticated and beautiful as most of her friends and family had thought of her, she was haggard and beat down.

"School," Lucy said as she passed Linda and headed for the kitchen.

"You liar!" Linda jumped up from the chair and followed Lucy into the kitchen. "What could you possibly be doing at school on Saturday? And where's Katie?"

Trying to sound calm while feeling the complete opposite inside, Lucy said, "Today is Thursday, Mom. You can check the calendar if you don't believe me."

"Don't talk to me like I'm an idiot! Where's Katie?" Her breathing was fast and heavy.

"She's at Kelsey's house." Lucy set her things down on the table and then moved back toward the living room. She struggled to keep her voice steady. "Her mom picked them up after school so they could work on a project."

Linda grabbed Lucy's arm as she was walking by her. "You call her and get her back here right now!" Their eyes met only for a second, but it was long enough for Lucy to see where this was going.

"No!" Lucy jerked her arm away and ran toward her bedroom. Her mother chased behind, but Lucy was able to shut and lock the door just before Linda grabbed the knob.

"You little bitch! You better open this door right now!" Linda banged on the door with a closed fist. "Don't you dare think you're in charge here. You're just a stupid little girl!"

Lucy slid down the back of the door with her hands over her ears. She knew the cycle, and she knew this outrage would eventually turn from anger to sorrow and then eventually, sometimes, pity. It was a standoff, and with her will, she knew she would win. She thought of prisoners in solitary. How long would they sit, staring at that door waiting for it to open? She'd wait forever if she had to. She wouldn't crack under pressure.

"I'm your mother...and you have to...listen to me." Linda banged a few more times, but her head couldn't handle the noise or the force. Her arm fell to her side. "You're not in charge of Katie. She's my...baby!" Her body slumped to the ground and propped against the door. "I'm in charge," she cried. "I'm the mom around here."

They both cried, Lucy silently, on either side of the door for twenty minutes before Linda made the first move. She went to the kitchen and began cleaning the mess from last night. Then she reached in her pocket, pulled out a wad of cash, and plunked it on the table. Lucy stayed in her position against the door. Her face and eyes were still wet, but she was past the emotional storm. Now she had to figure out what to do next. She could hear the rustling around going on in the other room but found herself still glued to the floor. After a few more minutes, there was a door slam, and then silence.

Still hesitant, she waited in her room until she felt safe, and then she opened the door a crack to peek out. She knew her mother was gone because that was the only thing Linda could do when she felt guilty. Lucy went to the living room and then into the kitchen and noticed the money on the table along with a small white piece of paper. She walked over and picked up the paper, which had only two words on it: *Forgive me.*

Lucy began to cry again as she crumpled up the paper and threw it in the trash. She couldn't take a chance that Katie would see it. As bad as things were, both Linda and Lucy tried hard to make things seem normal when Katie was there. Walking sullenly back to the living room, Lucy collapsed on the couch. She grabbed a pillow and pulled it tight against her as she closed her eyes in complete exhaustion.

Lucy had never felt more alone than she did at that moment. Not only did she believe there wasn't a soul out there who could help her, but she was also very confused about her life and where it was going. Was that how things were supposed to be? How much longer could she go on like that? She couldn't have known that it would be six more years of being on that emotional roller coaster.

Now the ride was over, but the aftermath was still very unstable. How could Lucy figure out who she was, or who she could become, if she didn't even know who she used to be? She couldn't find a place in her own family, let alone the world. At times Lucy had been a daughter, a sister, and a mother, but now she was nobody.

CHAPTER 5

"I'll drive," Anne offered as the two stood in the hallway about to leave. Anne was taller than Lucy, five foot seven to be exact. She had blonde hair that was long and straight. She was sweet and a bit naïve, and more on the cute side rather than pretty. It surprised Lucy how Anne was drawn to her even though Lucy was not very inviting. Anne was very laid-back and friendly, and she never took the things Lucy said personally. It didn't seem to faze her when Lucy was closed off or negative.

The club was about ninety percent full when they arrived, and the girls sat at a table more towards the front. Benny's friend Zach was on stage and about to finish up. They had missed the first guy, and there would be a short break before Benny, who was third out of five.

The girls chatted a bit, but it was mostly Anne talking and Lucy listening. She wanted to tell Lucy all about a guy she was interested in at the hospital. She spoke as if they were in high school, saying things like, "totally hot" and "awesome." Lucy was just about to excuse herself to the restroom when Benny came on stage.

To start the night, Lucy had a couple of beers at home before she met Anne outside Mrs. Allen's apartment. She added to that the two drinks that came with the cover charge. Before Benny was through with his bit, she was feeling pretty out of it. Not being able to sit there any longer, she told Anne she was going to leave.

"I just gotta get outta here," Lucy said, swaying in her chair just a bit. "It's too hot in here."

"Okay, let's both go then," Anne said. "I'll drive us back. I'm fine."

Laughter bellowed through the room as Benny delivered his quips and stories in a conversational voice. That was part of his style. He wanted the audience to feel as though they were just hanging out talking with him. The bright lights on stage made it difficult to make out any details in the audience, so he didn't notice that the girls were talking and not paying attention.

"No, Benny will be so bummed. You stay here and I'll take the bus." Lucy started to get up and tried to look totally in control.

"Are you sure, Lucy?" Anne sound worried.

"Really, I want to take my time going home anyway. I'll see you later."

Anne looked concerned but said, "Okay, be careful." She knew not to argue with Lucy. When she wanted to be alone, that was it, end of conversation.

Lucy walked to the back of the bar, out of sight, and stood for a few minutes. She couldn't quite leave yet because she actually wanted to hear some more of Benny's act. He was talking about his family being poor when he was growing up and how he and his brothers used to eat breakfast. He explained how they used to eat their cereal with a fork, and then they'd pass the bowl with the milk to the next person to use. She laughed and on impulse looked around at the other people laughing. She noticed a man at the bar staring at her. He looked vaguely familiar and mouthed a "hey" that seemed to say he recognized her.

While she was still looking at him, he got up from the bar and walked toward her. Lucy's first instinct was to take off. Caught off guard and with a pretty good buzz, she turned too slowly, and the man was suddenly in front of her. He was clean-shaven, wore a business suit, and had short, sandy-colored hair.

"Lucy...Lang." He snapped his fingers. "I thought that was you."

"Hi...uh," Lucy replied. She did think he looked familiar but still couldn't place him. She looked straight ahead as if she were engrossed in what was going on up on the stage.

"Kyle," he said, as if everyone should remember him. "Kyle Benson, Westen High School—we had Mr. Beamer's science class together." He put his hand out even though she wasn't looking at him.

"Oh, yeah, right, Mr. Beamer." She nodded and smiled but wasn't a hundred percent sure she remembered him. Then she took his hand and shook it.

"It's good to see you, Lucy," he said, as if they had been long-lost friends.

"Yeah, you too." Sure, she took that class, but that was a dozen years ago. And she didn't really date too many guys in her class. She had to give him credit though. He remembered her, and he still approached her. Maybe he didn't remember *everything* about her.

Kyle crossed in front of her and stood on the other side as if to cause a distraction. Their eyes met for a moment, and she noticed his deep blue eyes focusing tightly on hers, as if to get a read on what she was thinking. "How've you been, Lucy? You look great."

This was actually one of her better looking nights. Typically, due to her budget and motivation, Lucy's wardrobe consisted of mostly jeans and T-shirts. Tonight, she had her hair down and wore just enough makeup to show up on her light olive complexion. She had on black and silver croppy pants and a short-sleeve black shirt that fit snuggly against her thin body. She would have normally felt uncomfortable talking as if they were old friends, but she was in the mood to play along. "Good, and you?"

"Great. I'm working for a marketing company now. Some of us go out together after work...but everyone pretty much left." He gestured toward the door. "Were you leaving?"

"Actually, yeah. But good seeing you." She turned to walk away, half hoping he would stop her. It had been months since she had dated anyone and almost two years since she'd had a boyfriend. It would be nice to talk to someone new since she rarely had the opportunity to meet new people.

Reaching out and grabbing her arm he said, "You need a ride?"

Lucy stopped and smiled, trying not to let on that she was happy, or that she had been drinking. That was a skill she had mastered over the years. "I was going to take the bus...but sure, thanks."

CHAPTER 6

Kyle had a black Toyota 4Runner and was parked just outside the club. As he opened her door in the full gentleman role, she felt a hint of hesitation. These were the situations that parents warned you were dangerous. Lucy knew that, but she was in the mood to take chances. She got in, and while Kyle walked around to the driver's side, she took a quick look in the mirror. She felt a twinge of excitement as he rounded the back end of the car and opened his door.

In the car, there was a brief moment of awkward silence until he began to search for music. He pressed number three on the CD player. "You like Green Day?" he asked, looking straight ahead.

"Sure."

"I remember now…you never did talk that much in school." He chuckled.

That was an unsettling statement to respond to. She didn't want to just start rambling like an idiot to prove him wrong, or keep sitting there like some wallflower. The pressure of the silent seconds ticking in her head caused a sudden, yet casual, "Sor-freakin-ry."

Taken by total surprise, he burst out laughing. "Well I didn't expect that." He put a hand on her knee. "I'm the one who's sorry," he said. "Listen, I'm supposed to meet some friends for a get-together. Do you want to go? It's just a few people for drinks, and it's not too far from here."

"Sure, why not," she replied, surprising herself.

"I just need to stop by the store. I always hate walking in empty-handed."

Now at JP's Market, Lucy waited in the car while Kyle ran in to grab some wine for the party. Sitting there, Lucy suddenly began to feel that this was a big mistake. Her fight-or-flight was kicking in, and she thought the latter would be a much better option. She wondered why she had agreed to go with him. But she knew why. Did she really think she could make it through a party being nice and polite to total strangers? Enough for Kyle to like her and want to spend the night with her? Was she even sure that was what she wanted? The anxiety was rising in her, and she was starting to lose the buzz she'd earned earlier in the evening.

Nervously, Lucy looked at her phone, then out into the store window. She glanced around all the angles of the car to see who was around. For a second she almost opened the door to get out and leave. In the backseat she noticed a small bag that looked like it was for toiletries. She grabbed it and began to rummage through it. It seemed to hold the usual stuff: mini toothpaste, floss, shampoo. Then she saw a prescription bottle. She yanked out the bottle and turned it until she saw what it was: Vicodin.

Looking up, she noticed that Kyle wasn't at the cash register yet. What was she considering here? What would he think of her if he found out? At this point she didn't really care. Besides, he wouldn't miss a few, and it's always good to have a few painkillers around for an emergency. Not to mention the fact that she needed to ease her current tensions. Popping open the bottle, she poured four pills into her hand. Holding them tightly in her hand, she replaced the cap and put the bottle back in the bag. She opened her purse and pulled out her wallet. On the side there was a zipper, which she opened and tried to pour the pills in. To her dismay, only one pill fell in and the other three dropped between her legs. She looked up in a panic to see where Kyle was and found him paying at the counter. Now she really felt idiotic. She dug down and pulled one out and dropped it in the wallet. *Two more,* she thought. Kyle grabbed his change and headed back to the car as Lucy dropped her wallet in her purse and set it on the floor.

"Hey," he said as he slid in the car. He reached in the bag, pulled out a candy bar, and handed it to her. "Here, I got you a treat," he said, smiling.

Lucy took the chocolate and replied, "Oh…thanks." She couldn't decide if that was strange or sweet, but she was leaning more towards sweet.

Kyle set the bag on the backseat next to the little black bag.

Lucy smiled, trying to act casual, and put her hands between her thighs as if she was cold, which actually she did feel a little chill. In the dark he wouldn't notice her looking for the pills, so she began feeling around.

"Oh, I'll turn the heater on for you," he said.

"Thanks," she said, still running her fingers around. Then she felt them in the crease of the seat. "Mind if I have a sip of your water?" She gestured to a bottle with her head.

"Sure, but it's been there a few hours."

"That's okay. My throat is really dry." She turned her head to look out her window, popped the two of them in her mouth, and took a long drink from the bottle. "Thanks."

"No problem." He smiled but kept his eyes on the road.

Ten minutes later they arrived at a two-story home in a family-style neighborhood. Kyle grabbed the bag, got out of the car, and started to walk around to her side intending to open her door. Before he got there, she was already opening the door to get out. The cool breeze felt exhilarating on her skin and flying through her hair. She froze for a brief moment to enjoy it, and then her expression faded.

"Don't worry," he said as stood next to her. "Everyone here is really nice."

"Did I say I was worried?" She walked up the driveway towards the house as Kyle followed closely behind. She felt his eyes on her and knew he was trying to figure her out. And that eventually he may want to get to know her better. That was something that never seemed to work out very well for Lucy.

Walking through the door without knocking, they were greeted with "Kyle!" shouted in unison from half a dozen people. Lucy noted his obvious popularity. Like magic, a woman appeared from a doorway and handed them each a margarita. *That will work.* For the few cars that were outside, there were more people than she expected. The house was dimly lit, and there were several candles lit throughout the main living area. Most of the guests were standing in and about the living and kitchen area, and a couple was sitting outside, talking as if they were having a very serious discussion.

Kyle introduced Lucy as a friend to most of the guests, but she barely remembered anyone's name. They'd only been there for about thirty minutes, but the alcohol-pills-alcohol schedule she was executing caused her head to spin, fast! She spied a seat at the end of the sofa and went straight for it without letting Kyle know. She didn't want to interrupt his conversation with a beautifully dressed woman who appeared to be the hostess.

From the sofa, she watched as Kyle smiled and touched the woman's arm during their conversation. Instinctively it made her smile for a moment. All around her she listened to bits of broken chitchat on various topics, until Kyle finally turned and noticed her on the couch.

"I'll be right back," he said softly in her ear after walking over to her. "Do you need to go?" He gestured toward the hallway, and she assumed that meant the restroom.

"I'm fine," Lucy replied, taking note of the gentle way about him. It was like he was speaking to a timid child. She assumed he was that way with everyone based on her earlier observation; otherwise, she may have been offended. Or maybe he was treating her with kid gloves. She wasn't sure of anything at that point except that her head was starting to feel inflated.

Lucy watched Kyle as he walked off and disappeared down a hallway. *How the hell did I get myself into this one?* she thought. She figured that her best bet was to apologize and ask him to take her home. On the other hand, she absolutely hated asking people for help or being an imposition. Before she knew it, she was off the couch and headed for the door. Walking past a sea of blurry faces, the door seemed to be getting further and further away. An arm that didn't appear to be attached to anyone reached out to her.

"Are you okay?" a voice murmured in slow motion.

Lucy picked up the pace and started running. She finally reached the door and bolted outside. There was no way she could make it home like this. She wanted to puke it out of her, but she was well aware it was too late for that. Her head was blowing up, spinning, but if she could get to a bus stop she was home free. About a year ago, Lucy was without her own transportation and completely mastered the bus system. She slowed from her run to a speed walk until she got to a main road, and miraculously she tracked down a bus stop. After a few minutes of standing under the dimly lit bus sign, next to a thin Hispanic man, the bus finally arrived. She thought about jumping in front of it instead of getting on. How she made it back from there to the Sunset Vista Apartments was a complete blackout.

• • •

When Benny's set was over, Anne was there waiting for him with a giant grin. "You were so great," she cheered while doing little mini claps with her hands. She had explained that Lucy left, but saw most of his time. She also told him that Lucy had apologized and said that Benny did a great job. He knew better. That didn't sound like Lucy, and Anne was always trying to smooth things over.

"Thanks, Anne," he said modestly. "But I blew that bit about bosses."

Benny had insisted on them following each other home to be safe. He enjoyed taking on that big brother role since he didn't have any sisters of his own, just brothers. Normally he would be going out to continue the laughs with his buddies, but he had to admit he was tired from all the apprehension of the night.

Returning from the parking lot, Benny and Anne walked back to the apartment building. They talked and laughed about the show and hadn't even noticed that they were about to step right on top of Lucy. There she was, lying on the ground a few feet away from the stairs.

"Oh my God, Lucy!" Anne screeched as she ran and knelt down next to Lucy.

Benny was right behind her and took a swift glance around to survey the situation. "Lucy!" He grasped her shoulders and shook them slightly to see if she would jar awake. The night air was cool and thick, and the full moon seemed to be providing the spotlight they needed.

"Do you think she was attacked or mugged or something?" Anne looked desperately at Benny. She was not used to this type of situation. "Should we call 911?"

"Hold on a second." Benny checked her pulse and breathing. He was composed and acted as if he had experienced this many times before. "She's breathing. Let's see if we can get her conscious first." He shook her again, only a bit harder this time. "Lucy, can you hear me? C'mon, Lucita, wake up!"

"Benny! We're wasting time." Anne grabbed her purse and began searching hysterically for her cell phone. "I'm calling 911."

"Don't make me kick your ass," a slurred and quiet voice came from below. Lucy stirred slightly and groaned.

Benny and Anne shook their heads and smiled at each other.

"Lucy, you scared us," Anne said. "Thank God you're okay. I mean, are you okay?"

"God...kill me now," she moaned and rolled over to her side.

"C'mon, girl, let's get you inside." Benny picked Lucy up like a new bride and carried her up the stairs to her apartment. "Anne, grab her purse."

"Got it," she said, trying to sound helpful. She gathered up both purses and followed them up the stairs. Before reaching the top, Anne was able to find Lucy's apartments keys to open the door.

In Benny's arms Lucy's eyes were closed, but she spoke quietly. "I don't need you, Benny. I don't need anyone." A tear rolled down her cheek and landed on Benny's arm.

"I know," he whispered.

CHAPTER 7

Six-year-old Carly Moore walked along the tiled hallway, carefully placing a foot in each one of the outlined squares as she went along. Her hair was brown and wavy, parted on the side. The longer side was pushed back with a bejeweled pink bobby pin. Her big, beautiful brown eyes appeared even larger with her stylish pink prescription glasses.

Proudly following at a safe distance behind, her father Rick was not displaying the same carefree expression as his only daughter. He knew she felt somewhat at ease here as she had been to that hospital a half a dozen times over the last year. The nurses were always very friendly and made everything seem so normal. Rick knew better, though. Each trip to St. Vincent's seemed to signify a progressively worse situation.

"Wait, Carly," her dad called out just before she was about to enter an open door on the left.

Carly stopped and looked back at her dad. "We're going back to Mommy's room, right?" She pointed up ahead toward the open door. "It's that one!"

"That's right, honey, but Daddy needs to speak to Dr. Brady for a minute." He knelt down and motioned for her to come over to him. "Come give me a hug, and then you're going to wait here with Nurse Penny."

A woman dressed in light blue scrubs came from the side nurses' station as Carly ran to her dad. She flung her long, grayish white hair back behind her shoulder.

Carly wrapped her arms around her father's neck and asked, "Do I get to play with the gloves again?"

Rick gave the nurse a questioning look and a shrug. "It's up to Nurse Penny."

"Of course, sweetie." Nurse Penny flashed a comforting smile and reached out her hand to Carly. "C'mon."

Rick stood and watched as the two walked over to the nurses' station, both of their manes swaying in unison across their backs. He then turned and looked at the open door, pausing a few seconds before taking stride. Before he reached her door, he prepared his game face. He laughed in spite of himself, knowing that it was pointless. He could never fool her, and besides, he knew she was doing the same thing herself.

The first thing that Rick noticed when he entered the room was what he always noticed when he entered a room Katie was in: her smile. It always seemed to make everyone around her feel at ease. It was almost as though Katie was trying to put Dr. Brady at ease instead of the other way around. Katie was sitting straight up in the bed with her long, brown hair up in a ponytail. Her blue eyes were sparkling as she listened to the doctor speak. By the look on her face, those eyes would not give away to anyone that she was ill.

"Rick, Dr. Brady says it's about that time." She spoke as if she were talking about a business proposal. "Dialysis is not cutting it anymore. It's time to step up our game." Katie loved to throw in sports references for Rick's benefit. A completely guy's guy, Rick loved to watch, and play, sports. And he adored how Katie would memorize some obscure quote and then try to use it at entirely the wrong time. One time, Rick was watching a football game with his buddies and Katie walked by while they were arguing stats. She touted a player that she remembered Rick talking about, trying to be cool. Unfortunately for her, that player had retired eight years earlier.

"I know, babe. He told me this morning." Rick, tall and lanky, walked over to the other side of the bed. He reached out and put his hand on Katie's leg. He had short, black hair buzzed like he was ready to be deployed.

"These days, there is a really good chance of finding a live donor," she said with a reassuring look.

"I know," he repeated. "And we will."

Like most men, Rick stated his feelings in as few words as possible. Katie didn't mind this because, unlike most women, she didn't spend a lot of time talking about her feelings either.

"So what's the next step?" he said to Dr. Brady.

"First we need to have all your friends and family tested, even the ones out of town." He nudged his glasses up a bit higher on his nose. In his late fifties, Dr. Brady had been with Katie since the beginning of her diagnosis. "Kits can be mailed out, and they can bring them to their local physicians."

"Sounds easy enough," Katie said. "But...you know I don't have much family."

"I remember when you spoke about your family, Katie," he said. "These days we have a lot of options. And Rick can even have his coworkers get tested. Were you able to locate your mother?"

"No." Her smiled faded for the first time. "And I haven't spoken to my sister in years."

"I'm sure she'll want to help. Why don't you speak with Lucy, and then we'll get a kit out to her right away."

"Dr. Brady," Rick began as he was looking at Katie for confirmation. "Lucy's probably not the best—"

"Don't worry, Rick," Dr. Brady reassured. "Luckily we've made this decision at a good time. We're not waiting until the last minute, so if your sister-in-law is a match, then she'll have plenty of time to make a decision and get things *in order.*"

"Thanks, Doc." Rick reached out to shake Dr. Brady's hand. "We appreciate everything."

"No problem," he said. "I'll give you two some time to talk things over." Dr. Brady headed for the door and gave a smile and a nod as he exited. "Take care."

Rick looked down at Katie and smiled. He picked up one of her hands and squeezed it in both of his. "That's my girl." He bent down and delivered a kiss to her lips. "You are so strong, it's amazing."

"I couldn't do this without you," she said softer than she had been speaking with the doctor.

Rick was the only person with whom Katie could let her defenses down. Now both twenty-four years old, they had basically grown up together. They'd met at a football game when they were sixteen, but were on rival sides. Katie was sitting in the stands when Rick and a friend had walked by. They had gone over to talk to some kids that they had previously gone to school with. He saw her talking with her friends and convinced his buddy to stay on that side of the stadium. By the end of the game, and after several smile and nod exchanges, he finally got up the nerve to ask for her phone number.

Their relationship advanced quickly, and for the first time, Katie confided in someone about her problems at home. Rick was understanding and comforting. It was the kind of comfort that her sister Lucy could no longer give to Katie.

Just before graduation, Katie became pregnant. Both were able to finish out the year and graduate before it became totally obvious to everyone. Although Rick's family was understandably distraught, Rick's dad, George, wanted to help. He offered Rick a job and the two of them a place stay in Fort Worth, where he'd moved after separating from Rick's mother. Even now George was a huge help and took care of Carly whenever they needed him.

"I'm going to take care of everything—all the calls, anything that needs to get done."

"I just don't know if I can ask Lucy though. It was so awful in the end. I was awful!"

"It's not like you want to borrow money. This is your life we're talking about, and you are still family no matter what."

"I know, babe. And I know we'll find a match…somehow."

"You know, if this doesn't work out, we can always get one off eBay." Rick smiled, and Katie giggled.

In the doorway, a man appeared holding Carly's hand. "How y'all doin'?" he said with a concerned smile. Carly ran over and climbed on the edge of the bed.

"Look, Mommy, it's Papa!"

"I see that!" Katie said as she and Carly hugged. "Hi, George, thanks for coming."

"You know I gotta be where my two favorite girls are," he said as he walked over to the bed and patted Rick on the shoulder.

"Gee thanks, Dad."

Carly sang out, "Are you all better now, Mommy?"

"Almost, my little punkin pie."

"The doctors are taking good care of her," Rick said as he rubbed Carly's back.

"When are you coming home, Mommy?"

"Actually, I'm going home with all of you in just a little bit."

"Yay," Carly squealed. She ran over to George and grabbed his hand.

George was a handsome man of almost sixty. His voice was scratchy and made him sound like Clint Eastwood. He owned a successful real estate company and lived only about fifteen miles from Rick and Katie. The house they lived in was one of the first great finds George bought fifteen years ago. In this market, he was proud to say it was paid off and has kept most of its value.

Rick first started with his dad as an office manager until he was able to obtain his Realtor's license. Now Rick and George were partners, father and son, and George couldn't be more proud of his son. Things were rocky when he first found out about the pregnancy, but he had only to meet Katie to see that she was the right one for Rick. With his help, he knew they would make it.

"Papa, can you come with us?"

Rick looked at Katie, and she smiled and nodded.

"Yeah, Dad, why don't you come over and stay for dinner."

"We'd love to have you, George," Katie added. "And we can fill you in on the hunt for a new kidney."

"Alright," replied George. "But I get to do the cooking."

"Sounds great." Katie smiled.

CHAPTER 8

A hideously bright light shone through the small gap between Lucy's drapes and stretched right across her left eye. Turning her head from side to side, she attempted to escape the torturous beam. She rolled over on her stomach and put her face straight down into the pillow. She hadn't even realized yet that it was Saturday morning and she was already late for work. Voices started to drift in and out of her head. It sounded like two people talking, vaguely familiar. Was this some aftershock of last night's catastrophe? The voices started to become clearer, and she could make out some fragments: "…getting out of hand, needs to get some help…she won't talk to me." Lucy shook her head and then formed a taco against her head with the pillow.

"Don't worry, I already called your work," a quiet, sympathetic voice said.

Startled, Lucy flipped over on her back, put a hand across her face to shade the light, and saw Anne standing there.

"Anne? What are you doing here?"

"I stayed here last night."

"What—? Why?"

"Don't you remember what happened after Benny's show?"

Lucy ran her hands across her face and back through her hair. "What…Benny's show?" She searched her mind for an explanation. Images were flashing back into her brain as she attempted to put them together like a jigsaw puzzle. *The show, yeah, a Toyota, pills, a party, drinks.* It was coming faster now. *That guy...Kyle. Oh my God.*

"We found you lying on the ground outside."

Lucy turned her head away and closed her eyes. Just talking was painful. She whispered, "You shoulda just left me there."

"What?"

Lucy looked back at Anne and decided not to make this a pity fest. "I said...who found me there? You said *we*."

"Me and Benny. After we got back from the show." Her voice was calm and reassuring. "Remember, you left early? What happened to you?"

"I...don't remember," Lucy lied. "I think I had another drink in the back bar before I left. Maybe I just passed out or something. Maybe hit my head."

"Well, don't worry about anything right now." She reached for a glass of water on the side table. "Here, drink some water and rest. I called Amy's and told them you were really sick and in bed."

A knock at her bedroom door startled and surprised Lucy, and she looked up to see Benny in her doorway. Lucy sat up a bit, took a drink of the water, and set the glass back down.

"Hey, girl," he said. "How ya doing?" Benny walked over and sat on the corner of the bed.

"Well I'm doing just great!" she said sarcastically.

"You talk to her yet?" he said, looking back at Anne.

"She doesn't remember anything."

"So you guys were gonna give me a lecture, huh?" Lucy said defiantly. "I don't even know what happened. Maybe I got mugged or something. I'm lucky to be alive."

"Yeah, you are," Benny said sweetly, touching her face. "But you weren't mugged, Lucita. Your purse was still sitting right next to you. In this neighborhood, I don't think so."

"All I know is that my head is killing me." She scooted back down in the bed and pulled the covers up. "Thank you both for your help. I really do appreciate it, but do you mind if I get some rest? I just can't talk anymore." Lucy couldn't handle any more questions and was completely out of answers. She knew most of what had happened and why. It was a mistake. A big mistake. But there was no point in admitting it now. It was nice having Benny and Anne look out for her, but talking about it would be admitting that something was wrong. That she had a problem. She *wasn't* like her mother. She didn't need to drink, at least not every day. She just drank a little too much when she felt overwhelmed. That pills thing was just a fluke.

"Sure," they both said. Benny got up first and said in a parental tone as if she were about to be grounded, "But we'll talk later," and he walked toward the door. Anne followed behind.

"Oh yeah." Anne paused in the doorway. "Suzie said some guy named Rick was trying to get ahold of you. I guess the salon was the only number he had for you."

Lucy felt a chill wash over her entire body. There was only one Rick she could think of. Except, why would he be calling her? It could only be bad news. There was only one reason that she could think of, and she dreaded the possibility.

"Did you get a phone number?"

"Yeah, it's out here on the table," Anne replied as she walked into the other room.

"Who's Rick?" Benny shouted from the other room. Lucy detected a hint of jealousy in his tone, which made her wonder if he was concerned or maybe had other ideas. Knowing there was no way she could get any rest now, she got up and joined Anne and Benny in the other room.

Benny had already perched himself on the sofa, and Anne was standing holding a piece of paper.

"Here's the number."

Lucy took the paper and sat on the couch next to Benny. She was still wearing the outfit she had on last night, and of course she felt a chill as soon as she sat down. She reached across to the end of the sofa for a white, hooded sweatshirt that was draped over the edge. Lucy pulled the sweatshirt on and yanked it over her knees, which were tucked in and on the sofa. She sat for a few seconds and stared at the name on the paper.

"Well?" Benny said, looking at Lucy expectantly.

"What?"

"Who's Rick?"

"It's none of our business, Benny." Anne sat down in the chair next to the sofa. "Unless Lucy *wants* to tell us?" She smiled at Lucy, and both she and Benny stared and waited in silence.

"Rick is my sister's husband."

"Oh," Anne said, looking confused. "I didn't know you had a sister."

"That's because she doesn't tell us anything," Benny chimed in.

"Why do you guys care anyway?" Lucy said defensively as she got up from the couch and walked toward the kitchen.

"What do you mean, Lucy?" Anne said, sounding hurt. "We're your friends...or at least we're trying to be."

"Why?" Lucy repeated. "I don't do anything for you...except cause you trouble."

"Yeah, why?" Benny said under his breath.

Anne picked up a pillow and slammed Benny in the face. "Hey," he said, trying to deflect the blow with his hands. "I'm just kidding. Sure, you're kind of like an annoying little sister sometimes, but you're growing on me."

"You've done a lot for me." Anne tried to sound optimistic. "You help me with my aunt, and you're always scaring Dale away for me."

"You guys are being really nice, and I appreciate what you did for me…I'm just really tired from last night. And I feel like total crap."

"Want me to make you some tea or something?" Anne got up and joined Lucy in the kitchen.

"No…thanks. But I better call Rick back."

"We'll give you some privacy." Anne walked over to the couch and tugged on Benny's shirt. "C'mon, Benny. I hope you feel better, Lucy. And I hope everything's okay with your family."

"Yeah, feel better, Lucita."

Benny and Anne walked out the door. Lucy didn't move. She stood there thinking about Anne's words: *your family.*

My family? Lucy thought. She had only spoken to Katie once in five years, and she had no idea where her mother was. What kind of family was that? She thought about the time right before Katie had left home.

Lucy and Katie's relationship had evolved over the years from being sisters, to being as close as best friends, to being like mother and daughter. Although their daily lives were filled with strife and uncertainty, they always showed love to each other and even to their mother. Lucy taught Katie to be understanding and forgiving of their mother's problems even though at times she couldn't be forgiving herself. But in the end, Katie began to pull away from Lucy and rely more on Rick. To

Lucy, it was the ultimate betrayal. Everything she had done to keep the two of them safe and together, Katie threw right out the window by leaving.

Now Rick had called her…instead of Katie, which made Lucy angry. On the other hand, better to be angry at Katie for not calling than finding out there was another reason that Katie herself couldn't call—a horrible reason. She needed to find out now what was going on. No more stalling.

• • •

Lucy grabbed her purse off the table and pulled out her cell. Still holding the number, she hesitated just a bit and then dialed the number. Her face felt hot and her stomach was churning. She couldn't tell what was from last night and what was anxiety as the phone rang in her ear.

"Hello, this is Rick," he answered, sounding as if he were answering a business call.

"Rick, hi. It's Lucy."

"Lucy, I'm glad you called."

"Is…Katie okay?" Lucy asked, trying not to sound worried.

"Listen, Lucy, I didn't mean to scare you. Katie's fine, but she does need you. She was going to call you herself, but I wanted to give you a heads-up so you two could talk and get this part of it out of the way."

"What do you mean? What's wrong?"

"She's sick and needs a kidney transplant. They're asking us to get all our family and friends tested to see if they're a match to be a donor."

"A donor? You mean I need to give her one of my kidneys?"

"I don't know. We have to see if you're a match. We're asking everyone to get tested to increase our chances."

Lucy couldn't believe what she was hearing. She didn't understand how someone so young and seemingly healthy could be going through something like this. The thought of losing Katie flung her back in time and tore at her. She couldn't think straight and stopped listening to Rick.

"Lucy?" Rick said sharply. "Are you still there? Hello? Please, Lucy, Katie needs—"

"I'm sorry, I'm here." Lucy put her emotions in check, just as she had done all those years ago, and switched into guardian mode. "Where's my sister? I want to talk to her."

Rick told Lucy that Katie was asleep, resting after the recent episode that led them to the hospital. He explained that Katie was diagnosed with type 2 diabetes about a year after Carly was born. Then he updated her on what had happened over the last few years and the logistics of what was ahead. The conversation ended on a positive note, both feeling happy to have connected. Lucy was to expect a kit to take to her doctor, and Rick was to let Katie know to call Lucy when she felt up to it.

When she hung up, Lucy went over to a wooden end table next to the couch and opened the drawer. She pulled out a small square photo album, carried it into the next room, and climbed back into her bed. She opened the book to the first page. It was a picture her stepdad had taken of them at the beach just before his death. The girls were standing ankle-deep in the ocean with their backs to the camera. Linda and a twelve-year-old Lucy were on each side of little Katie, holding her hands. She remembered how Katie had squealed each time a wave came and they flung her up and over the splashing white wash.

Lucy's eyes puddled with water as she turned to the next page. Through her blurred vision, she made out herself and Katie painting on their matching easels with Katie wearing an oversized T-shirt as a smock. Back then Katie wanted to be just like Lucy. She wanted to do everything her big sister did and was so proud of her. Lucy sacrificed everything for Katie and didn't complain once about it. For all the responsibility she took on, she gave up just as much of her own life. Dances, boyfriends, parties—there was no time for those types of things.

Lucy was so hurt when Katie didn't need her any longer, leaving in an ungrateful rage. Did any of that really matter now? Katie needed her, and like any good mother, that was all that mattered. But how could she just push all those feelings aside? All the resentment that was never resolved? Somehow she would have to find a way. Lucy sat back against her pillow with the album pressed against her chest. She closed her dampened eyes and before long was sound asleep.

CHAPTER 9

....

After sleeping for the equivalent of almost an entire day, Lucy woke way too early for a Sunday morning. It would be a short day at Amy's since they were only open from twelve to five, but she had a lot to do. Her original plan was to work on the designs for the window display on Monday, since the salon was closed that day. But now she was expecting the test kit to arrive Monday and wanted to get the tests started right away. So today she would have to muster up the strength and get those creative juices flowing. After closing she would convince Mr. Chin and Amy to let her create her next *commercial* masterpiece. But first, she had something more important to do, something she hadn't done in years.

Opening the thick, heavy door to the cathedral, Lucy felt like she was stepping into an eclipse. It had been so many years that she had forgotten how dark and huge and beautiful the church was. There was a time when going to church was a comfort to her. She could see herself there, sitting in one big row, all squashed up between her family. Half the time she wasn't even listening to the sermon—she just loved being there, feeling safe in the heart of her family.

Ducking into one of the back rows, Lucy knelt down, then entered a pew. She noticed a white-haired man with a powder blue cardigan hanging loosely over his hunched back as he crept along the aisle. He took a seat three rows ahead, right across from a woman with a small boy. The woman had tired clothes and was shushing the curly-haired child for tapping his shoes on the echoing floor. The robed man at the altar turned for the shushing, not the tapping.

Lucy bowed her head, and before she knew it, ten minutes had passed. When she finally looked up, the old man had ambled out and had almost made it to the door. The boy was on his knees facing backward, staring right at Lucy. She smiled, he frowned. She frowned, he smiled. They both snorted. Lucy rose, causing an abrupt about-face from the boy. The flickering lights of the burning candles caught her eye as she made her way back down the aisle. Before pushing her way back into the light, Lucy turned for one last look at her younger, happier self.

• • •

"Lucy, so glad you're feeling better!" came Amy's cheery voice.

"Thanks, Amy."

"Listen, sweetie, please give out your cell phone. Mickey get mad you get too many personal calls."

"Oh, I'm sorry about Rick. Did he call again?"

"Rick? No Rick. Somebody name Kyle call for you." Amy shuffled away, leaving a fuzzy pink blur in her wake. Waving a hand at the cash register she said, "His number on the counter."

Lucy's face turned hot, and she felt her stomach drop like she was on a roller coaster. *How did he find out where I work? Did I tell him? Could he have noticed some of his pills were missing? Maybe he just wants to see if I'm okay since I left the party.* She walked over to the counter and saw the piece of paper with

Kyle's number on it. Once the feeling of shock and embarrass-
ment wore off, she felt a small surge of excitement. She planned
to call him back, but not until she got home.

The end of the day couldn't arrive soon enough. Lucy was
surprised that she was anxious to call Kyle. But whatever he
wanted, he would have to wait. Lucy's vision for the store's window was going to get its fighting chance tonight after work. She
would convince them that the entry to the store needed a fresh
new look. It was too bad she didn't have some fancy graphics
program to do mock-ups and print them out. Old-fashioned
drawing on paper would have to do. It got her other jobs, so
she was at least optimistic.

Sitting at the counter finalizing the receipts for the day,
Lucy felt relieved that Mickey had called to say he'd be late.
She did not want to do this in front of the two busybodies. Kim
wouldn't say anything, but Suzie would definitely add her two
cents. They were both finally ready to walk out, and Suzie shot
a final command at Lucy: "Don't forget to reschedule my ten
a.m. on Wednesday, Lucy. I don't want Mrs. Wallace getting
mad at me again."

"I said I would," was Lucy's only response even though
she really wanted to tell Suzie just what she could do with her
schedule. Behind the girls exiting, she could see Mickey walking
up. She sat around growing bored and frustrated waiting for
Mickey to do his regular routine. *Like he couldn't do that stuff
after I leave,* she thought to herself, sulking. Thirty minutes later,
all three were sitting on the front area couch. She spoke more
professionally than usual and showed her design ideas as well
as the designs of other projects she'd done. Amy asked why she
hadn't mentioned her other projects before, but she knew the
answer. They both listened intently, giving Lucy her fair chance.

Lucy thought she even saw a slim smile from Mickey. But after about twenty more minutes, they both simply said they'd let her know. Lucy was a little disappointed, but that was how most things happened at Amy's. No decision was ever made lightly. For a moment, she had a feeling it would go her way. But then again, how often did things really go her way?

It was getting late, and Lucy had wanted to get out of there. She was dying to have a drink and just relax. Being professional and upbeat certainly took its toll. It was something that didn't come naturally; Lucy had to work at it. But it would be worth it to do what she loved and get paid for it. The fact that painting was one of the only things that had made her happy the last few years was abundantly clear to Lucy. There was nothing else.

Lucy said a formal thank-you, gathered up her things, and headed out the door. Her hands were full with her designs, her purse, and an empty cup she was drinking from; Mr. Chin didn't want any trash left behind at the end of the night. After looking around to make sure she had not forgotten anything, Lucy crossed into the parking lot and headed to her car.

The sun was starting to make its way down, and in the distance she could see a car parked right next to hers that looked vaguely familiar. There was a man standing next to it, and it looked as if he was looking right at her. Lucy said aloud to herself, "Great, I wonder what the hell this guy wants." *Better not be money,* she thought. The ironic part about that was Lucy actually did help out strangers from time to time. To casual acquaintances, she might appear cold and uncaring, but Lucy had a soft spot for those in need. For some, those types of people seemed to fade into the scenery. But for Lucy, they popped out like vivid 3-D images in a movie.

As she got closer, the vagueness of the man became more evident, and the car she could tell was a black 4Runner. Her mouth went instantly to cotton. She was so nervous she couldn't tell if it was from fear or excitement. She had no choice. He had already seen her. Her best bet was to just walk right up and act casually.

"Well if it isn't Cinderella," Kyle yelled when he thought she was within earshot.

She didn't say anything, but just kept walking, shifting her load from one arm to the other. When she reached their cars, she smiled as she passed him and headed straight for her back side door. "Hi."

Kyle followed her and attempted to assist in getting her things into her car. "Let me get that." He reached for the back door and pulled it open. Lucy set the designs on the edge of the seat, pulled up her purse that had slipped down her shoulder, and slammed the door.

"I'm surprised to see you," she said, turning around to face him.

"Why, because you forgot to leave me a glass slipper?" he grinned.

He was better looking than she remembered, and his smile was kind of crooked and cute. "Well…yeah."

She walked around him to the driver's side door and stood as if she were waiting to get in. She wondered what he could possibly want after being ditched at that party. "So…how'd you find me?"

"That's it? You take off on me, and then I track you down and that's all you have to say?" His tone sounded more like a parent than a jilted boyfriend.

"Look, I'm really sorry about the other night. I wasn't feeling well, so I left." Instant lying. She hadn't needed to do it in a while, but it came back easily.

"Is that standard protocol for you? Just take off and don't say good-bye?" It was obvious to both of them he was just baiting her now.

"I didn't want to ruin your evening…with your friends."

Feeling uncomfortable after a few seconds of silence between them, Lucy yanked her keys from her purse, readied the appropriate key for the door, and said, "Thanks for stopping by, but I really have to get going."

Kyle stepped in close to her and put a hand gently on her arm. "Wait," he said softly.

She lowered the keys in her hand and pulled her arm away, and instinctively he took a half step back and gave her a reassuring smile.

"I don't know why, but I really want to see you again," he said.

"Gee, thanks."

They both laughed, and she dropped her eyes away from his.

"That came out wrong." He shook his head and gave a little chuckle. "I just meant—"

She decided to let him off the hook. She didn't know why he was trying so hard, but he was. "It's okay, I know what you meant."

"Could we please give this one more shot? How about next weekend, maybe Friday night? I'd love to take you out to dinner." He stood just staring at her as if he would wait an eternity for her answer.

Lucy couldn't figure out why he would bother with her after what happened and the way she acted. At that moment, she didn't care. All she knew was that this guy with the gleaming white teeth and sparkling blue eyes was being nice to her and wanted to spend time with her. So she opened her purse, took out an old grocery receipt and a pen, and wrote down her number.

"This is my cell," she said, reaching out with the paper.

"Great!" He reached out to take the paper, grabbing ahold of her hand in the process.

"Why don't you call me on Wednesday or Thursday and we'll see about the weekend." She smiled and pulled her hand out of his. Then she got in her car and started it up, while Kyle was still frozen in his position.

"Bye, Lucy." He waved as she drove off, holding a foolish grin on his face. When her car was out of the parking lot, he pulled out his cell phone. Staring at the piece of paper, he immediately programmed the number in. He didn't want to take any chances with losing that paper. Kyle already planned to call her Wednesday after work as he knew he wouldn't be able to wait for Thursday. In his mind he had already mapped out their date and was looking forward to finding out what this girl was all about.

CHAPTER 10

....

Could there be anything more humiliating than sitting on that loud, crumply paper, wearing that hideous gown and wondering if it was okay that you left your socks on? It had been nearly three years since Lucy had been to the doctor, and it was all she could do to keep herself from hopping off that table and sliding on out of there in her slippery socks.

Of course she had not received any reminders in the mail about her annual checkup, she told her doctor's office when she called for an appointment. Given the length of time since she'd been in, and the importance of what was possibly to come, Dr. Carlson insisted on Lucy going in and talking with her about the situation. She would need a full examination in addition to all the tests.

Lucy told Anne and Benny the night before about her sister and that she needed to get tested. Anne offered to drive Lucy to her appointment, and for once, Lucy felt like she wanted to accept an offer for help. The testing itself was no big deal, but the whole idea of what this all meant was just too much to handle alone. In the waiting room, she filled Anne in on some of the details of her family life. Since they had to squeeze her into the schedule, the two had plenty of time to talk. Lucy even let it slip about her possible date with Kyle. Opening up had always been difficult for Lucy, but with all of this mental and emotional stress, she just couldn't hold it back any longer.

"Oh my God!" Anne whispered and accompanied it with her mini claps. "That's awesome."

Lucy took a quick glance around to see if anyone was looking.

"I'm not really sure why I gave him my number. Apparently we went to school together, but I don't really remember."

"What's he like? Is he cute?"

"I guess so." Lucy shrugged. "I'll tell you more when or *IF* we go out."

"If!" Anne said a bit too loudly.

"Shh." Lucy looked around embarrassed and noticed the nurse standing in the doorway.

"Lucy…Lang," the nurse announced.

"We'll talk about this later," she said quietly as she got up from the chair.

"You're going!" Anne broadcasted as Lucy walked off.

With the only magazine in the room being a parenting book, Lucy grew bored. She was on her second round of reading the posters on the wall when she suddenly began to appreciate what her sister was going through. The uneasiness she was feeling was nothing compared to what Katie must be enduring. Being in those cold rooms, away from your cozy home, not knowing what was going to happen, worrying about Carly—they were all things Katie had to deal with regularly. Lucy could feel the struggle within her heart. She hoped that one day her feelings of love and concern would win the battle over hurt and anger. She wanted to understand what Katie was going through back then, but she couldn't. Lucy had never experienced true love, and she certainly didn't know what it was like to be pregnant.

Though she did understand what it was like to be a mother. She could still hear Katie's words during their final argument before Katie left.

"You're always trying to fix things! You can't fix this, Lucy!" Katie had shouted, holding her stomach. "It's done! And now we're trying to do the best we can to make it right."

"I just don't know if it's the right decision to leave. I can only help you if you stay."

"It's not *your* choice; it's mine and Rick's."

Feeling powerless and hurt, Lucy had said, "Do you even realize the sacrifices I've made to take care of you? I should be graduating from college right now, but instead I'm here. I've done my best to do what's right for you, and I'm not going to stop now!"

"I didn't ask you to be my mother. I have a mother."

"Yeah? Well where is she? And when was the last time you went to her for something, anyway? I'm the one who helped you with your homework, who talked you through all those tough times at school…and dealing with Mom."

"Well now I need to start making my own decisions. And maybe if I'm not around, you can finally get a life." Katie picked up a duffle bag that was sitting on the floor next to the couch. "I'm going to Texas with Rick, and we're going to have this baby. All I need right now is Rick." She'd walked out the door and didn't look back.

Lucy had stood staring at the door. That last comment had been like a knife through her heart. How could she have said Lucy needed to get a life? Katie was her life. She stood, hoping that Katie would come back, but knowing that she wouldn't. There had been other fights, other times Katie had stormed out, and she always came back. They would both apologize, then share a pint of Cherry Garcia while watching *Gilligan's Island*. That was Katie's favorite show, and they had all the old seasons on DVD.

The odd part of that memory was that Lucy had no recollection of where her mother was on that day. Probably because it really hadn't mattered at that point. All that mattered was that she felt so alone and helpless. A feeling that Lucy hadn't been able to shake all these years. Nothing had been able to fill the void left by her shattered family.

Now both Lucy and Katie were vulnerable and needed a way out. Lucy had prayed earlier for her sister to make it through this. She had hoped that she could help in some way. Even if she was not a match, she had to do something. Lucy planned to call Katie later that afternoon to let her know she had gone to the doctor. She hoped that just hearing Katie's voice would make her feel more at ease.

"Good afternoon, Lucy," Dr. Carlson said as she entered the room holding Lucy's file. She seemed especially young for a doctor. She had short brown hair that almost looked like a man, yet was very fashionable.

"Hi, Dr. Carlson."

"Well I'm glad you finally decided to come in. I know this isn't the best of circumstances, but we'll take a good look at you first and make sure everything's okay, and then we'll run the tests. Sound good?"

"Yep."

Dr. Carlson sat down in the chair next to Lucy and read the chart results from the nurse's preliminary checks. "Looks like your blood pressure's a bit low; nothing to be concerned about."

Dr. Carlson proceeded with the rest of the exam, including a gynecological exam, during which there was a bit of small talk. She asked Lucy about her sister and preached about the importance of regular checkups for Lucy. Then Dr. Carlson confirmed with Lucy everything they'd be looking for in terms of being a match for Katie. They would need to check blood and tissue type, general health including physical and mental, and of course health of her kidneys. Lucy had received all the information with the kit but didn't end up reading it all at the time. Talk about not doing your homework. Now she felt incredibly overwhelmed by it all and was concerned about some of the requirements.

"Are you okay, Lucy?" Dr. Carlson asked when she noticed the look on Lucy's face.

"I'm fine," Lucy replied. "It's just a lot of information. I didn't realize—"

"Are you sure this is what you want to do? It's a very big decision—there's a lot to consider."

"Actually, there's nothing to consider. I would do absolutely anything to help my sister. If I'm a match, I won't hesitate at all."

"That's nice to hear. I'm sure your sister feels very lucky to have you."

"I'm not sure about that. We actually haven't spoken to each other in years."

"Well, maybe this will bring you back together." Dr. Carlson smiled at Lucy, closed her file, and stood to leave.

"Can I ask you a question?" Lucy asked a bit hesitantly.

Dr. Carlson simply nodded and gave a, "Mmm-hmm."

"What if I'm a match, but I haven't really been taking care of myself for a while? What will happen? I mean, can I still donate?"

"Oh, well you don't have to be concerned about that now. Why don't you wait to see what the results show. Anyway, if you are a match, the process could take a while. And if there are some lifestyle changes you can make, Lucy, there's no reason you shouldn't start doing that now."

Lucy nodded as if she were a child being directed by an adult. "Okay."

"It will just be a minute, and a nurse will take you to another room for some tests," Dr. Carlson said, moving toward the door. "Take care, Lucy. We'll see you soon."

CHAPTER 11

Katie stared at the computer screen on her laptop, reading over the last few sentences she'd written. *I can't believe how amazing you are. Right now your favorite game is poker, and you love deuces wild. You are so smart, Carly Jean. BTW, you lost your first tooth yesterday.*

This was what made Katie feel at peace. It was what made her forget about what she was going through. She started Carly's journal when she was just eight months old. Katie had two reasons for doing this. One, she didn't want to forget a single moment of the precious gift she had been given. That's also why she was always taking pictures. The other reason was she wanted to be able to give it to Carly when she was older. Katie herself had very few memories to enjoy. The best times were when she was much younger. There were a couple of unfinished photo albums, but it was difficult for her to put the pieces together.

There could be one more advantage to having this documented keepsake for Carly as she got older, but that was something Katie did not want to think about. And although Rick thought about that in the back of his mind, he never brought it up.

Katie continued typing and then paused for a moment. Usually at some point she would hear tiptoeing little feet trying to come in for a peek. Katie always told Carly it was a surprise and she had to wait until she was older. This time the feet she heard were louder and much heavier. Coming from around the corner, Rick entered the room. He walked over to the bed where Katie had the computer balanced on her crisscrossed legs.

"Hey," Katie said. She looked up from her writing with a cheery smile.

"Hey, babe." Rick walked over to the bed and leaned over, then gave her a quick kiss on the lips. "Writing about our little genius again?" He sat down in a chair next to the bed, sliding himself all the way down with his long legs stretched out as if he were settling in for a while.

"Of course." She stopped typing and set the computer to the side. "I just wrote about her tooth and how cute she was when she spit it into her hand."

"*You're* cute," Rick said. He looked sweetly at her.

"What?" she asked, a little embarrassed.

"You love her so much."

"Yeah?"

"It's just cute that's all. You were just beaming when you were talking about her."

"So I'm proud and excited about our daughter."

"That's why you are such a great mom. And that's why you deserve a whole day to yourself." He sat up, reached into his pocket, and pulled out a small, square box and handed it to Katie. "Happy Mother's Day."

Caught totally off guard, Katie said, "Oh my gosh." She took the box in her hand and laughed. "I totally forgot. Thank you so much." She opened the box and found a gold heart locket on a chain. The front of the heart had two gems embedded in it, a ruby for her birthstone and a clear diamond for Carly's. "I love it!"

"Open it up."

Katie wedged open the locket with her fingernail and revealed a tiny picture inside. It was her favorite shot of her holding Carly in the backyard when she was just a few weeks old. Katie's eyes welled up, and a couple of tears escaped down her cheek. She held the locket by the chain in one hand and reached out with both arms to Rick.

"You're the best, you know that?" She held on tight for a few more seconds and then released him and said, "Let me put it on."

"Want me to do it?"

"I got it," she said, reaching behind her neck and clasping the necklace together.

"It looks great on you."

"Thank you." She sat up straight and sported a proud smile as if modeling a new dress. About a second later the smile faded some. "Hey…it's Mother's Day."

"Yeah?" Rick said. He looked confused.

"So where's my special girl then?"

"Well, she had a little plan of her own." He pointed toward the window behind her where the blinds had been just slightly open. "She said she would be here in a minute."

Katie turned to look out the window and saw Carly in the backyard. She was holding a combination of flowers and weeds in her hand and was sitting on a short brick wall rummaging through a plant with her hand. Katie enjoyed the moment and then fought hard against the unpleasant thoughts that often seeped into her brain. She had worked hard over the years to savor every memory and take each day as a blessing. That was getting tougher now that her situation was getting worse. She turned back to her husband, her rock through it all. "Am I doing the right thing? Not just for me, but for you…and for Carly?"

"Yes. *We* are doing the right thing." Rick got up and sat on the small space on the side of the bed next to Katie. "I thought we both agreed that dialysis was running our lives. It's just too much for you to take. It's too much for anyone. And like Dr. Brady said, it's not being as effective now."

"I know you're right." Katie turned to her side facing Rick and scooted right in and under his arm. That was a place she felt safe. His arm landed tight around her for the finishing touch. "I'm just scared of the surgery, let alone the thought of not finding a match. There're just so many things to consider and so many things that could go wrong."

"Let's just worry about one thing at a time. That's why we're doing it now. So we have the time to find someone…and even if we don't, you will be on the list. But I have a really good feeling we're going to find someone. Hand me your computer for a sec." He took his arm from around her and pushed himself upright. "I've got something to show you."

Rick put the computer in his lap and double-clicked the icon for the Internet. After a few more clicks, he arrived at his destination.

Katie looked over his shoulder interested and engaged, and when he stopped clicking and started typing she said, "What? You said you would never join one of those sites."

Rick entered his e-mail and password and hit enter on the keyboard. "Check it out, babe." He made a sweeping motion with his hand as if he were a model on a game show. "We already have thirty-four friends. And some have already agreed to get tested and will give us all their updates through status postings."

Katie was speechless and stared at the screen with a wide-open mouth. She wrapped her arms around Rick's neck and gave him a kiss on the cheek. "I can't believe you did this."

"I know, I'm a genius." He turned his head and looked directly in her eyes. For a few seconds neither moved nor spoke. They did not need words, for at that moment they both knew they were thinking the same thing. Together they could make it through anything. Rick laid his arm across her hip and gave her a long, gentle kiss. The moment could not have been more perfect, and then, suddenly, they felt a cannonball land on the bed.

"Happy Mother's Day, Mommy!" Totally unaware of her unfortunate timing, Carly thrust the flower/weed bundle right up to Katie's face.

CHAPTER 12

"Dude! What are you doing?" Kyle's brother Alex asked as he looked over Kyle's shoulder. Kyle was sitting at the kitchen table looking through his yearbook. Alex sat down next to his big brother and leaned in. "What's up, bro?"

"Oh, hey, Alex," Kyle said, not even looking up with his greeting. It was late morning, and Alex was wearing navy blue sweat bottoms and a white undershirt.

"Uh…hello?" He stretched out the "o" sound.

"What?"

"What are you doing?"

"What does it look like I'm doing? I'm looking at my yearbook."

"Yeah, but why?" Alex reached across the table for the opened box of cereal and carried it over to the counter. His hair was a shade darker than Kyle's sandy locks, and it always seemed to have that *I don't care* look to it. With his eyes still on his brother, he reached back and grabbed a bowl from the cupboard. He'd already made himself right at home though he had only been staying with Kyle for three days. Stuck with a giant student loan and no job prospects, and not wanting to live with their parents, Alex had asked Kyle if he could move in "for a while." Kyle wasn't too worried about what that meant.

The two got along well enough, as far as brothers go, and Kyle was actually looking forward to a little change in his life. He himself would admit that things had been pretty mundane as of late.

"Just wanted to see what someone looked like back then." Kyle flipped through the pages, carefully combing each side, then finally stopped and pointed to a photo. "And there she is." He skimmed his hand across the top of his hair, ran it down around his head, and then rested it under his chin with his elbow balanced on the table.

Alex set the cereal box down, did a side hop around the counter, and slid perfectly into the chair. "Who is she?" Alex always had women on his mind, but those days there wasn't much else, so he was game for a little female intrigue.

"Lucy Lang," Kyle said with his finger and his gaze still on the picture.

"Not bad. So what's the story?"

"No story...yet."

"There's always a story."

"Not for you, little bro." Kyle gave Alex a little puppy pat on the top of his head.

"C'mon, is that all I get?" Alex sighed. Then he got up and went back to making his breakfast. "I hate it when you do that."

"Do what?" Kyle asked defensively.

"You dig through all that crap in the garage to find your yearbook to look up some chick and there's no story? You gotta give me something. Did you guys hook up or what?"

"I really just met her a couple of weeks ago, but I plan to ask her out."

"Plan to?" Alex grabbed a few pieces of cereal and popped them in his mouth. "Is that a long-range plan?" he asked sarcastically. "C'mon, bro, what are you waiting for? You worried about Shannon?"

"Definitely not. Shannon has been over for months."

"See, you never tell me anything." Alex walked over to the table with his cereal and gave Kyle a smack on the back before sitting back down. "We're roomies now, bro. We gotta tell each other crap like that."

Kyle smiled and appreciated his brother's pushiness. He didn't mind that he was the one who was supposed to be giving the advice since he was four years older. Charm was Alex's biggest asset. Two inches shorter than Kyle, his five-foot-ten frame was pretty solid. He had about eighty percent of Kyle's looks but a hundred and ten percent more personality. Neither was jealous of the other, and Kyle didn't mind benefitting from Alex's talent for getting what he wanted.

"Now let me tell you something. Get on the horn right now and give her a call."

"This girl is different though. I already called her once, and she hasn't called me back yet."

"Oh, so you mean she's a bitch?" Alex said with a sly smile. "You have been known to be attracted to those."

"Shut up, man." Kyle got up from the table and carried his bowl to the sink. He washed the bowl and spoon sufficient enough to be clean, but he still placed it in the dishwasher—a habit he'd learned from his mother. He leaned up against the counter and pulled his cell phone out of his pocket. "There's just something about her. I don't know what it is yet, but I can't stop thinking about her."

"Well, there you go. Let's go pick out a ring."

"You're an ass!" Kyle said more slyly than with anger. Alex was lucky Kyle was in a good mood since that comment should have landed him a backhand on the neck. He knew this was a sore subject, and sometimes he pushed things too far.

Kyle's three-year engagement to a girl he met in college ended with her cheating with his then-roommate Michael. They met their sophomore year at UCLA, and Kyle was happy to finally be dating someone who was more driven than he was. They were engaged the next year, and both agreed they should wait until they graduated to get married. After another year passed and Kyle was still stalling, Shannon became frustrated, and while Kyle was out of town at a recruitment fair, she sought comfort with his roomie. There'd been no other serious relationships since then, and no roommates to boot, until now.

"Well, I'm outta here." Alex jumped up and headed for the door, grabbing a banana as he passed Kyle. "You keep staring at that phone. Maybe you can send her a message with your mind."

This is so stupid, Kyle thought to himself. She must have had a good reason for not calling him back. He should just give it another shot, and if she wasn't interested then fine, end of story. He punched in the number, hesitated for just a second, and then hit the green send button.

CHAPTER 13

Every time the phone rang, Rick and Katie both wondered if it was her doctor with news about a donor. It had been several weeks since they made the decision, and they were nearing the end of their search. No possible matches had turned up from Rick's small but dependable family, or from their close friends and neighbors. Even some of the local Realtors that Rick and George knew got tested. Her doctor had told her not to get discouraged because there was plenty of time, and she was still on the donor waiting list. But somewhere inside, Katie sensed that she could have less time than they originally thought. She knew her body, and in the last few months she just didn't feel as good as she should have.

It was about seven thirty, and Rick was loading the dishwasher while Katie was helping Carly with her bath. Actually, she was pretending to be organizing the sink area since Carly insisted she could do it herself, but Katie didn't want to leave her alone. The phone rang, and only Rick heard it; he picked it up after the second ring. Dr. Brady said he was working late and finally got to his afternoon messages, which brought some incredible news. Rick couldn't get off the phone fast enough and raced to the bathroom.

"You're not going to believe this," Rick announced, standing in the doorway.

Katie, kneeling down next to the bathtub, just stared at Rick. Carly was trying to gather up the last of the faded bubbles in the tub.

"What, Daddy?" Carly said for her mother.

"Well, it's not a hundred percent yet, but it looks like Aunt Lucy is Mommy's match!"

Katie still didn't move. The news was taking some time to register in her brain. She was supposed to be happy, relieved. "Wow," she finally said anticlimactically.

"This is great news." Rick knew she'd need some convincing at first. "Look, babe, your sister is the one…and you need to just forget about all that other stuff. This is incredible!"

"What other stuff, Mommy?"

"Oh…well Aunt Lucy and I didn't always get along so well. Remember, I explained that to you before."

"Oh yeah." Katie scooped up some bubbles and made a pile on top of her head. "Look at my crown!"

Rick grabbed Katie's hands and pulled her up. He wrapped his arms around her waist and lifted her into his hug.

"C'mon, baby, let's just be happy with what we've got."

"You're right. I'm sorry, babe. I'm sure everything's going to work out. And yes, I am happy." Her voice sounded as if she were reading dialogue from a script.

"Yeah, you sound ecstatic." He let her down but still held her waist.

"Does this mean Mommy's going to get better?" Carly interrupted.

"There's a good chance now, sweetie." Katie looked at Rick with a genuine smile. "Seriously, I'm happy. How could I not be?"

"Yay! I'm happy too!" Carly threw both her hands in the air, flinging water that splashed onto Katie and Rick.

. . .

Lucy felt a soft tap on her shoulder and turned to the elderly woman sitting two chairs over from her. The woman was trying to get her attention, but Lucy hadn't heard her, given that she was lost in the therapy of her iPod. Music was like medicine to her, and when she had both ears connected, eyes closed, she could usually free herself, even if for a few moments, of the loneliness and regret she felt. But this time she was ingesting the news that, so far, all the tests she had taken indicated that she would most likely be a match for her sister Katie. And once confirmed locally, she would need to go there for final confirmation and eventually the surgery that would save her sister.

"Excuse me, but your phone…it's ringing." The woman wore a white fuzzy sweater that matched her hair. She pointed to Lucy's cell perched upon her purse in the seat between them.

Lucy pulled out one earbud and let it dangle. It took a second to realize what the woman was saying until she heard the faint buzzing of her cell phone. She had put it on silent when she arrived at the doctor's office for her psychological evaluation.

"Oh, thanks." She fumbled with the phone and was able to hit accept just before the last ring sent the caller to voice mail. The old woman smiled, content with herself.

"Hello?" she said quietly. She looked around to see if anyone was annoyed by her answering the phone, even though there were only two other people in the room. The receptionist was the only one to look up, but just for a second.

"Hey, Lucy, it's Kyle."

There was a minor delay, so Kyle repeated, "Kyle Benson, remember me from the—"

"Of course I remember you. I gave you my number."

"Yes, you did." His voice sounded friendly yet put off. "That's why I called you last week."

"Oh…I'm really sorry." Lucy got up from her chair and walked to the open doorway where she could stand and still listen for her name. "Things have been kind of crazy lately."

"Sorry to hear that. Is this a bad time?"

"Actually…it kind of is," said she apologetically. The old woman watched her and smiled. Lucy wondered why she wasn't looking at a magazine or even watching the TV. She wished she could be that relaxed and patient.

"I can call you back later?" His voice stuttered and strained, but he said what he thought she wanted him to say.

"Well, the thing is…that I'm right in the middle of something and it's going to take a while. And actually…I should probably say that right now I really don't have the time to—"

"Eat?" he interrupted her.

"Eat?" she repeated in confusion.

"Yeah. I mean I know you've got a lot going on, but everyone's gotta eat, right?" His words were spilling out fast, hoping that she wouldn't be able to get a word in to say no. "We could meet somewhere for lunch or dinner…or breakfast. I just thought…well…you gave me your number, and I really—"

"Okay!" she jumped in abruptly. "How about Friday night?" She wondered if the old woman just gave her a nod of approval or if she had imagined that.

"Uh, yeah, great!"

"I'll text you my address later tonight. You want to pick me up at seven?"

"Sure, that's great, Lucy. I'm really looking forward—"

Noticing the woman behind the counter waving her over, she hurriedly said, "Oh, I'm sorry, gotta go!" She walked toward her holding up a finger. "Let's work out the details later. Bye," she said as she closed her phone. "Sorry about that," Lucy said as she arrived at the counter. She felt bad about cutting Kyle off, but she did not want to be a problem today. As much as she dreaded going, she was fortunate to get an appointment. They'd agreed to fit her in at the last minute due to her particular circumstances.

Lucy had hoped the meeting wouldn't be anything like her experiences with the school counselor. Mr. Anderson drilled her like a witness in a Supreme Court trial. Lucy figured the school must have had some idea how bad things were at home, and he was just trying to get some information. "I have nothing to say to you," she would tell him time after time. Mr. Anderson used words like "loner" and "withdrawn" and told her she was "much too smart for the grades she was getting." She wasn't about to trust him. She couldn't trust anyone. She just sat there staring at the picture on the corner of his desk: Mr. Anderson, his lovely blonde bride, and two little girls, both in matching lavender dresses.

Today she would play the part of the loving, concerned sister. Lucy knew what they were looking for, and she would deliver. She had to. If she didn't show that she was sure about her decision, that she was a perfectly sane person, they may decide she couldn't donate to Katie.

"No problem. I have one more paper for you to fill out." She handed Lucy a clipboard with a paper attached to it. The woman's long blue nails clicked against the board, and Lucy cringed. They were tacky and reminded her of some of the type of work Suzie did for her clients.

"Thanks." Lucy took the clipboard and went back to her seat.

She finished the last paper and gave it back to the receptionist, who repeated her standard, "Thanks, it'll be just a few minutes." Lucy remembered her saying that to the fuzzy-haired woman about half an hour ago, but she was still there. Returning to her seat, Lucy spent the next half hour listening to her iPod, doodling on an old grocery list that was in her purse, and watching CNBC talk about the immigration situation. She wondered why they had such dry and depressing stuff on the TV given the mental state of some of the people waiting in the room. It was about fifteen more minutes before the patient door opened again. In the last few minutes, Lucy grew stressed. For only a brief moment, she actually thought about walking out. She had come so far. She had to see it through. So when the nurse called her name, she gathered her things and headed for the door.

CHAPTER 14

The need to let off some steam led Lucy to Kelly's after her appointment—a semi-regular destination spot for her. It was where she went when she couldn't be alone but didn't want to be with people either. Kelly's was a small Irish tavern with a few casual tables and a bar, which is where Lucy preferred to make her perch.

She walked in the double-door entrance and as usual scoped out the bar area to see if it was worth staying. The longer side of the L-shaped wood bar was optimal so Lucy could have her back to the tables. It was only a little after four, so most of the tables were empty. She noticed only one man sitting at the bar, but regrettably he was right smack in the middle. She'd have to choose either end and decided on the left side against the wall. As she walked toward the bar, she noticed the bartender look up at her, causing the customer to follow his gaze. The man looked to be about in his mid-fifties. He wore khaki pants and a polo-style golf shirt, and he had a pale face with light eyes. He gave a nod and raised his glass as Lucy passed.

"Good afternoon," the bartender said in a mellow voice. It was as though he had a sixth sense, to read a person's mood and respond with the particular tone of his greeting. He slapped a napkin down in front of Lucy as she took her seat. She recognized the bartender as the young, scruffy-faced guy who had served her before, but she wasn't sure he recognized her. Maybe he knew she wasn't looking for friendly banter. "What can I get ya?"

Lucy could feel her neighbor's eyes on her and wondered how many drinks he'd had. Guys like that didn't faze her, but she wasn't in the mood to deal with some drunken idiot. Over the years, she had developed a sort of loser radar, especially since that was mostly the type of men that she encountered around her mother.

Once when she was seventeen, her mother was supposed to be taking her and Katie to stay with one of Linda's friends for the weekend. She wouldn't say why, only that she had to leave town for a couple of days. On the way they stopped at a house. "Just some guy I know," Linda explained in the car. Said she had to pick something up before her trip. Katie sat on Lucy's lap for about fifteen minutes while Linda was back in another room. When they started to hear arguing, Lucy got nervous. They could hear the man calling Linda names and telling her to get out. Lucy sent Katie to the car, and in a wave of panic, she took her mother's car keys, forty bucks from the guy's wallet, and ran out the door. Lucy drove them back home since she didn't know where Linda's friend lived. She couldn't believe she actually did that. The bizarre part was that Linda came back a few days later and there was never a word spoken about it.

"I'll have a Crown and Coke," she said to the bartender, finally snapping out of it but without making eye contact. Beer and wine were fine for home, but she needed something a little more effective. A sudden noise, and she made the mistake of looking to her right and met eyes with the man.

He raised his glass again and said, "How's it going?"

Lucy smiled and turned away. She didn't want to give a false aura of friendliness. But the middle-ager didn't take the cue. He stood as if wanting to stretch his legs. Then he looked over at Lucy, cupped his napkin around his drink, and slid it across toward Lucy. She lifted her eyebrows and gave him a look that said, *Don't even think about it.* What could he possibly see in her anyway? No makeup, wearing faded jeans and a white long-sleeve shirt, not to mention drinking alone at bar.

The man slid his drink right back and immediately sat down. "Ookaay."

The bartender smirked as he brought Lucy's drink and set it down in front of her. "Here you go." Then he turned to the back counter and began drying glasses.

Lucy took a big sip of her drink, hoping to instantly drain the pressure from her brain. The last few weeks had finally caught up to her. Until now, she had basically been running on autopilot—forms, needles, exams had all been formalities. None of it seemed to be for any real purpose. She was going through the motions, full bore—until today. The psychological evaluation had really made all of it seem so real. Her mind was racing. She took another drink, this time almost finishing it. The second the bottom of the glass touched the napkin, she raised it again and finished it off. She sat still for a while, watching the bartender as he hung the last of the glasses he was drying. She could see his face in the huge mirror that hung on the back wall, and she slouched slightly to avoid seeing herself.

"Another?" he asked when she caught his eye in the mirror.

Lucy nodded in agreement, and he went to work preparing another drink. The door behind her opened and closed over the next twenty minutes, and the ensuing patrons filled in vacant tables. Lucy didn't take notice of the increasing volume of clinking dishes and glasses, and muffled conversations.

After her third drink, she started to feel guilty. This was not the effect she was seeking. The pain was supposed to be decreasing, not increasing. She tried to sort things out in her brain, but nothing was clear to her. *Why am I doing this?* she thought. *Is this how I help my sister? By saturating my kidney with alcohol?* But she wasn't just feeling guilty, she was angry too. Why did everything seem to fall on her shoulders? Why had she gone through all that with her mother and taking care of Katie, only to have Katie run out on her?

Now all of a sudden Katie needed her again. Lucy wasn't sure she could take seeing Katie again, taking care of her again. *I can't help her...because I can't help myself.* That was it. She finally realized that it wasn't just the feelings you would expect when a loved one was sick. Lucy was bitter and scared and frustrated. She remembered the days when she thought she couldn't go on. Now...she had to. She had no choice. That was a frightening thought.

Suddenly the room started to spin, and she felt like she couldn't breathe. Digging through her purse for some cash, Lucy stuck a pile on the counter. She needed some air and had to get out of there. On instinct, she looked for help from the annoying man at the bar but was confused that he was no longer there.

She walked around for about an hour before she finally decided to call Benny for a ride home. He didn't hesitate, knowing that was something Lucy just didn't do. Plus, he didn't mind a chance to be around her. Even though he joked about what a pain she could be, he found himself growing fonder of her, and Lucy sensed it as well.

In the car Lucy didn't say a word for a long time, and she was grateful Benny didn't ask any questions. She gazed out the window and was in such a trance she didn't realize that a single tear started to roll down her cheek. An old man on a bicycle watched her as they slowed to turn the corner. She took a deep breath and tried to hold it all in. She'd become an expert at that back in school when teachers used to ask what was wrong. At first she would cry and then make up some story about someone teasing her or a test or something. Eventually she had learned to control it. She would simply say that she was just tired. They were just about home when the dam burst. Lucy began to sob. Tears were flowing, and her chest began to heave. Benny looked over, startled, but he still didn't say a word. He didn't know what to do or say, but fortunately they were just about home.

In the parking lot, he reached for her, put his arm around her, and held her. They stayed still in that position. A salty wet spot formed on the corner of Benny's shirt, which didn't matter much since there was already a hot sauce stain from lunch. Lucy could not comprehend what was happening to her. Out-of-control emotions were not her thing. Could all this be about Katie? Was it just the illness? Maybe it was the first time in a long time that she had someone she could trust enough to let go. No matter what it was, it was all powered by frustration: terrible things that should never have happened, dreams that never came, love lost. Lucy felt lost.

When she finally reached the end and the storm was blowing over, she still remained on Benny's shoulder. It felt safe there. After a few minutes she lifted her head. "I'm sorry, Benny," she said. Her voice barely came to her.

"You don't have to say anything to me, Lucy." Benny rubbed her arm and brushed her hair from her face. He wished he could do something for her, but he knew it was up to her. "I'm here for you, girl." He tried to make his voice sound lighthearted. Looking into her big brown eyes was starting to take effect, and he worried that he wanted to kiss her. He resisted, knowing that would be a mistake. He didn't want to ruin things, but more than that, it was just wrong. You didn't take advantage of a crying girl.

CHAPTER 15

Even though Lucy still had thirty more minutes to be ready, she still felt like she was running late. Her bed looked like a discount table at the end of a big clothing sale. She had already tried on four outfits, and she was wearing possibility number five. She looked in the full-length mirror on her closet door and wondered what this outfit said about her. The first two choices were simply too outdated. They had been her standard "going out" outfits for about four years. The next one was a tight blue dress that just seemed way too desperate, and number four was a skirt and top that had a big stain right on the front of the skirt. She forgot that she had brushed up against one of her paintings a while back and could never get the spot out.

Walking over to her dresser, Lucy picked up her cell phone. She scrolled through her received messages and selected the last one from Kyle so she could double-check what he said about the restaurant. *Nice, but not too formal,* his message stated. She walked over and looked in the mirror one more time. She was wearing long black, non-pleated pants and a sleeveless black and lavender shirt. The pants touched the floor, but the black heels she just picked up to put on would bring the hem to just above the floor. She knew she would be cold in that outfit, but she didn't have a cute enough jacket to match, and the look was the priority over comfort. Just as she was about to slip on the first shoe, the doorbell rang.

"Shit!" Still holding her phone in one hand and the shoes in the other, she checked the time on her phone. She still had about twenty more minutes and was hoping to recheck her hair and the little amount of makeup she had put on. She swiftly shoved her feet into each shoe, turned her light out, and shut her bedroom door. Skidding past a mirror on the living room wall, she took a last look at herself and then opened the front door.

"Benny?" Her voice sounded surprised and stressed.

"Ooh...check it out, mama caliente!" he said in his best Mexican accent. He was trying to be funny even though he really did think she looked great.

"I'm sorry about the other day." Her voice trailed off as she walked away from the door and Benny followed.

"No worries, girl. You know you can always count on me."

Hearing that made her happy. She was starting to believe it.

"You got a hot date tonight, I see." He walked in a circle around her. "Who's the lucky guy? Hey, is it that Kevin guy you told Anne about?"

"What? She told you about that?" she snapped, sounding embarrassed. "Look, Benny, I don't want to be rude, but I don't have much time. He'll be here any minute."

"Hey, I'm just here being a good neighbor." He pulled an envelope from his back pocket and handed it to Lucy. "This was in my mailbox by mistake."

Lucy took the envelope and examined it.

"It's got your last name on it...but it says Linda," Benny said curiously while Lucy continued to stare at the letter.

"Did you just get this?" she asked when she noticed the postmark on the envelope.

"Uh…well, I've actually had it for a week or so."

"What? Why?"

"It looked like it was from a collection agency, and well, you know I'm used to getting those. I usually just pile 'em up on my desk. I didn't think to look at the name and didn't notice it until I was going through my stack and went to open it."

"Geez, Benny." She tossed the letter onto her kitchen table. "Well, I don't have time to deal with this now, but thanks for bringing it over." She walked over to the door and grabbed the knob. "I really need to finish getting ready."

Benny didn't move. "I know I'm being nosy now, but who's Linda? Is that your sister, the one who's sick?"

"She's my mother. She owes some money, and they don't have any contact information for her, so they're hassling me."

"That stinks, Lucy. So your mom is avoiding them, or she doesn't have the money? I know how that goes," he said, trying to sound sympathetic.

"My mom is avoiding everyone. I haven't seen or heard from her in over three years. I had to deal with all her crap then, and now I have to deal with this!"

"I'm sorry, Lucy." Benny walked over to her. "I didn't mean to get you all worked up again and ruin your…*date*." He reached out to give her a hug, and she accepted halfheartedly. "I shouldn't have asked," Benny said, rubbing her back just a little too low for her comfort.

With one of Benny's arms still around her shoulder, Lucy pulled open the front door and led him into the doorway. "It's okay, Benny. I'm fine…*really*. Thanks for coming over."

Just then Kyle walked up and was standing inches away from Benny and Lucy arm and arm.

"Oh, hi," Lucy said casually.

"Hi, Lucy." Kyle quickly stopped in his tracks to avoid running into them.

Benny took his arm off of Lucy's shoulder and reached out to shake Kyle's hand. "Hey, man, you must be Kevin."

"It's Kyle." He shook Benny's hand. "How's it going?"

"Good, man. I was just leaving." Benny sidestepped past Kyle and gave him a quick slap on the back. "You kids have fun tonight." Benny was halfway down the hall when he yelled, "Not too late, Lucita!"

"Sorry about that," Lucy said, embarrassed. "That's just a friend of mine who lives down the hall. Come in."

"You look great, Lucy," Kyle declared as he walked in and stood in the middle of the room. He had on khaki pants and a dark blue button-down shirt that had faint gold stripes running down the sides. She envied the color and smoothness of his skin even with the tiny bit of five-o'clock shadow. "I hope I'm not too early, Lucy."

Was it her imagination, or did he tend to say her name a lot when they were speaking? Either way, she liked it. There was something about the way he said "Lucy" that sent a charge right through her. Maybe it was due to the fact that she hadn't had many dates in her life and even fewer boyfriends. Most men didn't have a chance to make it to a second or third date.

"No, I'm totally ready." Lucy remained standing awkwardly at the door. "Just give me one sec." She walked by him close enough to leave a trace of her aroma. He knew it wasn't perfume, probably her hair, and almost instinctively he wanted to follow her.

"Great, I'll just wait here then." Planting his feet down, Kyle appeared to convince himself he was being totally cool.

In her room, she urgently picked up her purse and gave her hair a couple of flicks. She didn't want Kyle out there alone too long. She figured his place was probably a lot nicer than hers and definitely bigger. *Just try to have fun tonight,* she thought to herself. A good way to not be disappointed is to not expect too much. But as she walked back to the living room, she found herself hoping for more.

CHAPTER 16

Didn't he say, 'Nice, but not too formal'? Lucy thought as they walked through the door of Moretti's, an Italian restaurant. Even though her attire made her feel a little uncomfortable, Kyle's hand resting on the small of her back gave her an unexpected boost of confidence.

The hostess led them to a roomy, high-back booth in the back of the restaurant, which suited both of them just fine. Kyle wanted to feel alone with her, and she wanted to be away from the crowd. Kyle asked the server to start them off with a bottled Evian, which he courteously poured for the both of them, and then set down a bread basket. Along with the basket came a plate with an oil mixture for dipping the bread into.

"How do you feel about wine?" Kyle asked, gesturing to the extensive wine list.

"Sounds good," she responded as she took in the full atmosphere of the beautiful Italian décor. "Whatever you pick is fine with me."

After getting one last nodding approval from Lucy, he ordered a pinot noir. She enjoyed and appreciated his confidence, and she could tell that he liked the fact that she was easygoing. Unlike most of the high-maintenance women he'd probably dated before. Lucy sensed Kyle's eagerness to get to know her and wondered if she would be able to open up and let him see who she really was.

Lucy felt surprisingly good that night and made a mental note to enjoy the rest of the evening and not simply *get through it* as she tended to do when going out. Then, as she glanced around the room, something caught her eye. She noticed an elderly couple sitting at a table in the middle of the dining room. They had just sat down and were positioned right next to each other, close enough so their chairs touched. Lucy wondered if it was so they could actually hear each other or if it was because they wanted to be close. By the way they looked at each other when they spoke, she believed it was the latter. After a prolonged silence, she realized Kyle was watching her watch them. He was smiling and waiting for her to look over at him.

"You're very real, you know that?" he said with a genuine smile.

"As opposed to what, one of those plastic blow-up dolls?" Lucy said with a smirk.

"No, I didn't mean…hey, I'm definitely not that guy. I just meant that you're…very different from most of the women I've dated."

"Oh, so you've dated a lot of women, huh?"

"I wouldn't say a lot." Kyle shifted in his seat. "Wow."

"What?"

"You're not going to make this easy, are you?" He gave a tiny chuckle and shook his head.

"I didn't realize I wasn't." Lucy held her ground and kept eye contact with him.

Up to the challenge, he met her gaze and said, "You're very beautiful, Lucy." He reached out and placed his hand gently over hers as it rested on the table. "Ah, I got ya. So what have you got to say to that one?"

"I'll just say…thank you." Lucy slid her hand from beneath his and put it in her lap. "There's something else I need to say too, Kyle." She took a drink of wine and fiddled with her purse in her lap. "You seem like a really great guy, and I'm glad you asked me out…"

"Please tell me you aren't on the road to the 'let's just be friends' speech," he interrupted.

"No…I mean I do want to be friends, but I'm not sure how much more I can be right now. The thing is…I may be leaving town for a while."

"How come?" He took another drink of his wine, finishing off the glass to catch up with Lucy.

"Well, there's a very good chance that I'll be donating one of my kidneys to my half sister who lives in Texas."

"Are you kidding?" He laughed, his sparkling blue eyes fixated on her. She continued to amaze and fascinate him. Before she could answer, he took the wine bottle and poured them each another glass. "Well, are you pulling my leg here or what?"

"I'm totally serious. I've been going through all these tests, and so far it looks like I'm a match."

"Whoa, that's pretty amazing."

"Yeah…but it's also very complicated. They have to make sure you're physically and mentally sound, you know, to make such an important decision. You can't believe all the questions they ask. I mean it's my kidney, and I should be able to do what I want with it, right?"

"Uh, yeah. I guess I never really thought about it. So when do you know for sure?"

"Probably in a few days."

"Well, it's an incredible thing you're doing for your sister, but to be honest I'm not happy about the timing. I was really looking forward to getting to know you better."

"Then why don't we just make the best of tonight and worry about the rest later?" She lifted her glass to him and took a drink.

The remainder of the dinner was spent with each of them telling their life stories as quickly and painlessly as possible. Lucy tried to leave out most of the more depressing details, but she couldn't believe how much she told him. The more she spoke, the more impressed Kyle was with her. He made comments about her strength and compassion and loyalty—all characteristics he admired. But for Lucy, she didn't feel like those were accurate descriptions of her. On the other hand, she felt like a different person when she was around him.

Kyle was open about his previous engagement, but he focused more on his career and family. They laughed about their connection of having to take care of their younger siblings: her with Katie, and Kyle with Alex. Before they knew it, two hours had passed. They felt guilty about keeping the server, so Kyle left a twenty-five percent tip, and they left the restaurant.

• • •

"Thank you for extending the night with me," Kyle said as he opened Lucy's door. "I know we didn't really plan this, and neither of us is dressed for it, but I thought it was the perfect night for a walk on the beach."

They had both taken their shoes and socks off at the car. Kyle found a place to park where they wouldn't have to walk too far before getting to the sand. "Do you think you'll be cold?"

He shut her door after she stepped out. "I have a sweatshirt in the back if you want it."

Lucy chose fashion over comfort. "I'm fine," she answered. All she could think about was how good it felt to just be around someone and enjoy their company. As soon as they reached the sand, Lucy took a deep breath and took in the smell of the ocean along with all the beautiful memories that it brought. After a few steps, their hands brushed closely by each other's and Kyle grabbed Lucy's hand. It made her feel young and giddy, but at the same time she felt sad. This was something she hadn't done, or felt, in a very long time. She laughed to herself about how such a small thing could evoke such a range of feelings in her.

Kyle noticed her giggle and laughed along with her, obviously not knowing why. "What?"

"Nothing," she whispered.

Lucy figured it probably wasn't easy for Kyle to get used to her unexpected silences, but he was patient and told her he didn't mind. He was happy to watch her walk along, the low breeze bouncing and puffing her long curly mane. As much as they talked at the restaurant, there was quiet now, almost as if they seemed to be reading each other's minds. For the most part, Lucy looked straight ahead or out to the choppy ocean. A few times she looked up at him and smiled. They both seemed to be thinking the same thing—that they didn't want the night to end. But at the same time neither wanted to get too close. The uncertainty of what the next few weeks, or even months, held loomed over them like quiet rain clouds. Then suddenly, Kyle stopped and grabbed Lucy's other hand.

"You *are* coming back, aren't you?" His voice was quiet, and he searched her eyes for the answer.

"I hope so."

"I wish we knew each other back in high school."

Lucy laughed and shook her head. "No you don't."

"I guess we're both different people now." Still holding both her hands, Kyle pulled her in closer. "I just hope I get the chance to know you better."

Lucy looked down at the sand. "Me too."

Kyle released one of her hands and gently lifted her chin until he saw the moonlight magnifying her shimmering brown eyes. Lucy was completely focused on him, and that moment, for once her mind was free from what had happened in her life—her regrets, her disappointments. It seemed like an eternity before he leaned down to her and their lips finally met. With waves crashing toward them, they both knew this moment could only last in their memories. For Kyle and Lucy, only time would tell if they had a chance for anything more.

CHAPTER 17

"Scrambled okay for you, Lucy dear?" Mrs. Allen said from behind the kitchen counter in her apartment.

"I thought you said you were making waffles," Lucy replied from the couch in the living room.

"Oh, I am." Mrs. Allen turned to the counter behind her and pressed a timer button on a black waffle maker. "But I wanted to make eggs too. Since I couldn't get you over here for a nice dinner, I want this to be a special treat." She went to the stove, picked up a bowl of beaten eggs, and poured them into the warm pan.

"Please don't go to any trouble for me, Mrs. Allen." Fidgeting around on the dark green tweed couch, Lucy tried to find a spot that didn't itch her or have cat hair on it.

"Besides, Anne invited that nice young man Benny. I sent them out to get some tea right before I ran into you in the laundry room." She continued to work busily and cheerfully around the kitchen as if she were a line cook in a diner. "So you see, this is turning out to be quite a little party now that you're here."

"That's nice, Mrs. Allen. Thanks for inviting me." Lucy could see that having people around and feeling useful was what made Mrs. Allen happy. She knew better than anyone how incredibly lonely it could be without family in your life. Lucy scooted to the end of the couch to grab a closer look of a framed photo on a wooden end table. It was in one of those ancient-looking wood frames that looked like spray-painted gold. She recognized a younger Mrs. Allen standing next to a handsome man with salt-and-pepper hair. They were surrounded by half a dozen other people of varying ages all wearing Hawaiian shirts and leis.

"That was our twenty-fifth wedding anniversary," Mrs. Allen said, noticing Lucy studying the photograph. "It's one of the happiest memories I have from when my Stu was alive. There's nothing better than having all those that you love around you." Balancing glasses on a stack of plates, Mrs. Allen made her way to the table and set the stack down.

"Your family looks very nice." Lucy jumped up and walked over to the table. "Here, I'll take care of this." She had begun doling out glasses and dishes around the table at each seat when she heard her phone text alert. She reached into her back pocket and pulled out her cell. It was a text from Kyle. Just the thought of him brought a rush of overwhelming feelings that confused Lucy. She pressed the "view" button to read the short message: *Can't stop thinking about you.* She didn't even have time to consider what to say back before she heard the door open. Startled, she pressed the message away and jammed the phone back into her pocket.

Benny bounded through the door with his usual big smile and loud greeting. "Honey, I'm home!" He was holding one grocery bag, and Anne was behind him with another. They both walked over to the kitchen counter and set the bags down.

"What else did you get?" Mrs. Allen asked.

"We got some fresh strawberries to go on the waffles," Anne said, pulling them out of the bag.

"And we got some lightbulbs," Benny said, proudly holding up the package. "I noticed one of your kitchen lights was out."

"Thank you, Benny, you're such a gentleman." Mrs. Allen scraped the pan full of eggs out and into a big bowl.

Benny showed a mischievous smile to Lucy, grabbed a strawberry out of the basket, and popped it in his mouth.

"Okay all, let's start getting this stuff over to the table, and then you kids can have a seat."

All three worked together to get everything from the kitchen over to the table. There was a stack of waffles with a warmer over them, a bowl of eggs, the strawberry baskets, a big pitcher of juice, and the bottle of iced tea from the store. Once they were all seated, they simultaneously looked over at Mrs. Allen and waited.

"Well don't wait for me," she said, grabbing her coffee mug. "Dig in. I'm just getting my kick start for the day." She poured herself some coffee and spooned in a little sugar.

"Ladies first," Benny said, looking over at Mrs. Allen for approval.

"Suck-up," Lucy said under her breath while snagging a waffle and putting it on her plate.

Anne went for the waffles too and topped them with a few strawberries before adding the syrup. Benny went for the eggs first and poured himself some juice. Mrs. Allen brought her coffee to the table and sat down with the others. "So how's your sister, Lucy? Anne tells me she's ill with diabetes."

"She's doing fine, thanks. In fact, she is going to be doing much better pretty soon." Lucy peeked up from her plate to see if anyone caught on to her hint.

"Why, did they find a kidney donor for her?" Benny asked and then shoveled a pile of eggs in his mouth."

"Yes, they did."

"That's great news, Lucy!" Anne cheered.

"It's me." Lucy continued eating as if the news had been nothing to pause for.

"What?" all three seemed to say in stereo.

"So *you're* the match, Lucy?" Anne set her fork down and sat back in her chair.

"So far, I'm the only option, and I've decided to do it. They can't say a hundred percent until I get there, but looking at the tests I've done here, they're saying everything should be a go."

Benny finally swallowed and chimed in. "Wow, that's crazy." Then he went back to eating as if someone were waiting to clear the plates.

"But doesn't your sister live in Kentucky or something?" asked Anne.

"Texas. Fort Worth."

"So you just have your kidney taken out, and they fly it over there in one of those coolers?"

"No. I'm going to drive there and have the operation in the same hospital as my sister."

"All that way, by yourself? That doesn't seem safe. Why don't you fly?" Anne asked.

"I don't fly."

"I'm with you on that one, Lucy." Mrs. Allen held her coffee in one hand and stirred as she spoke. "I don't fly either. Just can't handle it anymore. Not since before Stu. But I agree with Anne. You, driving alone…" She shook her head. "That doesn't sound like the best idea."

"Why don't I drive you," Benny said suddenly as if a lightbulb had gone off in his head.

All three women looked at him as if waiting for further explanation.

"What? I was just offering." He turned to Lucy to speak to her directly. "I mean, my car is much more dependable than your heap, Lucy. I really wouldn't mind. Plus you know I have a flexible schedule."

"Thanks for the offer, but I don't know if that would work," she said, thinking it out in her head. "I'll need to be gone for a while…maybe a couple of weeks."

"It's no problem. And you know what, I got cousins in Dallas," Benny said, jabbing his idea out with his fork. "It's only about an hour away. I could take you to your sister's and then go back and stay with them for a while. They'd be so stoked to see me."

"Would I have to listen to your jokes the whole way?"

"Very funny, Lucita."

"Let me think about it?"

"Sounds like a plan," Mrs. Allen said as she finished her last bite of eggs. "Now finish up, you slowpokes, 'cause I got Bunco this afternoon."

Not hearing a word of what her aunt said, Anne stared aimlessly over her shoulder. "I want to go," she mumbled, still in a trance.

"You never wanted to go to Bunco before, sweetie," Mrs. Allen replied.

"No!" Anne shook her head into alertness. "I want to go with Benny and Lucy." She turned to the two of them. "Oh, it would be so fun."

"Here we go," said Lucy.

"Fine with me," Benny declared.

"Oh please, Lucy," Anne pleaded. "I haven't really been any-where, and I don't start nursing school until the fall." Anne got up from her chair and walked over between Benny and Lucy. "And since I already planned to give notice at work for school, it couldn't be better timing." Anne held her breath, put her hands up in prayer, and then stared at Lucy.

"I swear, if you two yell, 'Road trip!' and then high-five each other, you can forget the whole thing."

"Thank you so much, Lucy!" Anne gave her a hug around the neck. "Do you think your sister will mind if I tag along? Maybe I can help out, you know, since you'll both be having surgery."

"I'm not saying yes for sure," Lucy warned. "I'll talk to my sister and Rick, but I don't see why they would mind since I *am* saving her life."

Anne was done listening by that time and was already pac-ing the living room with wheels spinning in her head. "This is going to be so awesome," she said to nobody in particular. She seemed to be forgetting that the purpose of this trip was of a serious nature. To her it was an opportunity to do something that most people her age had already done.

From age fifteen to twenty, Anne Preston had worked for her father, Henry, in the family business located in Buena Park. It was a casual clothing store that sold mostly T-shirts and shorts, hats, and accessories. Anne loved being there and working with her dad, who had hoped she would one day run the business. Her good-natured ways made her agreeable to her father's plan, but the older she got, the more her heart was somewhere else.

Anne wanted to help people. Her true dream was to become a nurse, but she never had the heart to tell her father. Then, with the economic downturn, the store was struggling financially. Eventually, Henry had to sell the business. He and Anne's mother moved to Detroit so Henry could work for his brother at a used car lot. That left Anne and Henry's older sister, Mary, behind. Being the only two in the family still left in California, Anne and Mary Allen had grown close and formed a very strong relationship.

Lucy leaned back in her chair trying to get Anne's attention. "Anne, hello? Uh, maybe you shouldn't make such a big deal about this. Being on the road can be kind of boring."

Still on her own track, Anne shimmied back toward the table. "Oh...my...gosh! What if we stopped in Vegas on the way?"

"What?" Lucy exclaimed.

"Uh, that's slightly off our course," Benny remarked thoughtfully. "It's more direct if we head straight towards Arizona."

"Thank God." Lucy was surprised at Benny's knowledge and sense of direction, and she was starting to feel a little better about the whole thing. Maybe it would be a good idea to have a man along, even though she hated feeling so dependent. Anne, on the other hand, was a different story. Lucy didn't know how she felt about Anne going along, but it seemed to be too late now. One thing was for sure, though, it was bound to be interesting.

CHAPTER 18

Packing for a trip was one thing, but getting ready to spend countless hours trapped in Benny's Durango, alongside the cheerleader, was completely mind-boggling to Lucy. And that wasn't even taking into consideration the fact that she had to improve her lifestyle, let some strange doctor slice her up, part with a vital organ, and then spend time with her estranged sister, after she saved her life that is. *No problem,* Lucy thought. *I'll just throw a suitcase together.*

She made lists upon lists so she wouldn't forget what needed to be done in the next few days before they left. There was a list for clothes to bring, services to stop, bills to pay, errands to run, and even a list of CDs and things for the car ride. She had so many lists that she actually made a checklist for her lists.

At the top of her to-dos: call Katie. As unbelievable as it sounded, the two had yet to speak on the phone. Lucy had plenty of correspondence with hospital staff both locally and in Fort Worth, and she had spoken to Rick once more. But Lucy had only tried Katie two times on her cell. The first time Lucy hung up, and the second time she left a voice mail, short and casual, asking for Katie to call her back. When Katie did call her, Lucy couldn't get up the nerve to answer the call.

Then last week, Lucy had received a letter from Katie. An actual, 3-D piece of paper with words and sentiments on it. At first she thought it was some logistical detail that needed to be taken care of or a test result, or maybe even correspondence about the trip. As soon as she unfolded it, her eyes scanned across the full-length letter, and she knew. Spilled out of her heart and onto the page was everything Katie had been thinking and feeling since the moment Carly was born. She finally understood about sacrifice and wanting to protect your child. She realized that Lucy had done that same thing for her all those years ago.

Lucy couldn't slow down her pace and was gliding across the words to make her way to phrases like, "I'm so sorry," and "I realize now," and "You were always there," until the words grew blurry from a flood of tears. The last two lines said, "I don't even know if I deserve to take this from you, but I have to do whatever I can to make sure I'm here for my daughter. Thank you, Lucy, for giving me this chance."

Lucy flipped through her lists and other papers as she leaned against the kitchen counter. At the bottom of the stack was the letter. She wanted to read it once more and bring it with her on the trip. Halfway through and the doorbell rang. She wasn't expecting anyone and didn't feel like talking, so she ignored it. Next came a loud knock. Looking up in annoyance, she set the letter down and crept to the door. Through the peephole she could make out that it was Dale, but she had no idea what he could want.

"I'm a little busy right now, Dale." She stepped back, shouting from behind the door.

Dale smiled up to the peephole and waved, thinking she was looking. Then he bent down and picked up something from the ground. "I thought you might want this package." He held it up. "I signed for it yesterday."

Lucy unlocked the door and opened it a foot. Creepy Dale was never to be trusted.

"It's pretty heavy. Wonder what it is." He turned the flat square package sideways as if he needed to slide it through a chained door.

Lucy opened the door all the way and grabbed the package. "Thanks for bringing it over." She tucked the box under her arm and started to close the door.

"Need anything else, Lucy?" Dale gleamed his gray-gold smile through the closing space of the door.

"No thanks," Lucy said just as the door closed.

She walked over and set the package on the counter. Her initial guess was that it was something from the hospital, until she saw the return sticker: *DST Marketing*. That sounded vaguely familiar. The weight was sufficient enough to be something exciting, so she ripped open one of the end flaps and revealed a clump of bubble wrap. Holding the box with one hand, she gripped the protected object and slid it out onto the counter.

It can't be, she thought. *Who would be sending me a... laptop?* She unwrapped the portable computer and stared dumbfounded. Could it be some sort of mistake, or maybe a marketing gimmick? *Marketing!* It hit her like a bolt of lightning. DST Marketing is where Kyle worked, but it still didn't make any sense. They had spoken at dinner about technology and how completely out of it she was. Maybe she mentioned she didn't have a laptop, but that was no reason to send one over. She would have to call him for an explanation.

Lucy went over to her purse to get her cell phone and the business card Kyle had given her. With her eyes still glued to the mystery gift, she dialed the number.

After only one ring, she heard a young male voice answer: "Good afternoon, DST Marketing."

Although it was perfectly fine for her to call Kyle, she still felt a sense of nervousness. She tried to make her voice sound professional. "Hello, could you please connect me with Kyle Benson."

"One moment please. May I say who's calling?"

"This is Lucy Lang."

"Of course, Ms. Lang, I'll connect you."

Expecting to hear some kind of boring Muzak, she was impressed by the upbeat tune transmitting in her ear. Within seconds she recognized "Pressure" by Billy Joel, but she didn't get a chance to enjoy it.

"Hey." Kyle came across sounding happy and surprised. "I'm glad you called."

"I think you were expecting me to call."

"Why do you say that?"

Lucy could hear the smile behind his words. She thought it was cute but was impatient and wanted answers to come more quickly. "C'mon, Kyle. I got the computer…but I don't get it."

"Didn't you open it?" he said, a bit confused.

"What do you mean? Of course I opened it—that's how I knew it was a laptop."

"No, I mean the laptop itself."

"Oh, hold on a sec." She walked back over to the counter and balanced the phone against her ear with her shoulder. "I'm opening it now." It took a couple of tries before she found the piece that released the top, and then she popped it open. Lying on the keyboard was a piece of paper: *kbenson@dstmarketing. com. Please take care, Lucy, and keep in touch. Kyle*

The long silence triggered some second-guessing from Kyle. "I hope you don't think I'm...a stalker or something." He flapped his green and blue tie against his desk. "I got a new laptop and thought you might want my old one."

"Oh..."

"It's still pretty new. You can use it for a lot of things, maybe even write about this unique experience you're about to have. And...we could keep in touch through e-mail...if you want to."

"It was very nice of you, and...of course I want to keep in touch. The funny thing is, I don't even have an e-mail."

"Oh, well they're free and very easy to get."

"I'll have Benny set it up for me." Lucy took Kyle's note and added it to her stack of lists. "He's kind of a computer geek, which will work out great if I have any problems while we're on the road."

With surprise in his voice, Kyle said, "You mean Benny is going with you?" He leaned back in his chair and ran his fingers through his sandy locks.

Lucy didn't pick up on Kyle's disappointment and was inexperienced when it came to male jealousy. "Yeah, he offered. My car's kind of a dud, so it's much safer."

Not wanting to sound like a jerk, he replied, "Right, that does make sense."

A screeching halt in the conversation, followed by an awkward silence, prompted Lucy to say, "Well, I'm leaving in three days, so I guess I'll...send you an e-mail from the road."

Suddenly, a short, plump female popped her head into Kyle's office, and he held up a finger to buy some time. "Lucy...I just wanted to say that I had a really great time with you last week, and I know we didn't have much of a chance to get to know each other…" the woman caught her cue and bowed out with an apologetic wave, "…but I hope we can do that when you get back."

Lucy didn't let her voice reveal her smile. "I hope so too. And thanks again for the computer."

"Bye, Lucy."

And she was gone.

Kyle leaned forward on his desk and tried to dissect the conversation. There was no sense in worrying about when he would see Lucy, or if she'd come back, or even about Benny. His only choice was to wait and hope that the magic of the Internet would keep them connected.

This one definitely caught Lucy by surprise. It was a smart move on Kyle's part. He knew Lucy didn't like to talk on the phone much. He also knew she wasn't very open with her feelings, and most people tend to express more in writing. She had to give him props for thinking of that one. On the other hand, writing wasn't really Lucy's thing either. Her sister Katie was the one who liked to write. Lucy's outlet for how she was feeling was her artwork. When things went her way, which was not too often, her paintings were bright and beautiful. If she felt down or lonely or frustrated, her creations were dark and sad. But Kyle didn't know her well enough yet to figure that one out.

Lucy pulled out one of her lists and reached across the counter to snag a pen. At the top in all caps she wrote: GET E-MAIL.

CHAPTER 19

....

Rick drummed on the steering wheel and bobbed his head while belting out a Scorpions hit from his favorite CD. His serenades never got old to Katie. She sat in the passenger seat with her feet up on the dash as Carly giggled in the backseat. Rick beamed and glanced between the road, Katie, and the rearview mirror to catch a glimpse of his other favorite girl. Any onlooker would say this family was returning from the beach or a fun family gathering, and not another arduous trip to the doctor's office.

"Come on, girls, sing it with me." Rick sang along, hamming it up as usual, and when the girls tried to join him, he obnoxiously sang louder. Katie laughed and wiggled her pink painted toenails.

Always the hero, Rick knew when Katie needed a laugh... or a hug, or whatever it happened to be at that time. He was always very in tune to her, and actually to females in general. Although he was truly a guy's guy, he was also very comfortable in a woman's world. In school, he always noticed when girls got a haircut, or he would compliment them on a new blouse. Sometimes he even helped them with their boyfriend issues. Thankfully, most of them took it as flirty and not feminine.

"Why don't we have family movie night tonight?" Rick suggested cheerfully. It was a tradition they started when Carly was almost three. They put a big blanket in front of the TV and ate dinner on it while watching a movie. The older she got, the better the movies got. Both Rick and Katie were relieved to be out of the *Winnie the Pooh* stage.

"Yeah," Carly squealed from the backseat. "Can we, Mommy?"

"I guess so." Katie turned to the side to face Carly. "First you have to finish making that card for Papa's birthday."

Carly folded her arms and cocked her head to the side. "Mommy…do you think I would forget my special Papa?"

Katie and Rick exchanged glances and held in their snorts.

"Of course not, sweetie. I was just making sure."

Rick pulled into the driveway, avoiding the paper that was still flattened to the ground after he ran over it on the way out that morning. They had slept in and didn't get to their usual routine of trading the paper sections. Rick liked the sports section, of course, and Katie always started with the local section. The problem was that many times the "Back Page," a section that had interesting tidbits from around the world, was on the back of the sports page. So Rick would try to hurry and finish reading all the stats before Katie finished reading about the schools and communities.

"I'll get her," Rick said as he hopped out and slammed his door. He opened the back door to Carly already freeing herself from the seatbelt. She greeted him like they had just been reunited and attached herself like a spider to his body. They had grown so close. She had become so attached to him with all of Katie's medical problems. That both comforted and upset Katie. She couldn't have been more thankful for the bond they were forming, but at the same time, she was jealous that Carly wanted Rick more and more. Her friends told her that it was just a phase, that most kids cling to one parent at some point. "Alright, you freeloader…ride's over." Rick started to lean over to put Carly down. Her arms and legs were locked around him.

"Carry me in, Daddy."

Rick walked up the cement path where Katie was waiting up ahead.

"Got your keys?" Rick shrugged as if he had no choice. He rubbed his free hand across Katie's shoulder to let her know he understood her feelings.

Katie reached in her purse, pulled out a set of keys, and stuck one in the door. Walking into her home was always a pleasure. It was her sanctuary. When she returned there, it meant things were good, or at least better because she was home and not at the hospital. She set her keys and purse on a small antique desk at the entry. Above hung a decorative mirror she used to have in her bedroom growing up. It was one of the few furnishings she took with her when she left. Rick could see her reflection, but he didn't need it to know that she was not enjoying her usual homecoming.

"Why don't you be a big girl and go to the den to pick out our movie for tonight?"

Carly released her grip and took advantage of the opportunity. "Any one I want?" Carly looked up with a mouthful of teeth and gums.

"Any one," Rick replied.

"Yay!" She did a little celebratory dance and ran out of the room.

Rick and Katie both walked into the living room and sat down on a big beige couch that puffed up when you sat on it. Katie leaned on one arm and tucked her legs up and to the side.

Rick wasn't ready to get comfortable yet and leaned his elbows on his knees.

"You know how much she loves you, don't you?" His voice was soft, and he watched her face for the answer.

Katie's smile let Rick know that it was something else that was upsetting her. "Of course I do."

"Alright then, spill it."

"What?"

"I know something else is wrong."

"I don't know…"

Rick fell back against the couch and jumped into place right next to Katie. His light brown eyes stared right into hers as if he were reading her mind.

"Well I do." With one hand behind her head holding it in place, he transported the information from her mind to his. "You're nervous about seeing your sister coming." His confident smile sang triumph.

Katie closed her eyes and tilted her head forward until their foreheads touched. "It's not just that."

"Then what?"

"The whole thing is just too weird." She lowered her head further and leaned it on his shoulder. "I haven't even spoken to her, and I don't know how she feels about doing this."

"What do you mean? She wants to do it or she wouldn't be going through all of this."

"You know that's not true. Maybe she feels obligated. Maybe she's still mad at me and that's why she hasn't returned my calls."

"First of all, who cares! This is only your life we're talking about."

"Rick!"

"What? If she's still upset, she'll get over it eventually. But I bet she wouldn't get over losing you." Rick popped up and went over to a black end table where a portable phone sat. "Secondly, I say we take care of this mystery right now." He swiped the phone from its station and glided back to the couch, gently placing the phone in her lap on the way.

Katie shrugged and picked imaginary lint from the sofa. "I don't know…maybe I shouldn't push her."

"Chicken."

"I am not." She pulled her hair together in a bunch and tied it in a bun. "I guess I just feel bad…for blaming so many things on her and then just leaving. I was so wrong…about everything."

"Hey, you were just a confused kid."

"I was a brat."

"Was?" Rick displayed his poker face, then readied himself for the blow Katie would surely deliver.

Katie let him off the hook this time and sat still, staring at the phone. "The thing that makes it so hard—that makes this so confusing—is that I'm not sure about a lot of things. You know how when you're a little kid and you remember some place a certain way and then when you go back it's nothing like you pictured?"

"Yeah."

"Well, my whole life kind of seems like that. I try to remember my mother and Lucy, and things that happened, and now that I'm older…some of those memories seem different." Katie touched her fingertip to the corner of her eye, attempting to stop the flow that would certainly come. "Why do I have to deal with this now? I almost wish…I wish that it wasn't…"

"That is wasn't Lucy?"

"Is that wrong?" Katie used her sleeve to dab at the tears before they made it down her face.

Rick put his arm around Katie and smiled. "It's not wrong to be scared. But you can't put this off any longer. She'll be here in less than a week, and it will be even more awkward if you wait until then to talk. Now, I'm going to go keep my other little girl busy…" Rick's voice changed into his *baby talk* voice, "and you're going to be a big girl and call your sister."

Katie laughed and slapped Rick's behind as he got up from the couch. Then she started punching in numbers on the phone. Her heart raced and her stomach sank as two rings went by. Then…

"Hello?"

"Lucy…it's me, Katie."

CHAPTER 20

Benito Enrique Garcia grew up with five brothers. He was number four, and he'd always hoped for a sister. Benny reflected on that wish and came to the conclusion that he must have been *muy loco*. After loading what he thought was the last of the suitcases, bags, pillows, et cetera, into his Dodge Durango, he suddenly spotted Anne walking up with a small piece of luggage. Her long hair was wrapped into a bun at the back of her head, and she wore beige knee-length shorts with a light blue strappy top. The weather was getting warmer each day. Texas would be even hotter, so Anne was prepared with lots of cute, summery outfits.

"Ah, c'mon, you're killing me, girl!"

Anne shrugged and gave a closed-mouth grin. "I promise this is it." She handed Benny the bag and walked back toward the stairs to the apartment, leaving Benny mumbling to himself and trying to rearrange the load that was already too much.

"I got like one bag here. What else do you girls need besides some underwear, T-shirts, and jeans?" In fact, that was Benny's uniform. Hot or cold, it didn't matter. He set the bag in the back on top of a black vinyl suitcase. When he turned and saw that Anne was already on her way back up the stairs, he yelled, "No problem, I got this!" He closed the back and continued to talk to himself. "I guess I'm not just the chauffer, but the butler too. I wonder what else these little *niñas mimadas* will get me to do." Deep down he wasn't really mad, though he figured it wouldn't be the last time he would call them *spoiled brats*. But he was actually looking forward to spending some time getting to know these girls and visiting with the cousins he rarely got to see. Benny also felt proud. He was going to take care of Lucy and Anne. He hadn't had a chance for his own family yet, so having this experience really meant something to him.

With the car ready and a schedule to keep, Benny headed back up to Lucy's to get the girls. It was just about noon, and the three had agreed to grab some lunch on the way out. Luckily everyone was in the mood for Mexican. Benny was always in the mood for Mexican, and his favorite stop-in place was just down the road. "Where's Anne?" He threw his hands in the air. "We gotta get a move on, chiquitas!"

"She was crying," Lucy answered. "She went back to her aunt's."

"She's still going, right?"

"I guess so." Lucy looked around the room, as if surveying the room and its contents. Her black leggings stretched to just below her knees and were covered by a long, but tight-fitting green shirt.

Benny sensed her uneasiness and walked over to her. He put an arm around her shoulder and gave one big squeeze. "What about you, Lucita? You gonna be okay?"

"Of course. Just making sure I took care of everything."

"So you're feeling alright with this, and you got everything you need?"

Benny knew Lucy had mixed feelings, but she didn't acknowledge the question. Maybe because she didn't know how she felt. The whole thing was just crazy to begin with. And now she'd agreed to let these two, whom she was just getting to know, join her on this peculiar mission. She released herself from Benny's grasp, picked up her purse from the couch, and walked toward the door. "Let's get Anne so we can go."

They both walked outside and paused for a moment for Lucy to lock her door. They could see down the hall, Anne in the doorway hugging Mrs. Allen. "Will you go already," Mrs. Allen chirped. "You're just being silly now. I'm going to be fine." Mrs. Allen craned her neck to see past Anne. "Will you two please tell her that I'm not an invalid?" Her white splotchy ankles peeked from beneath her faded blue housecoat.

Lucy and Benny walked down to Mrs. Allen's door. "C'mon, girl, your auntie's going to be just fine." Benny put a hand on the back of Anne's shoulder blades. "You should see what she does when you're not around. This girl is over here lifting weights and doing push-ups." Anne giggled, and Lucy smiled and then checked her cell phone for the time. "I saw her through the window," Benny added.

"Okay, but call me if you need anything," Anne warned. "I mean it, anything."

"Right, right," Mrs. Allen answered, then moved backward into her apartment and started to shut the door. "Goodness, at least I'll enjoy a bit of peace and quiet. Now you three be careful on the road." Mrs. Allen was always grateful for the time she had with Anne, but she was even more thankful that Anne was taking some time for herself. Between working at the family shop, going to school, and then helping her out, Anne didn't seem to have much time for fun. Ever since she started spending time with Lucy and Benny, that had started to change, so this trip seemed like a perfect idea. Mrs. Allen would be fine.

"We will," both Anne and Benny answered together as all three began walking down the hall to the stairwell.

• • •

Worrying about who sat where was not a problem. Lucy offered to sit in the back. This way she could avoid small talk, bury herself in her music, or use her new laptop. Not that she would already be e-mailing Kyle, but she could find something to keep her busy. And maybe Kyle was right. It might help her to write in a journal.

Except for the one at work, it had been a while since Lucy used a computer. Two nights before she had Benny set up the e-mail account and show her how to use it. It was actually quite entertaining for Lucy to watch. When Benny was at a computer, it was like he was a pianist with ADHD. He was always tapping his foot or jiggling his leg, and when he wasn't typing, he was tapping his index finger somewhere on the keyboard. He said he learned everything from one of his older brothers who had some kind of major computer technology job. Benny could have gone on the same path. He had the talent and the opportunity but not the motivation. Laughing, meeting people, entertaining—that's what drove Benny. That's probably what attracted most people to Benny as well, including Lucy.

"Did you hear from *Kevin* yet?" Benny inquired sarcastically.

Lucy closed the laptop and leaned forward. "Will you stop calling him that? You know his name." She sank back into her seat and stared at the mini Lakers basketball hanging from the rearview mirror. "And just so you know, I wasn't checking that."

"Will you leave her alone?" Anne slapped Benny on the arm. "What, are you jealous or something?"

Lucy looked up into the rearview mirror and locked in on Benny looking back at her. She was searching for the answer in his eyes, but he looked away too abruptly. It hadn't dawned on her before. He *had* been giving her extra attention lately, but she thought it was just his way and that he felt bad for her. *God, this could be really awkward,* she thought to herself, staring out the window. And then she remembered that time in the car, when she had cried on Benny's shoulder. Things did feel a little…intense between them. She had felt a connection, but there was no way she was going to acknowledge it, especially at that moment.

"No!" Benny reached up and clicked on the stereo. Each of the three had brought their own favorites for the trip and agreed to take turns making selections. "Alright you two, I'm going to pick first," he said, completely changing the subject. "Let's start with some Lenny. Here, check this out," Benny said as he handed Anne the Lenny Kravitz CD.

Anne opened the CD and began examining its contents. "Oh, awesome! This is one with all the words. Now I can sing along too."

Both Lucy and Benny cringed at the thought, but at the same time, Lucy enjoyed how young and innocent she was. She envied her carefree attitude, especially given the responsibility and maturity she'd shown to her family over the years. This trip meant something different to all three of them. For Anne it was having an adventure. Benny would fulfill his need to be a caretaker and protector. And Lucy, along with saving her sister's life, hoped to finally unload the baggage that was holding her back from creating a new life—a life of her own.

All three sat staring straight ahead listening to Lenny, while Anne attempted to sing by following the lyrics sheet. None of them said a word through the entire song, lost in the thoughts of what was ahead.

CHAPTER 21

First stop was to be Tucson, Arizona. By the time they got lunch—they ate in the car while Benny drove—it was after one. They wanted to arrive around seven thirty or eight, eat a late dinner, and get a cheap room they could all share. They were making good time, and both girls complimented Benny on his planning and timing of the trip—so far, that is. There was certainly a long way to go.

"What did you girls think? That I was just some joke-telling clown or something?" Benny gave a quick glance over his left shoulder and then switched into the fast lane. "I do have other skills you know."

"Of course we know, Benny," Anne reassured. "We knew you'd do a great job, right Lucy?" Anne turned sideways and looked back at Lucy.

"He's here isn't he?"

Anne displayed a disapproving look.

"I mean yes…that's why I wanted you here, Benny."

"Thanks!" he said in the rearview mirror. He sat up tall so she could see his face.

Small talk was exchanged from time to time, but for the most part, it was strangely quiet. Although the three had spent time together, they were beginning to realize that they didn't know each other all that well.

Anne searched through the pile of CDs, asking about the ones she hadn't heard of. Lucy gazed out the window, thoughts drifting, trying to make out the words and names of the rock formations people had spelled out on the side of the one-lane highway. She fought her natural urge to doze off in the car. This was something she'd actually forgotten about herself. There weren't many occasions where she was the passenger instead of the driver.

Lucy imagined what it was going to be like seeing her sister for the first time in so long. Would they just go to each other and embrace, not needing to say anything? She created a few different scenes in her mind like a movie director, playing each one to see which she preferred. She kind of liked the one where Katie's eyes fill with tears, and then she runs to Lucy and says, "I'm so sorry for everything. I was so wrong and now you are saving my life. Please forgive me." Lucy does not say anything of course, she just opens her arms to Katie and holds her tight.

"Yo! Lucita." Benny's voice cut right into her daydream.

"What?" she answered, stretching her legs and suddenly feeling uncomfortable in the backseat.

"What do you want to listen to?"

"Yeah, you haven't picked anything yet," Anne added.

"You guys can pick, I don't care right now." Lucy got the laptop from the seat and opened it.

Anne looked back and saw Lucy holding the computer. "You probably won't be able to hold a connection on these roads."

Lucy looked up, confused. "Really, because I thought—"

"Oh yeah, she'll be online alright." Benny's voice was teasing and childish. "Not only did lover boy give her that laptop, he also bought her a mobile broadband card."

"Reeaally?" Anne perked up and looked intrigued.

"Hey, I don't know anything about this stuff, but he said it was no big deal."

Benny hung one wrist over the top of the steering wheel. Casually he added, "Right," giving Anne a perfunctory nod and a smirk.

"Could we *please* not make a big deal about this?" Lucy pleaded.

"Okay, just tell us one thing," Anne prodded as Benny listened intently. "Do you like him or what?"

Lucy was quiet, punching keys on the keyboard as if she had not heard what they said. After a moment she looked up and said, "I...think he's a nice guy...and that's all I'm going to say about it right now." She clicked on the e-mail icon Benny had showed her to check if any messages had arrived. "Oh my God..." Her voice trailed off as she stared at what appeared on the screen.

"What is it, Lucy?" Anne leaned over and tried to take a look at the computer, but she couldn't quite reach.

"I can't believe it," Lucy whispered.

"C'mon, Lucita, what is it? Did Kevin send you a love note?"

There was no answer from Lucy. She just stared at the screen, then ran her hands through her hair and down to rest on her shoulders.

"Dirty pictures?"

"It's not from Kyle. My sister e-mailed me a picture of Carly."

"I want to see," said Anne. "Is she cute?"

Lucy spun the keyboard on her lap so Anne could see.

"Ah, she *is* cute," Anne squealed. "Her hair looks kind of like yours."

Lucy turned the screen back to face her and said, "She looks...exactly like my sister did at that age." She turned to look out the window seeming to be only speaking to herself. "It's so strange how an image, or thought, can just bring you instantly back to a memory. You find yourself feeling the same feelings you felt back then, like they never left. Feelings you thought you'd buried a long time ago." Realizing she'd shared too much, Lucy turned back to Anne and read pity in her eyes. Benny fiddled with the buttons on the stereo and acted focused on the road as the girls talked. Anne laid her hands on the shoulder of her seat and then rested her chin on top. "You don't talk about your family much, but it sounds like this is going to be hard for you."

Lucy grabbed her purse and began aimlessly rummaging through it. "I'll be fine. Getting my sister well is all I need to think about right now."

"I know what it's like to not have family around. It can be really hard...and really lonely." Anne's voice was sincere and caring, but she could tell from Lucy's face that her attempt was not having the desired effect.

"Your *family*," she said as she closed her purse and looked right into Anne's eyes, "and your situation are nothing like mine."

"I'm sure they aren't, Lucy, but I don't really know because you never share that stuff with us." Anne looked over at Benny and caught a glimpse of *be careful* in his expression. "Maybe if you talked about it, you would be able to move on...or at least feel better."

"You already know the gist of it. The details don't matter much."

Finally deciding to jump in, Benny insisted, "Everything about you matters to us, Lucy."

"That's so sweet, Benny." Anne reached over and gave him a little tap on the arm.

"Yeah, for a funny guy, you sure are warm and fuzzy." Lucy was happy for the segue and hoped the conversation would continue in a lighter direction. She wasn't in the mood to give her life story. She decided to finish checking her e-mail and see if maybe there was something from Kyle. She felt a quick flutter in the pit of her stomach when she saw another message waiting and recognized that it was from Kyle. She smiled as she double-clicked to open the message.

"I saw that!" Benny accused. He had been glancing back to see if she was okay and noticed the change in her expression when she looked down at the screen. "I knew he wouldn't be able to wait. I could tell when I met him that day. He's the type that gets whooped easy." Benny was laughing when he spoke, which seemed to make Anne nervous about his ability to joke and drive at the same time.

"Keep your eyes on the road, mister," Anne scolded.

"Yeah, Benny…look who's talking, *mama's boy*! I heard you calling her when we stopped for gas."

"What, she asked me to. Hey, I was just being polite." His voice became frail and immature. "I didn't want my mamacita to worry. Who knows what could happen to me alone with you two?"

Anne and Lucy laughed, while Lucy gave Benny a tiny thump on the back of his head. The quiet empty highway started to turn into a busy freeway with signs and buildings dotting the sides of the road—an indicator that the first leg of their journey was about to end. Benny had scoped out two prospective hotels, but he hadn't made reservations. Neither was close to being full, so they planned to drive by each and see which one looked better.

Lucy diverted her attention back to the e-mail and read:

Lucy,

I hope you are off to a good start on your trip, and that you don't mind me sending you a message so soon. Think of this as a test to make sure everything works fine. Now you have my e-mail too. This is a little strange for me, and I'm guessing it is for you too. It is a good way to get to know each other, though.

Lucy, I had such a great time with you at the beach (and at dinner) and just had to tell you that ever since I've been thinking about it a lot.

Take care.

Kyle

BTW: Don't think you can't give me a call just because we are exchanging e-mails. I won't either.

Lucy read the e-mail in its entirety one more time and thought about replying, but Benny announced they were already on their way to the first hotel "drive-by." He was really getting into this new "big brother" role. She didn't want to be in the middle of typing and have to stop to get out. This would actually give her some time to think about what she wanted to say, and then she could write back later tonight. What else did she have to do anyway? She would be stuck in a hotel room with nothing to do but worry about how many other bodies had touched those same sheets.

Lucy thought it was funny that even in his e-mail, Kyle said her name twice. She still liked that.

CHAPTER 22

The drive-by on the first hotel validated Benny's reason for having two choices. Both girls made faces and shook their heads when Benny turned into the parking lot. The outside was very poorly lit, and there was a big rig truck parked along the long side of the lot. Two men leaned up against a small car with the door open playing music. You could barely make out their figures, but you could see the glowing of their cigarettes as they went from down by their sides to up by their mouths.

The second choice wasn't Park Avenue, but it looked safe. It had a big drive-through entryway were you could park by the door for loading and unloading. Benny pulled up and ran inside to make sure they still had vacancies. The price was actually cheaper than they had originally thought, so they decided to get two rooms. The girls would share one, and Benny would have the advantage of getting his own room, although he may not have seen it that way. It was almost seven, and Benny took the opportunity to point out how *right on schedule* he was.

The Motel 6 in Tucson was conveniently located right across the street from Perry's Pizza. Once all three were checked in and had their things settled in their rooms, they headed across the street on foot for dinner. "This is so cool." Anne commented on how this was only the third time she'd stayed in a hotel room.

Benny and Lucy laughed as they all headed down the sidewalk to the light where they would cross. "You crack me up, girl," Benny said, tucking his hands in his jeans pockets. "You are so easily pleased."

"What? I'm just enjoying being here…with you guys."

"Yeah," Lucy added. "I just love walking the streets at night in a strange town."

"That's what's so great." Anne was a step ahead, so she pressed the button on the crosswalk. "We have Benny to take care of us."

Benny puffed out his chest and wore a huge smile. "That's right, girls, I'll protect you if anything happens."

"Oh brother!" Lucy shook her head. "Look what you got started, Anne."

"Well it's true." Anne slipped an arm through Benny's arm as if he were escorting her across the street. "Don't you think so, Lucy?"

Benny was loving the attention, and Lucy's uneasiness was an added bonus. When they reached the curb, he put an arm around her and gave her a good shake. "It's okay, Lucita, I know I'm your hero. You don't have to admit it."

Lucy rolled her eyes, but she couldn't help smiling just a little.

• • •

The pizza place was bathed in lacquered wood, with high-backed booths and octagonal tables. It was seat-yourself, and there were plenty of open tables. Of course Benny headed straight to a booth facing one of the two televisions in the place. Anne followed while Lucy headed to the bathroom. Both stalls were occupied, but she was the only one waiting.

When Lucy returned to the table, she found what appeared to be three iced teas already deposited in front of Anne and Benny. Anne was on the phone, so she asked Benny, "What's with the teas? Don't they have beer here?" Benny shrugged and pointed to Anne, who held up one finger and made an apologetic face.

"I'm so excited for you, Aunt Mary," she said into the phone. "I wish I was there, though. Promise me you'll be careful." She tilted the bottom of the phone back towards her neck and whispered to the two of them, "Auntie's got a date." She gave a breathy giggle and spoke back in the phone. "I know. Okay. Love you...bye."

"You ordered these?" Lucy asked Anne when she hung up.

"Uh...I hope you don't mind." She could tell Lucy didn't get it by the confused look on her face. "I just thought...well, you really shouldn't be drinking, right?"

"So you didn't think I could make that decision for myself?" Lucy sat back against the booth and folded her arms. The truth was that she was probably angry because she really wanted a beer.

Anne leaned forward with her elbows rested on the table trying to muster up the right words. Benny was torn between the baseball game on the TV hanging from the ceiling and refereeing his own match right there at the table. Add to that the smell of melted cheese that was probably gnawing at his severely empty stomach.

"I'm sorry, Lucy. The server was here, and...I was just trying to help. Please don't be mad at me," Anne pleaded.

Lucy's anger melted away with those last spoken words. That was the same thing Katie used to say to her when they were growing up. They both knew when their mother was angry that the consequences would most likely be disastrous. Katie worried that one day Lucy would lash out in the same way. There were times when Katie had done something wrong or was acting like a typical sassy child, and Lucy would begin to get frustrated with her. Katie always knew the exact right moment to utter those same words: "Lucy, please don't be mad at me." Lucy never wondered or even cared if it was a child's tactic. She just took Katie in her arms and held her, telling her over and over again, "I could never be mad at you...I love you." Lucy wished that had continued to be true. And she hoped that at least this visit—this situation—could help bring them back together.

"It's no big deal," Lucy said calmly. "You're right. I'm just *really* hungry...and tired. I *do* need to be taking good care of myself now. So who's the date with?"

"Oh...it's Mr. Ahern." Anne's tone jumped right back to its normal pep. "It's so adorable. She made him muffins when his parakeet died, and now he's asked her to lunch. That counts as a date, right?" She didn't wait for an answer. Benny shrugged but kept his eyes on the game. "I told her that definitely counts." Lucy had stopped listening and didn't even notice Anne's phone ring again. "Yikes," Anne said with a surprised look. "It's Auntie again...better take this." She shrugged an apology and walked toward the bathroom with the call.

The mention of dates made Lucy think of a time when her mother had a date. It was almost like Linda was her old self again, but it didn't last long. The two days leading up to the date, she was home a lot—cleaning, painting her nails, and she even spent some quality time with Lucy and Katie. Lucy remembered how strange it was that her mother said, "This guy's a real sweetheart. You're gonna love him." But the night of the date, Linda just stared out the window until she saw his car pull up, and then she ran out to meet him. All Lucy could see was a shadowy figure in the front seat of a blue jeep. The next day it was like it never happened. Lucy knew not to mention it, but she didn't get to Katie in time to stop her from asking. "He was a jerk—most men are," was the only thing her mother would say.

The three ordered their pizza and salad and talked about the drive over the next two days. Benny would try to get the girls dropped off in Fort Worth by dinner on Friday night. Then he would drive the hour to his cousin's place in Dallas.

While they were still at dinner, Benny's mom called to check in on him, Lucy sent a text to Katie updating their ETA, and Anne went up to get quarters for the arcade. They were trying to prolong going back to the hotel as they knew they would just be sitting around talking and watching television. In the corner of the restaurant was a small room with about six games including one pinball machine, a dance simulation game, and one of those claw machines that never seemed to pick up anything but your quarters. There were two children, who appeared to be brother and sister based on the arguing that was going on, pretending to play a car racing game. A teenager wearing shredded jeans and flip-flops was playing the pinball game, throwing out quiet swears every few seconds. He had one of those Beatles-type haircuts that was a bit longer in the front, and he kept flicking it back with his head.

Benny and Anne played a few games, with Lucy watching from her seat pretending to be busy on her phone. Anne gestured toward the teenager as she passed, shooting a *he's cute* look to Lucy. But there was something else about the boy that fascinated her. He didn't seem to be having fun playing, but was more focused on working something out in his head. Lucy sensed he was trouble, but then again it could have just been her cynicism. She reached over and grabbed the happy hour flyer that was on the table and a pencil from her purse, and she began sketching the boy. She seemed to look more at the boy than the paper, her hand moving automatically around the paper. Within minutes, a sketch appeared depicting a tall teenager with his hair accentuated across his face. She stared at it for a moment, then simply folded it up and put it in her purse. Then she walked over to join Anne and Benny.

After about thirty minutes, it was unanimous. They couldn't deal with the game noises any longer, so they decided to head back and see what movies were available to purchase back in the room. It had gone from dusk to dark while they were inside, but the cool air felt nice, even to Lucy. As they walked they talked about their favorite type of movies; Anne liked the romances of course, and Benny was all about the thrillers. Lucy said she didn't have a preference as long as Benny didn't select from the "Adult Favorites" section. Anne confirmed that was a good point, and Lucy added that she probably would be on the computer for a while anyway.

• • •

Back at the hotel, all three gathered in the girls' room. Benny relaxed in a black and green cushioned chair, plopping his feet on a small, fragile end table. Anne lay down on her stomach across the green and gold checkered bedspread, while Lucy was propped up with a pillow on the other bed. The laptop was closed and lying beside her as she ostensibly watched *The Breakup*, which was a compromise on Benny's part. He was pushing for action, but he settled since he had heard the movie was funny and had one of his favorite actors, Vince Vaughn. He admired him for his genuine comedic presence.

Benny and Anne were enjoying the movie and exchanging looks and laughs during funny scenes, but Lucy was looking right through the screen. She couldn't help thinking of Kyle and wondering what he was doing. She drafted her e-mail response to him in her own little computer brain. She had several ideas down and had almost worked out the final wording, so she reached for the computer and opened it up on her lap. She clicked on her e-mail and went right to the message from Kyle. She read it again just to make sure. Anne and Benny both pretended not to notice.

Kyle,

Thanks for your message, and again for the computer. So far everything has gone right on schedule. I'm writing you from a hotel in Tucson. You're right, this is kind of weird, but it works well for me since I won't have much privacy on this trip. I was thinking about our date too. I had a great time with you. It's too bad that was our only date—if you don't count the night we met. I still feel bad about that and appreciate you not bringing it up.

Talk to you soon,

Lucy

CHAPTER 23

Waking up in the same room with someone was strange for Lucy. The first time she woke up, she wasn't sure where she was. The thick, double-lined drapes were like an iron curtain blocking out any hint that daylight had arrived. Lucy assumed it was five or six in the morning until she squinted over at the clock that was between the two beds—ten after seven. That's when she noticed Anne and reality set back in. Yes, this was all real. She *was* going to be reunited with her estranged sister, the one who'd abandoned her, who'd left her to deal with their absentee mother. Save Katie's life by giving her one of her vital organs? No problem, Lucy was used to having her insides ripped out.

She thought about the day she'd finally moved out of the house. Her whole being had felt about as empty as that house. Lucy actually had a bit of hope on that day though. She tried to convince herself that it was a new beginning. Everyone and everything she had was gone from her life. Nowhere to go but up. Or so she let herself think. Only it didn't quite happen that way. That's what happens when you think you can do it all alone. She hadn't built any friendships, no alliances to help her. Any money she made was spent on technician school and paint supplies. She hadn't saved a dime. So her only choice was to take whatever job she could get and move into an affordable apartment.

Lucy turned over and decided she needed a few more minutes, even though falling back asleep was hopeless. It wouldn't matter anyway because after five minutes there was a knock at the door. She closed her eyes and pretended not to hear it. Two seconds later and the knock was even louder, followed by, "C'mon, chiquitas, let's get a move on!" She wondered how Benny could sound so cheery after spending the night in that place. In fact, he was always that happy, and she couldn't figure out why. Yanking back the covers, she slipped her sock-covered feet into some sandals. She wore black leggings and a long white T-shirt. "Just a sec," she said loudly as she tried to smooth down her hair on the way to the door. As Lucy opened the door, she noticed Benny's arm raised up toward the door. He had been covering the peep hole.

"Hey, you don't just open up the door like that." Benny walked in and shut the door. "What if I was a serial killer?"

"That's right, a serial killer with an accent that sounds just like a Mexican comic I know," she said sarcastically. Then she sat back on her bed with her legs crossed Indian style.

Benny plopped down on the edge of Anne's bed with an extra jolt, but she didn't budge. "What's with her?"

"I don't know, I guess she's a heavy sleeper."

"Well I want to get down to the continental breakfast before it's all picked over. Maybe stash a few things for the road." Benny got up and headed toward the door. "Mind if I meet you girls downstairs? I'm starving."

"Fine with me. I don't eat much in the morning anyway." Lucy didn't bother to get up.

• • •

Benny entered the tiny café with a low grumble in his gut. He absolutely had to start every day with breakfast, and preferably something hearty. He was relieved that it wasn't too crowded and there was someone looking after the stations. At least that's what Benny hoped when he noticed an elderly woman rearranging a pastry tray, which was exactly where he was headed. He figured he could pop something in his mouth while he was preparing everything else. Looking like a man on a mission, he whipped down the line, piling on scrambled eggs, bacon, and a small mound of cantaloupe.

He was still chomping on a mini muffin when he snaked a cheese Danish in his free hand. He took a quick spin around to see where he should sit. Among the available options there was a long table that was only being used at one end by a young couple with a gooey toddler, and two smaller tables that were empty but would be tight when the girls arrived. Not in the mood to have food flung at him, Benny headed for one of the two smaller tables. Sitting alone at the adjacent table was a young kid who somehow seemed familiar. Benny stared at the young man as he approached, trying to place him. Then, he watched as the pastry organizer walked over and said to the boy, "Excuse me, but only registered guests may enjoy the breakfast." She wore blue polyester pants that looked a couple sizes too big for her mega-petite frame.

Pushing the mouthful to the side of his cheek, he replied, "I am a guest here."

"Oh, may I see your room key?"

Benny arrived at the table and sat down right next to the boy. "Yo, bro, why didn't you wait for me?"

Caught off guard by Benny's presence as well as his words, the boy just continued chewing and stared at Benny in confusion.

"Here's our key, ma'am." Benny reached into his pocket and pulled out the room key. "Sorry about that. My cousin got here late last night. I forgot to give him one."

The boy flicked his brown hair back just like he'd done the night before while playing the pinball machine.

"No problem." The woman smiled. "Sometimes we get people in here, try and sneak in for free food." She gave the boy a quick pat on the shoulder, and the two watched as she walked back to the food area.

"Thanks, man. I'm Chad," he said, holding his hand out.

"Hey, it's cool, Chad." Benny took his hand and gave it a firm, quick shake. "I'm Benny."

Strangely the two ate for a minute or two without either of them saying another word. Then, finally, Chad looked up and said, "Aren't you curious?"

"About what?"

Chad smiled. "About me?"

"Naw...I been in your place before. I got a feelin'." Benny understood having hard times, but he hadn't been that young. He did wonder how old he was, so he decided to ask that.

"I'm seventeen," Chad replied.

"Forgot my juice...you need anything?" Benny got up and headed back to the drink station.

"No thanks."

Just as Benny sat back down, Chad looked up at the two women coming from the corner of the café walking towards the table, staring at him curiously. When they got to the table, they just stood there as if waiting for something.

"Hey, girls, grab some grub and join us," Benny said.

"Us?" Lucy said, looking straight at Chad.

"Yeah, this is my buddy Chad," Benny said, gesturing with his head.

Anne immediately stuck out her hand and smiled. "Hi, Chad, I'm Anne...and this is Lucy."

Chad smiled and shook both their hands.

"C'mon," Lucy said to Anne, nudging her arm. The girls walked off, leaving Chad following them with his eyes as they left.

"They're too old for you, bro," Benny chided.

"Hey, man, I was just lookin'. So what's your story? You guys don't seem like you're on vacation."

"It's a long story, but we're on our way to Fort Worth." Benny's plate was just about empty, and he contemplated seconds. The girls came back, and Benny noticed that both of their plates were about a third of what he just ate, and he decided against getting anything more.

"I'm actually headed that way too," Chad commented. "Mind if I catch a ride with you guys?"

Everyone stopped eating and froze in time. They searched each other's faces to see who would be the first to speak. Obviously it wouldn't be smart to give a stranger a ride. *But he does seem like a nice kid,* Benny thought to himself. He looked at Chad and then to Anne, who appeared to be warming to the idea. But Lucy's expression told him that she didn't think it was a good idea.

"Well..." Benny spoke up first. "You said you were seventeen, right? We could get in trouble giving you a ride without your parents' permission."

"My parents don't give a crap about me, and I'm almost eighteen…two more months. Hey, I'll show you my license if you want."

"I don't know…" Lucy said to nobody in particular.

"Hey, it's cool," Chad said. He finished the last of his water and stuffed a wrapped muffin into a backpack he had on the floor. "I don't want to cause any trouble." He got up from the table and patted a hand on Benny's shoulder. "Thanks anyway."

"Hey, man, I wanna help you out…" Benny's voice was apologetic. "But I gotta look out for these girls too."

"That's okay. Nice meeting you guys, and good luck on your trip."

Chad took two steps toward the door, and then Lucy's voice caught him. "Wait a sec."

Chad turned and faced the three at the table. "Yeah?"

"We'll give you a ride, but Benny has to search you." The words seemed to surprise Lucy herself.

"What?" Benny and Anne said in unison.

"Your backpack, pockets, everything. We need to make sure you don't have any weapons or drugs or anything. Is that cool?" Lucy seemed to enjoy being in control.

"Yeah…sure. I got nothing to hide." Chad sat back down and displayed a very toothy grin, which spread around the table. "Thanks, guys, I really appreciate this. You don't know how hard it is when no one wants to help you out."

"I think I've got a pretty good idea."

CHAPTER 24

Two energy bars, a notebook, two pairs each of underwear and socks, a T-shirt, a few pages of sheet music, a bottle of water, a wallet that contained forty-eight dollars, and a license that confirmed Chad William Gordon was indeed two months away from turning eighteen. That was the contents of the frayed black backpack that he'd been carrying around for four days since he left his home in Oro Valley, a suburb six miles north of Tucson.

Staring out the window from the backseat, Chad tried to think of the good things he had going for him. At least he was able to stick it out until he graduated. And after four nights of uncertainty, of going from a friend's couch to a park bench, he now had some allies. Three strangers who took a chance to help him make a fresh start in life. He thought about his mother and hoped she would leave his stepdad now that Chad was finally gone. He felt guilty. But not enough to go back.

He looked around the car at his three new travelling companions. They'd told him a little about themselves, filling him in on the purpose of the trip. It sounded like an unbelievable story to him, but they had no reason to lie. Chad appreciated that they didn't pressure him to do the same, but he actually wanted to talk about it. He needed to talk about it. And he was happy they listened.

It was a pretty typical story that most had heard before. Chad's mother had been raising him alone. When Ed came along, she thought he would finally make their family whole and take care of the two of them. At first he treated Chad with kindness and respect, but as soon as he married Chad's mother, everything changed. Chad looked away when he talked about how Ed belittled him in front of the other employees at the garage where Ed worked and got Chad a part-time job. His mother justified it by saying, "That's just his way." That justification probably helped her make it through as well, since he treated her even worse. He was constantly putting her down and making her think she would be nothing without him.

Before leaving, Chad snuck a letter into his mother's purse, begging her to leave and go live with her sister. It was risky, knowing she might show Ed the letter, but he had to try. Watching the endless strip of white flowing down the highway, he wondered if his mother would someday forgive him. Then with the hum of the car mesmerizing him, the white strip began to blur and suddenly he fell asleep.

That's it, Lucy thought to herself. She'd finally figured out what was causing her to sneak endless peeks at their new guest. There was something familiar about him that she couldn't quite place until that moment, when they were talking about Katie and Rick. Chad looked a lot like Rick did back when he and Katie were dating. A tall, lanky kid with a laid-back disposition—cute too.

She stared at him as he slept, and suddenly she was smiling. Not because of something familiar in his face though, but because of a familiar feeling. It was something she hadn't felt in a very long time. The feeling you get when you do something nice for someone. Lucy had gotten used to being needed, and she realized how much she missed it. She wondered why she felt it now, with this strange boy. And why she hadn't felt it when she found out what she would be doing for her sister. Maybe because it didn't seem real, and Katie wasn't there. But Chad was; he was right there needing someone to take care of him. She was relaxed in her thoughts, and before she knew it, she was asleep too.

• • •

The problem with diabetes is you can't have an off day without worrying about what else could be wrong. Katie knew the warning signs. She was always on top of things, in terms of checking her blood sugar levels. But she also knew she had to be vigilant in keeping herself healthy on a daily basis, and getting enough fluids, even with just a cold. The consequences could be minor, or they could be life-threatening. Lying on the couch with a lightweight blanket over her, she sped through the channels not really paying attention to what each show was.

"Mommy, you're going too fast," Carly announced, resting on her knees in a pale blue princess dress. The outfit was a security blanket of sorts, which she would put on when she was worried about her mother. It had started a couple of years back when she was first read the story of Cinderella. What she got out of it was that nothing bad happens when you're dressed like a princess. Ever since then, Carly would don the dress when things seemed uncertain with her mother. Strangely, there were times when Katie was in the hospital, but she didn't feel the need to put it on. It was like she had a sixth sense, knowing when things were just routine and when they were really serious.

"Sorry, sweetie," Katie replied, handing her the remote. "Why don't you do it? Find something good for us to watch."

Katie took the remote and went straight to the three hundreds, where she knew there would be several good choices. "How 'bout *Max and Ruby*?" The show about a girl rabbit and her younger brother was one of Carly's favorites, because that was what she one day hoped for—a little brother she could take care of. She looked over at her mom for confirmation.

"Sounds great to me." Katie smiled and took a deep breath. "You know, I'm feeling much better!" Her voice sounded perky. She knew that with the combination of Rick being gone for the day and her not feeling well, Carly would need the reassurance.

Carly got up and sat at Katie's feet at the end of the couch. She watched her show with one arm resting across her mother's legs. Katie watched her daughter, trying to permanently implant the image in her brain, drifting in and out of sleep.

• • •

It was the grinding sound of metal that jolted both backseat passengers awake, first Lucy and then Chad. Lucy quickly sat upright and tried to survey the situation. Looking to the front, she noticed Benny with both hands on the wheel, leaning forward and looking from side to side. She felt the car begin to slow. Anne's right hand gripped the handle above the window.

"What's wrong?" Lucy spoke in a calm voice not wanting to make the situation worse.

Benny scanned over his right shoulder and passed into the next lane. "Not sure, but I'm pulling over."

"All of a sudden the car started…like stuttering or something," Anne added. "Then this awful grinding noise started."

Chad didn't say a word. He looked around through the back window to make sure there were no cars coming up too fast.

"Great!" Lucy instinctively looked back with Chad. "That's all we need."

Once they reached the shoulder of the road and Benny turned the car off, they all looked at each other questioningly. Then all eyes turned to Benny.

"Uh...I'm guessing none of us have triple A?" Benny shrugged and looked to see if it was clear on his side. "I'll get out and take a look." Unfortunately for Benny, that was one male stereotype that didn't apply to him. He knew nothing about cars. As he got out, a look of uneasiness spread across his face. Then he seemed to remember something—something Chad had said in the car. "Chad!" he yelled to the closed back window. "Didn't you say you worked in a garage?"

"Yeah." Chad gave a self-assured nod to the girls and got out, flicking his hair back.

Anne shot a flirty smile back to Chad, and then sensing Lucy's stare she turned to her. "What?"

Lucy just shook her head and sat back in the seat.

Anne's gaze was like a dart aimed right at the bull's-eye on the back of Chad's jeans as he walked to the front of the car.

"Don't forget, he's not even eighteen yet," Lucy said.

"I was just looking. C'mon, don't you think he's cute?"

"I guess...in sort of a little brother way."

"No way, he's totally hot...and sweet too." Anne could see Lucy getting that serious look on her face, and she did not want to hear a lecture. "Don't worry. I know he'll be gone soon. I'm just having some fun. So do you think they'll be able to fix the car?"

"I hope so."

"Should we get out and help them?" Anne tried to hide her smirk.

"I'm sure you'd like to have Chad look under your hood, but he's a little busy right now. He needs to stay focused, 'cause you know Benny doesn't know jack about cars. Did you see his face?"

"Yeah, it's like fate or something that we picked Chad up. Maybe he'll save us. I mean, who knows what could happen to us stranded out here."

"He hasn't done anything yet."

"He will," Anne said with a confident smile.

The girls continued to talk but made sure they watched out the back window for approaching cars. They realized it would probably happen too fast for them to do anything, but they wanted to make themselves feel useful. Thankfully the road was not too crowded, and if their estimations were correct, then they weren't too far from the next town if they ended up having to walk for help. With the engine off, the sun was starting to penetrate the windows, sucking up the last of the cool air the AC had been providing. It was close to four thirty, so the hottest part of the day was behind them, but it still had to be mid-eighties outside.

Just when they were about to get out for some air, they noticed Benny and Chad walking back to get in.

"It's already like an oven in here," Benny commented as he slammed the door. "Why didn't you roll down the windows?"

"Well why didn't we think of that?" Lucy replied sarcastically.

"We didn't want to turn the key while you were under there," Anne explained. "So what's the deal?"

The girls both looked at Benny expecting an explanation.

"Here's the deal with the car..." Benny looked confused, like he suddenly couldn't remember what the heck Chad had just said about the car. "Tell 'em what the deal is, Chad."

"The thing is," Chad explained, "we could actually keep driving, but it would most likely cause serious damage to Benny's ride. Could be five hours...or five minutes."

Both girls sighed and waited for more, while Benny nodded in agreement.

"I don't think we should chance starting it up again. I'm pretty sure I can fix it, but I need some parts and a few tools."

Benny cringed and fidgeted like his manhood was being threatened. He pulled out the map and unfolded it about half-way. "Looks like we are about seven or eight miles from Las Cruces."

CHAPTER 25

With all four windows down, a slight breeze wafted in and out of the car. Lucy and Anne rested with their backs against a door, facing each other with feet stretched out in front of them, Anne in the front and Lucy in the back.

"I didn't realize it was that bad for you, Lucy," Anne said after Lucy gave her some insight into her family history. "I wish you would have shared this with us sooner…or does Benny already know?"

"No…I mean not really. I just don't like to talk about it. There's no point, anyway—it's all in the past." Lucy surprised herself that she let the conversation get to that point. But after an hour and a half of meaningless chitchat, her defenses were somewhat weakened. And she had to admit to herself that she was feeling closer to Anne and Benny because of the trip. "It's just…well, you were talking about your mom and how great she is and—"

"Oh, I'm sorry, Lucy. I wouldn't have brought it up if I knew."

"It's okay, you couldn't have known."

"I have an idea! Let's talk about something more exciting." Anne's phone rang, and she grabbed it from the dashboard. "Just a sec." She looked at the phone. "It's them." She nodded at Lucy and added an eye roll. "Hey," she said into the phone. "Yeah, we're still alive…uh-huh…How are you guys doing?…Okay, talk to you in ten minutes." Anne set her phone back down on the dash, and Lucy pictured Benny and Chad walking down a deserted highway that stretched into eternity. She was starting to rethink their agreement to check in every ten minutes. It was the only thing they could think of to ensure everyone's safety. Benny didn't want to send one of the girls on the eight-mile hike it would be to the next town. And he wasn't going to leave one of them alone in the car with Chad either. He seemed like an innocent enough kid, but these days you couldn't be too care-ful. Both girls knew what Benny had been thinking and agreed with their silence. Besides, it did seem as though Chad was the only one who knew what to buy to fix the car.

"Okay, so we've got ten more minutes until they call again. I was going to check in with my aunt, and I was thinking you should call Kyle." Anne's expression gleamed with pride at her brilliant idea.

"You go ahead, I'm good."

"C'mon, Lucy. You can't tell me you wouldn't like to talk to Kyle."

"We've been exchanging e-mails…and texts since before we even left."

"I said *talk*." Anne waved a fly away from her face, then tried to retighten the tired bun on her head. "Don't you want to hear his voice?"

Lucy knew Anne was right. With all that time on her hands, her thoughts did seem to keep drifting to Kyle. "Maybe you're right, but it's not really the right time."

"Well, you can make excuses all you want, but I say you better keep in touch if you want him to keep you on his mind." Anne gave a look like she was asking Lucy a question.

A big rig truck whooshed by the car so fast it sent a shock of wind and motion through the car and made Lucy jump.

"Call your aunt," Lucy said firmly.

Anne shrugged and pressed the speed dial on her phone. As it was ringing, she watched as Lucy picked up her own phone off the seat and stared at it. Anne smiled and gave Lucy a thumbs-up with her free hand. Lucy made a face and turned her body to the side as if to shield Anne from her conversation.

"Auntie, it's me," was the last thing Lucy heard when Kyle's line started ringing.

"Lucy, how are you?" came Kyle's voice into Lucy's cell.

"I'm good. How 'bout you?"

"Great! I'm so glad you called. Where are you?"

"Well, that's kind of a long story." Lucy didn't want Kyle to worry, but she didn't want to lie either. She told him that they'd had a setback and needed to get a part for the car, but the problem came when she made the mistake of saying, "They should be back soon."

"Benny and Anne left you in the car by yourself?" Kyle sounded concerned and angered.

"No," Lucy hesitated. She had no choice then. She had to explain about Chad and how they'd picked him up. She tried to sound reassuring and let him know they had taken every precaution and that he was just a kid really.

"Well, I'm sure everything will work out fine...just...be careful." Only Kyle wasn't sure things would work out. Lucy could hear it in his voice. But she appreciated that he didn't want to upset her.

"Can you do me a favor though? Call me when you get to the hotel. Not a text or e-mail. I want to hear your voice."

"Sure, I'll call you as soon as we get there."

"Great, but don't forget. As if I'm not already thinking about you all the time, now I'll be wondering and waiting until I hear from you."

There was silence as Lucy tried to figure out what to say. She was stumped. She didn't know exactly what she was feeling, and she didn't know quite what to say to make him feel better. On top of all that, her ten minutes would be up soon. The one thing she was sure of was that she did find herself thinking of him more and more, and not knowing when she'd see him again was frustrating.

"I won't."

"Just…please be careful, Lucy," Kyle said.

"Don't worry, I will…and I'll talk to you soon."

Just as Lucy hung up the phone, she started to hear a faint sound of pebbles grinding into pavement. Steadily the sound got louder, and closer. She wondered if that could be the boys back already, but as the sound clearly became footsteps, she was sure there was only one set. Lucy and Anne's eyes met as Anne said her own good-byes to her aunt. They both sat up straight and looked through the back window. About ten yards back, a man walked toward them from a car that was about twenty yards back. All they could make out was that the car was a light tan color and some sort of older looking model. The man was medium height, but thick. It was his heavy footsteps and not his oversized clothes that gave it away.

"Why'd he park so far back there?" Anne wondered aloud.

"Hurry up," Lucy whispered urgently. "Roll up your window." Lucy hopped to the front seat, turned the key, and they each rolled up their side windows.

"What's wrong, Lucy?"

Lucy felt around under the seat for the flashlight Benny kept there. It was one of those long, heavy black ones that could come in handy, but not just for lighting.

"He probably just wants to offer us help." Anne tried to sound convincing to Lucy, but also to herself.

"Put your phone up to your ear and pretend to be talking." Lucy looked back once again to find the man just rounding the back end of the car and about to reach her window. "Now!" she said in a strained whisper. Anne complied and faced forward, unsure of what to say.

Lucy could see the man's overly tan chest through his barely buttoned shirt as he bent down to knock on the window. His hair was very straight and looked like one of those bowl cuts a young kid would get, but this guy looked to be mid-forties. "You girls need some help?" the man yelled through the window.

"We're fine, thanks," Lucy said. She only looked at him for a second and then turned forward again.

"Want me to take a look? I'm pretty good with engines. This isn't too good a spot to be stranded." The man took a look up and down the highway. "Specially for two young ladies such as yourselves." He bent down again and put a hand on the door, smiling into the window. "My name's Mike."

"Well, Mike, like I said, we're fine. See, my friend here has already been talking with the tow service." Lucy gestured to Anne on the phone while Anne nodded and gave a couple of "uh-huhs" into the phone. "So thanks anyway."

"Oh…great. But I still wouldn't feel right leaving you all alone out here, with this heat and all." Mike ruffled his shirt casually to fan himself, then gently pulled on the door handle. "Got some cold drinks in my car you can have while you wait."

Anne's eyes widened as she realized what he was doing, and then she dropped her phone in her lap. "Lucy!"

Lucy's heart began to beat faster, but she didn't show it. She looked calm and put a hand on Anne's lap. Her eyes alone seemed to tell Anne to stay cool. Working against both of them was the instant temperature change that began the second the windows were closed. As Anne reached for her phone, Lucy picked up the flashlight.

"Look, Mike!" Lucy said sternly. "My friend is about to dial 911 if you're not gone in five seconds. And if you try to get into this car, I'll beat your fucking head in with this flashlight. Then *you'll* need 911!" This time Lucy stared right at him holding up the flashlight.

Mike's expression was surprised, but his hand was still on the car handle. He froze for a couple of seconds, then jerked his head to the side. They all heard it now—the sound of another car, a truck, pulling up. This time it pulled up right behind the Durango. It looked like there were three people in the front, and the driver started beeping the horn.

"Oh God! What now?" Anne said as she turned to look through the back window. Anne's phone still in her lap began to ring, and she answered it before it even completed the first tone. "Benny! Thank God, I think we're in some trouble here," she started to rattle off hysterically. "There's this guy here, then this other truck came. They're beeping now and—"

"What? You're in the truck?" Anne looked at Lucy with confusion as Lucy began to smile because she could see exactly what was going on.

"Look, Anne," Lucy said. She pointed to Benny, who was exiting the passenger side of the truck, holding a cell phone to his ear. He was followed by Chad, and then the driver exited as well. He was a gray-haired little man wearing blue work pants and a striped button-down shirt with the name Leroy stitched across the pocket.

"Great, help has arrived," Mike said to no one in particular. He quickly walked past the three, then took to a jog back to his car. The three men exiting the truck all stared as Mike ran past them to his car.

CHAPTER 26

"Oh my gosh!" Anne screeched. Both girls busted out of the car and ran to meet Benny, Chad, and the old man.

"You girls alright?" Benny asked as Anne clung to him, hugging him with her head against his chest. "Who's that guy?"

"Everything's fine," Lucy reassured. "Just some jerk saying he wanted to *help* us. What's going on with you guys? And who's your new friend?"

Anne looked up as if she hadn't even noticed the man driving the truck until Lucy mentioned him.

"This is Leroy," Benny said. "He owns a garage not too far from the place we were buying the parts." Leroy gave a nod and a smile. "It was lucky he was there the same time we were."

"It's nice to meet you, Leroy," Anne said. She walked over and shook his hand. "And thanks so much for coming to help us."

"You can thank your young friend here for that." Leroy gave Chad a pat on his back, which evoked a proud grin across Chad's face. "He talked me into coming…said there were two young girls left all alone on the highway. Not sure how he knew I'm a sucker for ladies in distress."

All eyes were fixed on Leroy as he stood with one hand on his hip and the other wiping his forehead. "Well, let's get to it," he said. "We only got about an hour or so more light to work with."

They all walked to the front of the car, Chad and Leroy each carrying a bag. Lucy grabbed ahold of Chad's shoulders as he walked and gave him a couple of shakes. "I knew you were going to come in handy on this trip, kid." She stopped him just short of the front of the car and looked into his eyes. "Seriously, Chad…thanks."

"Hey, it's no big deal." He flipped his hair back and walked around her to stand next to Leroy as Benny opened the hood. At first all three stood and stared at the engine as if waiting to see which one of them would make the first move.

Benny knew it wasn't going to be him, so he made a different move instead. He got the girls out of the way and led them back to the truck where there were sandwiches and chips that they'd picked up after they met up with Leroy. It was actually Leroy's idea based on his own experiences of having to keep women out of his hair when he was working. Benny watched as the girls sat on the tailgate and devoured the sandwiches, hoping they wouldn't finish them all. Even though he ate his in the car on the way over, he was still hungry.

"That was just what we needed, Benny," Anne mumbled as she chomped on some Doritos. Once she cleared her mouth, she added, "And thanks for taking such good care of us."

They both instinctively looked at Lucy, waiting for her to finish chewing.

"Yeah, thanks Benny." Lucy tried to hide her smirk behind her napkin, but Benny could sense her sarcasm.

"What?" Benny wondered.

Lucy wiped her mouth, cleaning a bit of mayo off along with her expression. "Nothing. It's just…it's so funny how Anne knows how to pump up your ego and you just eat it right up."

Benny's posture went from a straight arrow to a slumped-over sausage. He didn't have a chance to respond.

"Hey," Anne said defensively but with conviction. "I really meant that. Benny's done a great job on this trip, and we should really appreciate everything he has done for us." Feeling a little embarrassed by her display, she mellowed her tone. "Don't you, Lucy?"

Lucy was taken aback by Anne's reaction given that standing up to Lucy was not something she had done before. "You know I…I don't know why I said that. Anne's right. Benny, you've really been great on this trip, and…I wouldn't have been able to do it without you."

"Hey, it's cool, Lucita. The funny thing is that even though it's been kind of crazy, I'm actually having a good time."

"Me too!" Anne chimed.

"But…I can't accept your apology without a hug, girl." Benny opened his arms wide and stared at Lucy.

"Uh, I didn't apologize…I just said thanks." Lucy tried to keep a straight face, but she couldn't hold back a smile. She knew her friends were still trying to figure her out. "I'm kidding!" she added sharply. Lucy hopped off the tailgate and wrapped her arms around Benny's neck. Benny's arms almost doubled around her petite waist, and he tried not to lose himself in the pleasure of the moment.

"Hey, what about me?" Anne whined.

"Well, get your butt over here, girl." Benny took an arm from Lucy and reached out to Anne, who joined the hug fest.

He was big enough to hold both girls in his arms. "Now this is what I'm talkin' about."

"Hey," Chad shouted from the front of the Durango. "Why do you get to have all the fun, while we're over here doing all the work?"

"You guys are the experts!" Benny shouted back, laughing over Lucy's shoulder.

Then it all became a bit too awkward for Lucy, and she was ready to break free. "All right, people, that's enough."

Chad and Leroy worked on the car for about another forty minutes. There were a few false starts when they thought they had everything in place, but Leroy didn't feel confident that things were just right. Once he was satisfied and the engine roared with vitality, everyone got ready to move out. The sun was starting to set, and there was a beautiful orange glow floating towards them. Leroy commented on what a great job Chad had done and that he should definitely work with engines in his future. Benny offered to take Leroy out to dinner, but he declined, stating that his wife was expecting him. After many thanks and handshakes, they watched as Leroy climbed into his truck and drove off.

Back on the highway, the four passengers reviewed their options for the night as the sun slowly disappeared from their sight. Unfortunately, they had lost about three and a half hours back there on the highway, so sticking to the original plan would be more difficult.

"What do you think, guys?" Benny asked. "Should we still go for Midland? It's at least four more hours. Or we could try El Paso." No one spoke. "Tomorrow would be a longer drive though."

They all looked around to see what the general consensus was.

For the first time, Anne was looking tired and far from her usual energetic self. "I know I could use a good night's sleep after all that. What about you, Lucy?"

"I'm fine either way. You guys decide."

"Any thoughts, Chad?" Benny said to the rearview mirror.

"Hey, I'm just along for the ride. Whatever everyone else wants is fine with me."

"All right then," Benny responded. "I guess I'll make an executive decision. Let's see what we can find in El Paso. Then we'll get up early for the long haul to Fort Worth. Sound good?"

"Thanks, Benny." Anne patted his shoulder, then slid down in her seat, resting her head and staring at the ceiling.

"Don't thank me yet. Wait 'til we see what kind of rooms we can get."

CHAPTER 27

The door was wide open when Kyle arrived home that evening. Normally, his first instinct would be to walk in cautiously and take inventory of what was missing. But the way things had been going lately with his brother, he knew Alex was up to something. The moment he stepped in the doorway, he heard music and a blast of wind hit him in the face. That meant the back door was open too. His blood began to boil. As he walked past the front bathroom, the door opened, and he was about to let Alex have it, until he realized it wasn't Alex.

"Hey, man," an over-six-foot Asian man said. He was wearing loose jeans and no shirt. "You here to see Alex?"

"You could say that." Kyle tried to hold back and not take out his frustrations on a total stranger.

"Come on back." The man motioned for Kyle to follow and headed toward the living room.

Kyle could see the sliding back door was wide open and some people were sitting at the patio table in the back, three girls and one guy, and they all looked to be in their late twenties. There were drinks on the table, and everyone was dressed according to the hot weather of the day. Kyle wondered how many hours they had been there freely roaming around his home. Walking through the living room, he looked around to see if he could spot Alex. He noticed the refrigerator door open and immediately recognized the rear end sticking out of the side, so he stopped short of the unwanted houseguests and took a hard right to the kitchen. The Asian guy just kept walking toward the back as if he had forgotten that Kyle was even back there.

As if he sensed Kyle's foot heading toward his butt, Alex popped up out of the fridge and slammed the door. "Bro!" Alex's voice was surprised and nervous. He set the full beer he was holding down on the counter. "Thought you had that dinner thing tonight?"

"I decided to skip it."

"Great! Now you can hang with us."

"Are you kidding?" Kyle looked out to the patio, then back to his brother with a hard stare.

"What? These guys are great…and check out Jen in the green tank top." Alex smiled and nodded in her direction. The tall guy joined the others outside but sat in a chair off to the side and began texting on his phone.

Trying not to sound like a parent, but knowing that it would come out that way anyway, Kyle lectured, "Alex, the front door was open."

"Crap. John musta left it open. He just left a few minutes ago. I swear."

"And you know I don't want that back door left open either. I'll be cleaning up dead flies for days."

"Come on, man. What you need is a beer and some social interaction." Alex pushed the beer over to Kyle. "Ever since you met that girl, whatsername, you've been dragging your ass around her like Cocoa right before we put her to sleep."

"Sorry if I can't be your big *frat* bro, but I just don't like coming home to a bunch of strangers trashing my house." Kyle picked up the beer and took a long drink. He knew he needed to relax, but at the same time he did want his brother to get serious about getting his life together.

"They're not strangers, they're my friends. And you know they're not *trashing* the house. We're just chillin', man." Alex turned to the back counter and picked up his phone. "Check this out." He maneuvered through his touch screen for about thirty seconds, looking up once to see Kyle take another long one off the beer. "Here," he said, handing Kyle the phone.

"What's this?"

"It's my thank-you e-mail to BriarPort." Alex smiled proudly and waited for Kyle's response. A second later, they both froze and stared as one of the girls jogged past.

"Gotta pee." She smiled and waved as she headed to the bathroom.

It took them both a second to turn their gaze from the flowing blonde hair whooshing by. "You got an interview?" Kyle snapped back.

"Yeah, today. And I remembered how important you always told me the follow-up thank-you was. I think I nailed it. Then I met some of these guys for lunch and came back here to celebrate."

"Oh, man. Congratulations." Kyle put his arm around his brother's neck and gave a couple of quick jerks. "But why didn't you tell me?"

"I wasn't sure I'd even get the interview. They just called me yesterday...and to tell you the truth, bro, I didn't want to say anything until it was over. I was afraid you'd stress me out." He looked down, feeling a bit of guilt for his honesty.

"I'm proud of you, man."

"You're not mad?" With a sudden burst of relief and energy, Alex went to the fridge and got his own beer, popping it open on the way back to his brother.

"You did the right thing. I have been kind of stressed lately… and on your case. I guess I just thought since you were here and not with the parents that I had somewhat of a responsibility to help you out…you know, keep you focused. But I guess you're not as much of a *loser* as I thought!" Kyle laughed and held up his bottle. They clinked bottle tops, and each took a long swig, Kyle finishing his off.

Usually, Alex wouldn't miss the chance to return a dig to his brother, but at that time he had more important things on his mind. His expression was serious. "Now it's time for me to help *you* get focused. Let's work on getting you back on track… starting with Jen over there."

"Look, I know what you're saying, but I'm not interested."

"You haven't been interested in anything lately. Does she really mean that much to you?"

Kyle smiled, but before he could answer, Alex continued with, "I mean, is she even your girlfriend or what?"

"To be honest, we left it kind of up in the air. We didn't really have much of chance, but all I know is that I can't stop thinking about her…and I miss her. I don't know what's going to happen. I just know that I'm not interested in hooking up with anyone else right now. I just have to wait it out, okay?"

"I get it, bro. But what if she doesn't come back?"

"I'll worry about that when or *if* it happens. Now I've got some calls to make, so why don't you go ahead and get back to your friends. I think they're starting to wonder what's going on."

"All right, but don't worry, most of them have to work in the morning, so they'll be gone soon." Alex took his beer, grabbed a bag of chips from on top of the fridge, and headed toward the back door.

"Alex," Kyle said abruptly.

Alex stopped just short of the door and turned to look at his brother. "Yeah?"

"Good job..."

Alex smiled a thank-you and stepped out back.

"And shut that door!"

CHAPTER 28

Benny and Chad waited in the car while Anne and Lucy went into the office of the Coral Motel. Depending on the price, they'd either get one or two rooms. Ironically, none of the three adults had a credit card they could charge a room to, and cash was getting low. They'd all chipped in money to fix the Durango, even Chad, which just about wiped them out.

Even though the door said *push*, Anne pulled and the door jerked and stopped. They both giggled and said, "Push," then pushed the door open. A jingle above their heads triggered the sound of a wooden chair dragging on a hard surface. From behind a doorway came a heavyset blonde woman with a large ponytail sticking out of the top of her head. Her makeup was gaudy, but she had a sweet smile.

"Good evening, ladies," she said as she rested an elbow on the counter. "Can I get you a room?"

"How much?" Lucy asked.

"Seventy-five a night…includes free movie channels."

"We just need one room…with two beds though."

Back in the car, Chad and Benny listened to music and Chad tried to impress Benny with his knowledge of older music. He talked about playing the guitar back home and how he used to use his computer to play along with Van Halen, Slash, and Ace

Freely. By the time the girls got back, the radio was cranking and they were both singing and playing air guitar like a couple of kids, which was probably fine for Chad.

• • •

"What the heck!" Lucy stared in the open door of room 118 at the single king-size bed in the room.

"I thought you said two beds," Benny replied. He walked in and dropped his bag on a table that was in the corner under a hanging lamp.

"We did," Anne said and walked over and sat down on the bed. She picked up the phone. "I can call over?"

"Better not," Lucy interrupted. "They may not have it, and we said it was just us two." Lucy entered with Chad right behind, closing the door. "They charge extra for more people."

"I'll sleep on the floor," Chad said.

Benny added, "Yeah, it's all good. The Chadster and I will take the floor, and you girls can cuddle up in the bed." He sported a naughty smile that made Chad laugh and then turn away, pretending to look in his backpack.

Anne hung up the phone. "All right, let's make the best of it."

All four instinctively spread out to the corners of the room to get settled, trying to maintain personal space. It was a little after eight, which meant there would be some time to kill. Anne went through her bag on the bed, pulling out a book and a brush to tidy her hair. Benny sat in the chair at the table and leafed through the motel binder, pretending to be interested in whether or not they had room service.

"Hey, Benny, is there a TV guide in that stuff?" Anne asked.

"Uh…" Benny looked through the pile on the table and tossed her a folded cardboard directory.

"Thanks!" Anne said, delighted. She scanned down the listings for a few seconds. "Oh, *Shrek*'s on the free channel. Anyone want to watch it? I love that movie!" She grabbed the remote off the nightstand and stared at it for a moment, trying to make out which button was the power button.

"I'm in," Chad said as he dove across the room and landed on the bed.

"I think I'll go outside for a while," Lucy announced casually. "Get some air, maybe make some calls."

Forty minutes had passed, and Benny could still see Lucy on the phone through the crack of the curtains. He watched her as he pretended to be going through the Southwest-themed magazine that was in the room. The sound of *Shrek* hummed in the background and only became noticeable when accompanied by bursts of laughter from Chad and Anne. A few times Lucy paced back and forth, and from her side view, he could see she was not happy. When she was finally done, Benny hesitated to give her some time alone. He sent a few texts out to family, checking in with his mother and cousins, then headed outside.

"Hey, guys," Benny said to Chad and Anne. "I saw a vending machine downstairs. You want a soda?" Benny was amazed that they both ignored him like little kids tuning out their parents and zoning in on the television screen. Walking between them and *Shrek*, Benny headed outside, and neither acknowledged his exit.

"How 'bout a soda, Lucita?"

Between the thin crescent moon and the poorly lit motel lights, there was barely enough light to see each other.

"Sure, thanks," Lucy called to Benny, who was already halfway down the steps.

The night air was still, and the only sounds to be heard were the sporadic cackles from inside their room.

"We have to share," Benny said. He set the soda on the railing. "This cheap-ass motel! Damn machine stole my money."

Lucy was leaning forward, staring into the empty courtyard. She didn't say a word.

Benny popped open the can, but he set it back down without taking a drink. "Can you believe we're going to be there tomorrow? Seems like we've been on this trip forever." He looked at Lucy, waiting for a response, but when she didn't answer, he slapped a hand to his cheek and replied for her in his best girly voice: "Yeah, Benny, I'm so excited!"

With the poor lighting, he hadn't noticed it before. Lucy was crying. He wondered if it was something he'd said or if it was due to one of the calls she'd made. Usually he didn't press Lucy when she was upset, but this time he felt differently. He wanted to help her, and he knew that would mean getting her to talk. He brushed her hair back gently and rubbed her cheek with his thumb. "What's wrong? Are you nervous about tomorrow? Or...did something happen?"

"I don't know what's wrong with me," she said, barely above a whisper. "I don't do this."

"Do what?"

"I always keep it together. I always have. But these last few weeks I just seemed to lose it."

"You don't have to be so strong all the time." Benny put his arm around her shoulders. "Maybe you had no choice before. But now you have us. You have me."

"Yeah, that's just what you want. Someone blubbering around you all the time." Lucy wiped her tears with the back of her shirt.

"Hey, you're just going through a tough time right now. Anyone would be like this. Well...not me."

Lucy let out a tiny giggle and shoved her body against his. She looked up into Benny's eyes like a lost puppy looking for safety, for comfort. It happened so quickly and unexpectedly that Benny didn't know if she kissed him or he kissed her. Either way, something happened to join them together, both being lost in each other. After a few seconds, one of the two nearby lights popped and went out.

"Oh, man," Benny whispered, pulling back. "How wrong was that? I'm so sorry, Lucy."

"It's okay, really. We just got...carried away in the moment."

"Yeah...right." Benny's face fell, and he turned away.

"What's wrong?"

"I just care about you so much...and I don't want you to think I'm trying to take advantage of you or whatever."

"No way. You've done so much for me, and I know I don't show it, but I really appreciate it." She grabbed his arm and turned him to her. "I honestly don't know how I can make it through this without you. You're a great...friend." Lucy put her arms around him, and they hugged silently until Benny pushed back.

"Okay, then talk to me. Tell me what was going on with those calls out here."

Feeling a combination of defeat and obligation, Lucy realized she would have to spill it. Benny needed to be reassured that she would confide in him.

"Well, first I was talking with Kyle…and that one didn't go so well." She turned and leaned her back against the railing. "I think that was my fault though."

"Why?"

"I don't know. This situation is just so impossible, and I think he feels I'm shutting him out."

"Huh, I wonder why," Benny interrupted sarcastically.

"Seriously, how can you get close to someone you barely know when you're hundreds of miles away? And he wasn't too happy to hear about Chad and all the other stuff that's been going on."

"Yeah, it has been pretty crazy."

"Then I talked to Rick, and my sister had sort of an episode. She's going to be okay, but it doesn't always work out that way."

"I'm sorry, Lucy. But at least you'll see her tomorrow." Benny searched Lucy's eyes to see if something else was bothering her. He was getting proficient at reading the signs. "What else did he say?"

"He asked if I called the hospital to check on Katie."

"So you feel bad that you didn't?"

"No, I didn't even know she was there, so I couldn't have called. The nurse said a woman called asking about Katie. Said she was family."

"Who do you think it was?"

"I really don't know, but…I hope it wasn't my mother."

"You don't want her there? I mean, maybe it would help Katie, having more family there."

"That woman's never helped Katie, or anybody but herself. All she—" Lucy stopped herself before she said too much. She was tired and really didn't want to get into it. Benny knew enough, and maybe that woman who called the hospital, whoever it was, was just someone from Rick's family. She hoped that would be the case because there was no way she could deal with her mother on top of everything else. "Can we go inside now? I'm really tired."

"Yeah, me too."

"Great," Lucy complained as Benny opened the door.

"Should we wake them up?" he asked.

"No, just let them sleep there. I'm fine with the floor if you are." Lucy set her bag down on the floor while Benny quietly closed the door. Chad was on his back with his head propped up on a pillow, mouth hanging wide open. Anne was flat on her stomach with her feet to the head of the bed. One of them had slid over and landed right next to Chad's open mouth. The movie hadn't even ended yet, but the sound was turned way down.

"Hey," Benny whispered. "I can just kick it in this chair right here, so you can have more space on the floor. Use this blanket." He pointed to the comforter on the bed that had been pushed to the very edge and was about to fall off. Lucy wouldn't have to worry about being cold with four bodies in one room.

"Don't be a martyr. We can sleep together on the floor."

Benny smiled and cocked his head with a raised eyebrow.

"You know what I mean," she shot back.

While Lucy was in the bathroom, Benny had pulled the comforter off the bed and spread it out across the floor.

Lying in the dark next to each other was not something either of them had planned on this trip. At first, Benny was on his side and crammed up against the side of the bed. He didn't want her to feel uncomfortable.

"Stop being dumb," Lucy whispered, yanking on Benny's shoulder. "C'mon and get comfortable. Just sleep regular and stop acting like I'm so fragile or something. I trust you, Benny."

Benny turned on his back, and Lucy scooted in and put her head on his shoulder.

"Benny?"

"Yes, Lucita?"

"Thanks."

"Anytime, girl."

There was a part of Lucy that felt like she had betrayed Kyle by kissing Benny. She felt guilty, but she tried to convince herself that she shouldn't. After all, what was Kyle to her anyway? Not a boyfriend. They weren't committed. Then why was she so concerned? Lucy definitely didn't need any more drama at this point and fought hard to forget about it. As much as she cared about Kyle and didn't want to hurt him, Benny was there for her and she needed him too. She closed her eyes, and after a few minutes, she fell asleep. Benny lay awake long after, staring at the ceiling and listening to her breathe.

CHAPTER 29

....

"Katie?" Lucy was still sound asleep, and her words were barely audible. She mumbled something else, but Benny couldn't make it out. He had been lying there next to her, waiting for her to wake up. It was still early, about seven a.m., but he couldn't sleep any longer. Her face had a distressed look on it, and she started to breathe heavily, so he decided to wake her up.

"Lucy," he said softly, rubbing her arm. "Time to wake up, girl."

After a few seconds, she began to stir, then awoke startled. She seemed confused and gaped at Benny for an answer.

"You okay?" Benny rested his body on one elbow.

"Yeah…I just…what time is it?" She pushed her body up to a sitting position and glanced at the clock. It looked like Anne was still asleep, but Chad was no longer in the bed. Turning her head to the bathroom door, she could see the light on and heard water running. Surprisingly, she felt relief that he hadn't taken off.

"How'd you sleep?" Benny asked.

"Fine, how about you?"

"Oh, it was great for me."

Lucy shot him a look and got to her feet. She walked over to the bed and jabbed it with her knee a few times, shaking Anne's body.

"I'm awake, Lucy," Anne said, lifting her head. "I've actually just been waiting for everyone to get up."

"Good," Lucy replied and sat on the edge of the bed. "We should probably get going as soon as everyone is ready. Don't you think, Benny?"

"Sounds good." He got up, gathered the comforter from the floor, and tossed it in the chair. He noticed Anne watching him, and they exchanged smiles. Benny shook his head and tried to avoid a conversation about last night. "There's a donut shop across the street. You guys want me to go grab some coffee and donuts?"

Lucy nodded, and Anne added, "If they have chocolate chip muffins, will you get me one, please?"

"Sure." He grabbed his wallet off the table and headed out the door.

Both girls watched and waited for the door to slam.

"What happened last night?" Anne jumped in first, sitting abruptly up in the bed.

"Hey, I was just about to ask you the same thing."

"Absolutely nothing," Anne said, defeated. "I know it's stupid. I mean, I'm probably never going to see him again, but he's so cute...and sweet too. Don't you think?"

"Yeah, but you're right. After today, that's it. Besides, don't forget how old he is."

"I know, I know...but what about you and Benny?" Anne's demeanor suddenly brightened.

"Don't get so excited...nothing happened with us either."

"Really?"

"Really. We were just sleeping down there because you two fell asleep in the bed together."

"Oh, sorry."

"It's okay. I actually slept pretty well."

"Then what's wrong? You seem like something's bothering you."

"I'm fine." Lucy got up from the bed. She wanted a little more distance. She took the comforter from the chair, tossed it onto the bed, and flopped into the chair.

"You don't seem fine," Anne pressured. "Plus, I heard you talking in your sleep. You said 'Katie' and something about a painting."

Lucy stared across the room to nothing in particular. "Do you ever have a dream, and then wake up still feeling the way you did in the dream?"

"Yeah, totally. Once I had a dream that Shia LaBeouf was my boyfriend and for some reason he broke up with me. I was so devastated, and when I woke up I totally missed him. One time I even woke up crying from a dream." Anne finally noticed Lucy was not expecting the conversation to be focused on her dreams. "Oh, did you have a bad dream last night?"

Lucy curled her legs up under her on the chair. "It's actually a recurring dream that I've been having for a while now."

"Do you want to tell me about it?"

"Some parts of it I can't explain or even remember, like some things seem real and others are just really different. I think I'm a lot younger in the dream, because Katie's in it and it seems like she's about six or seven years old. I'm at home, only my house isn't the same house we lived in." Lucy's eyes were glazed over like she was trying to remember the details from the dream. "I'm looking all over for Katie. I can hear her calling me over and over, and I'm just following her voice. When I finally find her, she's in this room, painting a picture. She's wearing this cute sort of dress-up dress, but something is different about her. I can never figure out what it is."

"You mean the way she looks?"

"Yeah, she *looks* really different." Lucy wasn't looking at Anne. Her eyes were straight ahead as if she was watching the dream unfold. "Anyway, when I walk in the room she's smiling. She wants me to see her painting, but it's turned the other way. So I walk up to her, and as soon as I reach her I start to see her painting."

"What is it?" Anne asked.

"It's my mother. And every time I get to that point in the dream, every time I see that picture, it's like something grabs me and pulls me right out of the dream."

"Wow," Anne whispered. "I wonder what that means."

Just then they heard the door of the bathroom open. Chad poked his head out of the small opening he'd made. "Anyone waiting to get in here?"

"We're fine," Anne answered. She flashed her pearly whites at him.

Always the voice of reason, Lucy added, "But we should get going soon."

"No problem. I'll be out in five," Chad said and closed the bathroom door.

Then Lucy suddenly got up from the chair, signifying the end of the conversation. "Let's get our stuff together. You can have the bathroom next." Lucy tried to make herself look busy gathering her things even though she didn't have much to put back in her bag.

"Wait…what about the dream?" Anne sounded concerned. "Don't you want to finish talking about it?"

"Not really. It's better if I just forget about it and focus on something else."

"Are you sure?" she urged. "I mean, maybe if you talk about it you'll be able to figure out what it all means." Anne started pulling the covers back as if she intended to make the bed. "Isn't it supposed to be like unresolved issues are trying to send you messages in your dream, or something like that?"

"I thought you wanted to be a nurse, not a psychiatrist?" Lucy answered sarcastically. "And you don't have to make that bed, you know."

Anne laughed and dropped the blanket even though she was almost done. "Oh yeah."

A loud pounding on the door sent them both whirling around with questioning looks. "This is the manager!" a loud, deep voice came from the other side of the door.

Anne looked at Lucy, who just shrugged and walked slowly toward the door.

"Open up! We know you got a teenage boy in there…we know he has awesome hair, and he's cute too!"

Lucy reached the door and turned to look at Anne, who mouthed, *What?* They both giggled, and then Lucy opened the door, knowing that it could only be one person.

As Benny stepped in holding a bag from the donut shop and a carton of drinks, Chad walked out of the bathroom with jeans on but holding his shirt. "What's all the noise?" he said, looking around confused.

"Don't worry, kid, we'll protect you!" Benny said in a serious voice and then started laughing.

"What?" Chad whined. "I don't get it."

"Just forget it," Anne said, walking over to Chad and trying not to stare at his chest. "It's just Benny being Benny."

"Oh, so this is what I have to look forward to," Chad said. He pulled his shirt on.

"What are you talking about?" Anne asked.

"Didn't you tell them?" Benny jumped in. He walked casually over to the table and set everything down. He looked at Chad with a silly grin.

"No, I thought you would."

"Tell us what?" Anne sounded impatient as she turned and looked at Lucy and then Benny.

"I decided to take the kid with me. Mind if I eat since we're not ready to go? I'm starving." With only two chairs in the room, he politely stood next to the table and started munching on a chocolate old-fashioned—one of his favorites.

Lucy had a feeling she knew what he meant, but something this big needed clarification. "What do you mean? With you where?"

"He's going with me to see my cousins and then back to LA." Benny polished off the rest of his donut and began brushing crumbs off of his shirt. "We were talking about it last night when you girls were getting the room."

"Really?" Anne screeched. Lucy shot her a look that said not to overdo it on the excitement, so she calmly sat on the edge of the bed and waited to hear more.

"Yeah," Chad said as he walked over to the table to join Benny. "Pretty cool of my man, Benny, huh?" He pulled a random donut out of the bag, and without even looking at it, he took a bite. "He said I could crash on his couch for a while…figure out what I want to do, maybe check out the music scene…"

"That's great, Chad." Anne held her smile at about a medium even though a super-size was trying to get out. "And that is so nice of you, Benny," she added.

"Well, I guess my generosity is limitless."

"Great, then why don't you share those donuts," Lucy teased, finally succumbing to her own hunger.

Although she was concerned about how that bit of news would change things for everyone, she had enough things to worry about. Maybe Chad would be gone before they even got back home. He did seem like a great kid, and whatever happened, he made the trip a lot more interesting.

CHAPTER 30

Halfway through the last day in the car, the conversation made its way to sharing stories of growing up. Benny talked about having a big family and how there was always something to go to—a soccer game, a recital, or even just watching his little brother skateboarding in the local park. His best memories were the family barbeques where all of his relatives would go and cook something to share with everyone. At one of the barbeques, when Benny was around fifteen, he and one of his older brothers nabbed a six-pack of beer from the cooler. After they hid in the garage and drank it all, Benny went around the whole party telling all the guests just how much he loved them. Even though he ended up in deep trouble, everyone in the family forever remembered it and laughed about it.

Anne talked about the time just before her dad opened up their business. He was more relaxed and was able to spend more time with Anne and her mother. She loved going to the beach with them and staying all day until sunset.

Chad wanted to talk about his mother and how different she was before meeting his stepdad. Not just her personality, but also in appearance. He showed a picture of the two of them smiling at one of Chad's school functions. Her hair was dark brown, long and full, and her smile was rich and proud.

Without a doubt, Lucy could relate to Chad's situation. She understood how life can take a seemingly happy person and turn them into something so lifeless and self-destructive. But she didn't want to bring down the mood being shared by all. She had her own happy memories she could share, but at that moment, only one thing came to her mind.

Lucy shared a story about one of her best, and worst, dates in high school. She was supposed to be going to a party with Eric, a guy in her English class. She'd only been there for about half an hour when Katie called. Her mother had gone to the store, and Katie was afraid she wouldn't come back. Lucy wasn't with Eric at the time; he'd gone off to talk to some friends. When she couldn't find him after five minutes, she realized she was holding his keys in her purse. She didn't even give it a second thought, and she was out the door to go get Katie.

Once back at the party, they went upstairs and looked around until they found a quiet room to hang out in. They basically made themselves at home and did whatever they wanted. At one point Katie asked, "Are you sure we're allowed to use this stuff?" Lucy reassured her, "Of course, this is my friend's room." After a while, Lucy snuck downstairs and got some snacks. "It was kind of like a slumber party," Lucy remembered. They played games, watched TV, and even put on makeup. "The funniest part was," Lucy continued, "Eric finally called me after a couple of hours wondering where I was and saying he needed his keys. He was pretty nice about the whole thing and ended up driving us both home."

"That's hilarious," Benny laughed. "I guess that guy wasn't missing you too much on your date."

Lucy had to agree. "I guess not."

"Well I think it's a sweet story," Anne added. "Lucy took care of her sister back then…and she's taking care of her now too."

Chad agreed and told Lucy he thought she was brave, and then he asked her the question that no one asked her yet, which put an abrupt end to the happy memory phase of the trip. "Are you scared to have the operation?"

"Kind of. I guess it just doesn't seem real yet."

"Isn't there still a chance that you won't end up having the operation?" Anne asked.

"A small one. I have a feeling everything will work out and I'll be the one. Plus, the doctors say there are just a few more tests to do there, but it shouldn't change anything."

"I had my appendix taken out when I was six," Chad added, "but I barely remember it."

"I guess I spent so much time thinking about the trip and seeing my sister after all this time that I hadn't thought that much about the actual surgery."

"Nice work, Chad!" Benny teased.

"Crap…I'm sorry, Lucy."

"Hey, don't worry about it. Benny just can't miss an opportunity to make someone feel awkward. In a couple of hours we'll be there, and then that's all I'll be thinking about and talking about anyway. Might as well get used to it now." Her casual tone did not match her unsettled stomach or her overloaded mind. She reached down into her bag and plucked out her iPod and earphones. Lucy didn't want to seem abruptly closed off to her travel companions, but she also didn't want to arrive at her sister's mentally drained. So she closed her eyes, inserted her earphones, and slid back in the seat. When she needed to relax, she liked to picture a black canvas in her mind. Slowly the black would melt away and become beautiful swirls of red, purple, fuchsia. The colors started flowing to the music, and Lucy fought to stay focused on the canvas and not what was waiting ahead.

. . .

"Can I call her Auntie Lucy?" Carly asked her mother as she sat on her bed. She was watching Katie put her laundry away in her purple and pink painted room. Carly had felt like a big girl when her parents let her pick out the paint and the bedspread that had hearts and flowers to match the wall colors.

"I'm sure that will be fine with her." Katie scooped up a pile of socks and underwear from Carly's bed and stuffed them into her top dresser drawer. "Sweetie…I want to make sure you understand that Aunt Lucy might need some time to get to know you."

"But I don't even know her yet, Mommy," Carly answered, looking confused.

Katie smiled at the cleverness of her daughter. "I know, baby girl. What I meant was…you know how you are with Papa? Like how you guys give lots of hugs and play and stuff?"

"Yeah, my papa's the best!" She threw her fists in the air as if performing a cheer.

"Well, Lucy may not be that way at first." Katie walked to the closet and began hanging a few dresses she picked up from a pile on the bed. "She might be kind of…shy at first."

"That's okay, Mommy. I play with shy kids all the time at school."

"I know," Katie laughed, "and I'm so proud of you for that. Just be patient, okay?" When Katie came to the last dress, she hesitated. It was Carly's Cinderella dress, her security dress. "I was thinking maybe we should put this away in your special chest." She knew it wouldn't fly, but she thought she should give it a shot. This wouldn't be the first attempt. "It's getting a bit too small for you…and we want to keep it nice, right?"

Carly jumped up and stood on the bed in protest. "No, Mommy! It's my favorite…and I need that dress."

"Carly, I know you love it…but you know what?" Katie walked over with the dress and sat next to Carly.

"What?"

"You are becoming such a big girl, and this dress is kind of like a security blanket. You know, like the one Zoe carries around all the time."

"But it's not a blanket, it's a dress."

"Yes. But when do you wear this dress?"

"Just when I feel like it."

"No, you wear it when you are upset or worried and want to feel better."

"Yeah, and it works really good, Mommy, so why do you want to get rid of it?"

Katie could feel she was losing the battle and actually thought her daughter had a point. She was only in the first grade. No sense forcing her to grow up too quickly. She was well aware that there weren't many benefits to that. "Okay, smarty pants. We'll keep it a bit longer. At least until you can't fit into it anymore."

"Yay! Thank you, Mommy." Carly leaned over and hugged Katie and then ran out of the room as if she were late for an appointment.

CHAPTER 31

It sounded like it was coming from a faraway place in the corner of her mind. "Lucy, wake up." The voice was echoey and somewhat familiar. "Lucy, can you hear me?" She felt a hand on hers as she lay in a bed, and the voice came again. This time she knew. "Lucy, how do you feel?" Kyle said softly.

Is it over? her mind thought, but her voice would not cooperate. She felt tired, but whole. Not like someone who had just been cut open. She forced her eyes to open halfway.

"You did it...you saved your sister." He brushed the hair away from her face and stroked her cheek. Kyle's face looked warm and glowing. He was smiling with his mouth and his eyes. Lucy could see beyond his shoulder another bed in the room with someone lying next to her. She turned her head and instantly knew that it was Katie. Her eyes were closed, but Lucy noticed the rise and fall of her body beneath the blankets. It was almost as though she could hear Katie's heart beating, a reassuring tempo that meant she was going to make it.

Kyle picked up Lucy's hand in both of his and kissed her fingertips.

"I can't believe you're here," she whispered.

"I had to come. I couldn't stand being away from you...not knowing what was going on, or if you were going to be okay."

She started to smile, but it faded instantly when confusion finally set in and questions began to well up inside of her. She didn't understand what was happening, how she got there, or when Kyle got there. She could still hear what she thought was Katie's heartbeat, only it sounded as if it was getting faster. Lucy looked over at Katie. Her breathing was increasing with the pace of the heartbeat. The monitors on each side of Katie's bed began to hum and beep. She felt her hand slip from Kyle's.

"What's happening? Kyle—" When she looked back at Kyle, he was gone. The door opened, and a doctor and two nurses rushed in to Katie's bedside. It was at that moment that she noticed the little girl. She was standing against the wall in the corner by the door. It didn't make sense to her. "It couldn't be," she said to herself. It was little Katie, just like in her dream. And she was wearing the same dress-up dress. Again, there was something different about her, but Lucy still couldn't figure it out. While the doctor looked at Katie, the nurses were pressing buttons to quiet the machines. The little girl sank to the ground and hugged her knees. Her eyes were puddled with tears of fear. The nurses' lips were moving rapidly but without any sound coming out. Lucy suddenly felt as if she was slipping away and fought to keep her eyes focused on Katie. When one of the nurses turned to face Lucy, she could have sworn it was Anne. The nurse walked over and put her hand on Lucy's arm.

"It's okay, Lucy." This time Lucy could hear her voice, but she could no longer keep her eyes open. She felt like she was slipping away, dying, and everything was fading.

"Lucy!" Anne's voice got louder. "Lucy, c'mon wake up!"

"Yo, Lucita, *despertarse!*" Benny yelled from the front seat, jolting Lucy from her dream. "Now that's the way to do it."

"What?" Lucy looked around the car to find Anne, Chad, and Benny all looking at her. She couldn't believe something so real could only be a dream. Part of her was relieved, but another part of her was upset. She would have been just fine to have the whole thing over with.

"That's mean, Benny! Sorry, Lucy," Anne offered. "I tried to wake you up gently, but you wouldn't budge. You were really out of it."

"What's going on?" Lucy was still trying to get her bearings and bring herself back to reality. "Are we almost there?"

"Yep, 'bout forty-five more minutes. I'm pulling off to get gas though, and I figured you may want to get out too."

"Yeah, thanks."

In the bathroom at the gas station, Anne and Lucy took turns in the one stall that was decent enough to use, and then they adjusted their hair and makeup while trying not to touch anything inside.

"I know this sounds stupid," Anne said from inside the stall, "but I'm kind of nervous."

"It's not stupid," Lucy reassured. "You're going to a stay with a house full of people you don't know and be put in a pretty weird situation." Lucy looked for somewhere to set her bag down and decided to balance it between her legs while she washed her hands. "I know I should have said this a while ago, but…thanks for coming with me."

"I was glad to. I want to help you, Lucy." Anne flushed the toilet with her foot and came out. "Aside from being in this place, it's actually been kind of fun." Anne jumped back just in time to avoid getting hit with the door as it swung open. "Whoa."

"Excuse me," a dumpy looking woman said, ushering her little boy through the door. He was about seven or eight and had a big chocolate stain on the front of his shirt. "Now let's go," she ordered, shoving him into the stall. Anne and Lucy exchanged looks of sympathy for the boy, who looked very embarrassed to still have to be going in the women's restroom. Lucy held on to her paper towels and opened the door with them in her hand.

"I always do that too." Anne walked out as Lucy held the door open with her foot, tossed the towels in the trash, and scooted out the door. They could hear the woman nagging her son to hurry up as the door closed behind them. "I guess that's what kids will do to ya?" Anne shrugged. Lucy didn't answer, so Anne added, "I still can't wait to be a mom though."

"Oh yeah, with who? Chad?" Lucy teased as they walked through the minimart that housed the bathroom. Chad was at the register buying an energy drink. He flicked his hair back and counted out quarters to make up the rest after his two dollar bills.

"Lucy!" Anne shushed her and pointed ahead at Chad like a schoolgirl at lunchtime.

"Well?" Lucy asked.

"Well what?" Anne answered. She stared at Chad as they walked past and out the door.

They stood in the shade watching Benny pump gas and waiting for Chad to come out.

"He'll be legal and free by the time we get back…"

"Chad's cute…and I do really like him, but he doesn't really go with my plan."

Lucy folded her arms and gave Anne an inquiring look. "What plan would that be?"

Anne peeked in and could see that Chad was headed toward the door, so she motioned with her head for them to start walking to the car. "Well, when I become a nurse, I'll be in my mid to late twenties. Then I'll meet a lawyer or some type of business-man who's a couple years older than me. We'll date for a while, then have a quaint little wedding, then start a family...after two or three years of blissful marriage, of course."

"Blissful marriage?" Benny shouted from the other side of the car. "Who's getting married?"

"Never mind, it's just girl talk." Anne elbowed Lucy and gave her a look that said *conversation over.*

"That sounds like quite a plan...and you are just the girl to pull it off." They both climbed in followed closely by Chad, who was already gulping down his drink.

• • •

After twenty minutes of laboring through traffic in the city streets, they finally came to the point where they would enter the residential neighborhoods that led to Katie and Rick's home. Lucy had called the house phone when they got off the freeway, but there was no answer. She spoke to Katie briefly that morning and told her they would arrive somewhere between four and six in the afternoon. It was almost four thirty, so it was possible they hadn't gotten home yet.

Just a few blocks away, Lucy relayed left and right turns to Benny. The homes in their neighborhood looked pretty new to Lucy. She figured they were only about five years old and prob-ably had some type of home owners' association. The trees and other landscaping were beautifully manicured, the sidewalks were clean, and there were minimal cars on the streets. It's not like she thought they were living in the slums, but seeing what a pleasant and nice community Katie lived in was comforting to Lucy.

"That's their street, Coyote Lane. Turn right there."

About six houses down on the right, Benny pulled alongside the curb next to a one-story green and tan house.

"You think they're home?" Anne asked, craning her neck to look out the window.

"There are no cars in the driveway," Lucy answered.

"Maybe they park in the garage," Benny offered.

Chad just sat quietly, looking around the neighborhood like he wished he and his mother could escape together and find their way to one of the beautiful homes surrounding him. He was probably picturing himself arriving home after school, her waiting inside to see how his day went. No chance of that now.

"I dunno. I guess we'll go see." Lucy unbuckled her seatbelt and started to get out. Anne scooted over to get out, following Lucy.

"Wait, I'll help you get your stuff and walk you up," Benny offered. Unlike the small overnight bags they had brought into the hotel rooms, this time the girls each had a suitcase as well.

"I'll wait here." For the first time, Chad seemed to feel uncomfortable, out of place, like he didn't want to intrude even though Benny and Anne weren't family either. He did roll down his window so he could see better and hear what was going on.

At the door the three of them stood there while Lucy rang the doorbell several times, then knocked. A ceramic tile hung above the doorbell. It was decorated in lavender and yellow, and "The Moores" was written in flowing cursive with flowers surrounding it. The space at the front door provided some shade, but the heat still penetrated the area, and Lucy was starting to sweat.

"Maybe you should try her cell," Anne finally said to break the silence.

Lucy realized that she would have to do something. She couldn't just stand outside forever and avoid the awkward reunion that was bound to take place. "Okay." She had started to rummage through her purse when a car pulled into the driveway.

CHAPTER 32

It was a blue Ford F150 with a man in the driver's seat who appeared to be alone. The man noticed the three of them standing there and gave a nod and a quick wave after halting the truck in front of the garage. He climbed out holding a briefcase-style bag he picked up from the passenger seat. "Hey, guys!" he shouted as he slammed the door. "Sorry about that...hope you haven't been waiting long."

"No, we just got here." Lucy tried to sound casual and friendly.

Rick immediately walked up to Lucy and gave her a hug with his free arm. He obviously knew which one was her. "We're so glad you're here." Before Lucy had a chance to say anything, he turned to the others and said, "And you must be Anne." He gave her a hug. "And Benny." This time he held out his hand for Benny to shake.

"Well, you got all the names right, man. Nice to meet you," Benny said with a laugh.

"Looks like you got one more over there," Rick wondered aloud as he gestured towards Benny's car.

They all looked over to see Chad bobbing his head listening to the car stereo, and Lucy jumped in first with, "That's a new friend of ours, Chad."

"Well, let's get inside where it's cool." Rick went for the door with his keys. "What about Chad, is he coming in?" He opened the front door and stood to the side so the girls could walk in to the tiled entryway. Benny stayed on the porch.

"Actually," Benny interjected, "we should really get going, try to beat some of the traffic."

"Oh." Lucy suddenly felt like an insecure child being dropped off at kindergarten on the first day of school. She was aware of the fact that they weren't staying, but she didn't think it would all happen so quickly. She wanted a chance to say good-bye to Benny.

"I'm just gonna give Katie a call, let her know you're here, and give you guys some time to say good-bye."

Taking turns hugging each other, all three seemed to be sharing the same mixed feelings. The girls knew they'd eventually separate from Benny, but both were already feeling that separation anxiety.

"You guys better call or text me every day and let me know what's going on." Benny held one of each of their hands in his. "We'll probably only be at my cousin's until Monday, and then we're back on the road."

"Be careful!" Anne warned like a mother hen. "We've had enough adventure on this trip."

Reaching out for another hug from Anne first and then Lucy, Benny added, "You take care of yourself, Lucita. And if you need anything, you better call me."

Over Benny's shoulder Lucy saw Chad getting out of the car. He flashed a cute shy smile as he swaggered over. Anne met him halfway, and they said their good-byes first.

"I'm glad you came with us," Anne said, apparently not worrying about how it would sound.

"Me too."

They gave a quick hug and confirmed that each had the other's number in their cell. Chad added that he may not have that number long since his mom would probably, eventually, cancel his service. He was surprised his stepdad hadn't thought to make her do it already.

"Do me a favor," Lucy said when it was her turn with Chad. "Call your mom...let her know what's going on." She surprised herself at what she was saying to him. "She at least deserves to know you're okay."

"I will," he promised. When Lucy started to walk away, he added, "Thanks for taking a chance on me. I appreciate everything you guys have done."

"Don't worry, you can work it off when we get back," Benny chimed in, walking up behind them.

"It wasn't too risky, Chad." Lucy smiled and walked back up toward the house. She turned and gave a final wave as Chad and Benny got back in the car. Behind them Rick appeared in the doorway and picked up their bags.

"Ready?"

Walking in gave Lucy a strange feeling. This was not just a house, it was a home. Of course she should have expected that, but the reality of her sister having this whole separate life and family finally came through. The walls of the hallway were covered with various combinations of photos of the three of them, and a few included a friendly-looking older man. Inside, Rick led them to a family room with a matching beige couch and loveseat along with a huge bookshelf in the corner. She could tell the bottom two shelves belonged to Carly. The books were all shapes and sizes, and some were sticking out here and there.

They all sat down, and Rick explained that Katie went to pick up Carly at a friend's house and that they should be arriving home soon. He showed them to their room in the back of the house right next to Carly's room. There were two twin beds, which relieved them both, but they could tell that one matched the room and the other was added in for their visit. There was also a tall dresser and a closet with sliding doors.

"I hope this is okay for you girls. I know it's a little cramped—" Rick gestured around the room.

"It's fine," Lucy reassured him, although she did feel a bit like she was in a dorm room. The two beds were separated by a small nightstand that carried a lamp and an alarm clock.

"Yes, thanks Rick," Anne added. "And thanks for letting me come along."

"Sure, we thought it was great that you were coming. Katie and I are just really glad you're here…both of you. We also have a fold-out futon in the den if you decide you need more space."

"Thanks," they both said.

"I'll let you two get settled, and I'm going to go start dinner. It's my turn to cook tonight." Rick walked out and gave a last, "Let me know if you need anything."

Anne instantly jumped up and opened her suitcase. There were empty hangers in the closet, and she started to hang up a few blouses. On the shelf above the closet, there were two boxes that looked like storage items, a couple of photo albums, and a stack of folded clothes. The pile looked like a child's clothes, probably things that Carly had outgrown. Lucy sat down on one of the beds and appeared to be watching Anne, but her gaze was going right through her.

"Don't you want to unpack?"

"I will later. I don't really feel like it right now."

Anne stopped, with a look of guilt about her happy vacation mood. "You're nervous about being here, aren't you? About seeing your sister?"

"I don't know, maybe. It feels weird being here. I'm sure I'll get used to it."

"Lucy, what you should be feeling is proud. I'm proud of you. And I know Rick and Katie are so thankful to have this chance with you. Everything's going to be okay...you'll see." Anne tossed the shirt in her hand back into her suitcase. "Let's just unpack later."

Lucy got up and mumbled to herself as she walked toward the door. "I think I'd see a lot better if I had a drink right now."

"Yes, you did say that out loud," Anne laughed.

Back in the kitchen, Rick made good progress on the dinner. He had two big pots of water on the stove, a large one and a smaller one that had already started to boil. There were various plates and bowls lined up on the counter, and the table, which was in a small dining room off to the side of the kitchen, had been set with glasses and silverware only. Lucy noticed right away that one of the seats had a small yellow plastic cup in front of it while all the rest had glass. It was obviously Carly's seat, but she was taken aback at the reality of being around a child again. So much of her energy had been focused on the anxiety of seeing her sister again that she hadn't given much thought to what it would be like to meet her only niece for the very first time.

"If you don't think it's too rude of me, why don't you girls show yourself around while I make dinner."

"Not at all," Lucy offered first.

"If you're sure you don't need any help," Anne added.

"Naw, go ahead. There's not much to see, though."

The girls walked around together as if they were attending an open house, examining rooms and eyeing the photos and knickknacks scattered throughout the house. When they got to Rick and Katie's room, they barely stepped in and glanced around. Neither felt comfortable enough yet to invade their personal space. But as they turned to walk away, something caught Lucy's eye and she did a double take. They had one of those attached bathrooms with no door, just a walkway. Lucy could see through to the counter and noticed various medical supplies crowded up into the corner of the counter. She couldn't make out specifically what it was, but it obviously was not hairspray and makeup. It gave Lucy a feeling of guilt, almost like it was her fault that Katie was sick. She shook the thought from her brain like a just-bathed puppy.

In the outside bathroom, the one that they would probably use, they smiled at the ocean décor. The shower curtain had shells and starfish on it, and the toothbrush holder was a little umbrella on a stand.

The last room they came to was Carly's, with her pink and purple walls and butterfly bedspread. Her name was written with wooden blocks painted different colors and hung on the wall in an arch. Stuffed animals of every variety covered every inch of the room. Her bed was lined top to bottom with the little creatures, just barely giving enough space for her little body. There was a wooden shelf hanging on the wall crammed with about twenty miniature stuffed bears and bunnies. There were even animals along the walls on the floor and piled up in her walk-in closet. Lucy delighted in how wonderful it must be to grow up in such a cuddly room.

"Look at this cute painting," Anne said, pointing at a wall next to a window. It was held up by a piece of tape and was obviously Carly's depiction of her family. Katie was holding a flower in one hand and held Carly's hand with the other. Her scale of sizes was a little off, and Rick towered over both of them. His arm was around Katie, and there was a huge sun shining above them all.

Lucy felt a bit of pride zap through her as if she had handed down her artistic talents to her niece. "Hey, that's pretty good."

"Thanks, Aunt Lucy!"

In the doorway Carly stood watching them looking at her painting. When they saw her, she immediately ran over and wrapped her arms around Lucy, which caught her off guard. She wasn't used to little kids.

"Hi, Carly," Lucy said. She gave her back a little pat.

Not willing to let go yet, Carly said, "You're finally here… I've been waiting and waiting."

Lucy pried Carly's arms from her waist and bent down towards her face. "This is my friend, Anne."

"I know," she said, smiling and looking up at Anne. "You're a nurse, right? Maybe you can help my mommy."

"Well, I'm not a nurse yet. It's nice to meet you, Carly," Anne said.

Just then Katie appeared in the doorway of the room, and all eyes turned her way. Her hair was dishwater blonde, lighter than Lucy remembered. She wore loose capri pants and a baggy T-shirt. It was difficult to tell if she just wanted to be comfortable or if she had lost weight.

Carly ran over and grabbed her mother's hand.

"Look, Mommy! They're here!"

"I see that, sweetie."

They all stood frozen for what seemed like an eternity, but was only a few seconds, waiting for someone to do or say something. Lucy couldn't believe how different Katie looked. She'd expected change, but she wasn't quite prepared to see her sister was now a woman. After all, it had been almost seven years since they had seen each other. But her face looked older than she expected, more aged. She figured it was most likely from being a parent, combined with her illness. "It's good to see you, Katie," Lucy said, walking toward her sister.

"I'm so glad you came, Lucy." Her voice was soft and quiet.

The two embraced, and Lucy couldn't help feeling strange, like she was hugging a casual acquaintance. She pulled away first and took a few steps back, but before she could give the introduction, Katie said, "Hi, Anne, how are you?"

"I'm great, Katie. It's nice to finally meet you."

"Mmm, I smell something good. Let's go!" Carly smiled and ran out of the room, assuming they were going to follow her.

"It's nice to meet you too, Anne. Why don't we go into the living room. Otherwise she'll just come back for us." Katie laughed and exchanged a smile with Lucy as they walked out of the room.

CHAPTER 33

Was it a coincidence that Rick happened to be cooking Lucy's favorite dinner, spaghetti? Either way, it didn't matter. Lucy's stomach was filled with Caesar salad, pasta, and one too many pieces of garlic bread. The way Lucy and Anne were scarfing down the food, Rick and Katie probably wondered how long it had been since these two girls had a decent meal. And of course Lucy didn't question the glass of red wine that had been placed in front of each seat. Rick must have been reading her mind when he spoke up about it.

"I used to be a big-time beer lover, but we're a red wine house now. A good dry red actually has little or no sugar. So the health benefits are worth it...for both of us." He looked at Katie, and the pair exchanged a loving smile.

Sounds good to me, Lucy thought to herself.

Dinner conversation revolved mostly around the trip there and discussions on the differences and similarities between Texas and California. The topics of the surgeries, and Lucy and Katie's past, were tiptoed around like landmines. There was also little talk about Katie's health, mainly because Katie herself kept skirting around the subject.

At one point Anne had asked her how she was feeling. Lucy could tell Katie's response was only somewhat accurate since

Carly was listening intently at that point. She said she'd had some setbacks lately, but had been feeling pretty good that day. Of course she wouldn't bore them with the history and details of her illness. Maybe later, once they had settled in and they all got to know each other better.

Lucy couldn't help but to wonder about that. As she sat there listening to random stories about Carly as a baby or Rick and his dad's business, she felt like she was sitting across from strangers. That person, that little girl she once knew, was buried beneath the years, the experiences, and the burdens. Whereas Lucy felt like she was frozen in time, still stuck to that old life. How was Katie able to move on? How did she so easily leave and never look back? The answer was clear: Carly.

After everyone was finished eating, they remained at the table, except for Carly, for another half hour. She ran back and forth from various rooms in the house, proudly showing her aunt the things that were most important to her. First, there was Betty Bear, dressed all in pink, including matching shoes and purse. Next was a picture she'd drawn in class of her and her grandpa. She explained that they were supposed to draw a special person in their life.

"My papa is the most specialest person I know," she added, handing the paper to Lucy.

"What a beautiful picture. I like to draw too."

"I know, my mommy told me. I like to paint like you too. And guess what else?"

"What?"

"You get to see my papa tomorrow."

"I do?" Lucy looked over at Katie for confirmation.

"I hope you girls don't mind," Rick put in. "My dad really wanted to take us all out to dinner."

"No, it's fine," Lucy said.

"Not at all," Anne added. "That would be nice."

"He wanted to meet you, both of you," Katie said. "And there's this restaurant, Guadalajara's. They have the best Mexican food."

Lucy and Anne looked at each other, smiled, and in unison replied, "Sounds great."

Carly continued her commuting to and from the dining room, but after about three more interruptions to the adult conversation, Katie stopped Carly and wrapped her arms around her daughter.

"Why don't you show Aunt Lucy some more stuff tomorrow, okay? Now go get your jammies on and you can watch one show."

"Okay, Mommy."

As she ran down the hallway she yelled, "I can show Lucy my Tinkerbell nightgown, too!"

Katie apologized for Carly's complete bombardment of Lucy and explained how excited Carly had been the last few days before they arrived.

"You'll see soon enough how stubborn Carly can be," Rick added, getting up from the table. "Don't anybody move. This was my meal, and I'm taking care of the dishes too." He stacked a couple of plates together and carried them over to the counter next to the sink.

Katie must have noticed that both Anne and Lucy had that look of obligation and were just about to say something. "Don't even try to help him. He's just as stubborn as Carly. That's where she gets it from."

"Hey, don't blame me, it's my dad's fault," Rick shot back.

Rick and Katie swapped smiles and laughed, and then Katie said, "You're probably right." To Lucy and Anne she said, "They're very close. George helps out quite a bit with Carly, so they spend a lot of time together."

"That must be nice." Lucy heard her own voice come out sounding empty, but it was too late to stop it. Then she saw Rick and Katie glance awkwardly at each other, so she took a breath and added in a more positive tone, "She's a very lucky little girl."

Anne made the first move to change the subject. "Well, thanks so much for dinner. I'm so stuffed. It was really good though." Anne got up sluggishly from the table like she was carrying a heavy load on her back. "I promised my aunt I'd give her a call, so I think I'll go do that, maybe read a bit before bed." She had packed a couple of books from the nursing program, but she hadn't even had a chance to think about them while on the road.

Realizing that was the perfect opportunity for Katie and Lucy to talk, Rick insisted they head to the den while he did the dishes and kept an eye on Carly.

Lucy took a seat on the only spot to sit in the den—a small brown leather couch. She thought the room looked like it was fighting to find its identity. It had probably started out as some sort of office, but the older Carly got, the more it transformed to meet her needs. There was a weak looking black desk with an old HP desktop in the corner of the room. Next to that were a couple of black cases that held DVDs and a few old VHS tapes. All the way in the closet from her view she noticed there was a child's easel standing next to a small wooden tray that held art supplies. It kept her gaze and gave her a feeling of contentment.

"I know." Katie must have read her mind. "It's pretty cool, huh? I was never an artist like you, but Carly's a natural. And she just loves it."

She joined Lucy on the couch, turning her body sideways and cranking a knee up on the cushion. That's when Lucy saw it. It was startling at first, but she realized instantly what it was sticking out from beneath Katie's top. A thin, clear plastic tube, casually hanging there like earphones from an iPod. She imagined something like that would become second nature, but that it also had to be a constant reminder to Katie that her body needed help. Katie relied on the insulin pump to keep her feeling like she could lead a somewhat normal life. It gave her freedom.

"Why didn't you tell me?" Lucy asked when Katie realized what she was looking at.

That simple question alone caused Katie's eyes to well up. "I don't know," she whispered. "I don't know how or why any of this happened the way it did. You were everything to me growing up, and then suddenly, I didn't have you anymore."

"That's because you left, Katie." Lucy looked away, ensuring she wouldn't be swayed by Katie's tears. That was who she was, and she wanted to have her say. "You made that choice."

"I'm sorry, Lucy. I know I'm the one who made the decision to leave, but I honestly felt like it was my only choice at the time."

"You could have stayed...with me. I could have helped you."

"C'mon, Lucy, let's be honest. Would you really have wanted me there? Me and a baby to take care of?"

"Yes." She turned back and was looking straight at Katie now. "Of course I wanted you there. I took care of you, and I could have taken care of Carly too."

"But it wasn't your responsibility. It was mine...and Rick's. If it wasn't for him, I'd—"

Lucy stopped her by putting a hand on her knee. She could see the emotions building up in Katie and knew it wasn't good for her. Besides that, she was beginning to wonder if maybe it wasn't that Katie had left, but how she left and never looked back. "I can see he's taken good care of the two of you. That's all that matters now. We should just leave all this behind, at least for now, and focus on what's ahead of us."

Katie grasped Lucy's hand. "No. There's something else I have to say to you. I do think I made the right decision back then. But…I know the way I left hurt you."

Lucy couldn't find the words to respond. She was hurt, but she wanted to let it go. To be free from it all.

"I was immature and ungrateful, and I will never forgive myself for how I treated you, especially after all you did for me, Lucy. For that…I'm really sorry."

All Lucy could say was, "I know." She was confused. She thought about when Katie first left. She was hurtful, but it was more than that. Katie wasn't just leaving Lucy, she was leaving Lucy to deal with their mother. Alone. It was the first time Lucy realized her own selfishness. With Katie by her side, she'd had the strength and motivation to make things bearable at home. She was strong for Katie. Once Katie was gone, Lucy's whole mentality changed, and every day was a struggle. The impact of that insight cranked her heartbeat way up. Her natural fighting instinct kicked in, and she fought back the tears. Instead, she reached out and embraced her sister. "I love you, Katie…and I'm sorry too."

Clinging to her big sis, Katie replied in a whisper, "You have nothing to be sorry about."

"But I do." Lucy separated herself from Katie but looked her straight in the eyes. "I was selfish. I didn't want you to go."

Katie smiled with understanding.

"But look at you now. You have this beautiful family." Her voice was convincing and proud. "And Carly. She's a happy, healthy little girl. You are doing a great job…and you didn't need any help from me."

"But I do now, Lucy. You were always there for me when I needed you, and you're here now."

"Now…and always, little sis."

CHAPTER 34

Rick had sure earned his husband points that night. After getting all the dishes into the dishwasher and cleaning the table and counters, he successfully got Carly's teeth brushed and got her into bed. No matter how much of a daddy's girl she was, Carly always wanted Katie to brush her teeth and tuck her in first. Rick told her she would be helping her mommy a lot if she let him do it this time. He knew Katie would be exhausted and would appreciate swapping bedtime roles with him.

Rick was the one who usually sat on the couch when it was bedtime and yelled, "Let me know when I'm up." Which meant he basically wanted to fly in for a quick hug and a kiss when all the logistical stuff was done. There was the last-minute potty trips, the drinks, arrangement of stuffed animals, and whatever else Carly could think of to prolong the inevitable. This wouldn't be the first time Rick had to take over, though. Carly was quite mature for her age, and she was well aware of the fact that sometimes her mommy wasn't feeling well enough to do all things she needed and wanted.

Rick read Carly a couple of her favorite stories in bed while they waited for Katie to come in. With his elbows rested on the bed, Rick leaned against Carly's bed on his knees. Exhaustion from the day was starting to run down through his entire body, and he fought to stay awake. A few times his eyelids drooped and he slurred his words. Carly shook his shoulder with both hands and yelled, "Daddy! Stay awake." Thankfully, Katie walked in just as he was finishing the second book because he knew he wouldn't make it through another.

"Thank goodness. Mommy's here." Rick got up and gave his girl one last kiss on the forehead. "You're my special girl, right?"

"Yep."

To Katie he said, "You okay?"

"Yeah, everything's fine. I'll be there in a few minutes." Katie grabbed Rick's hand and gave it a squeeze before he walked out of the room, shutting the light off. Then she turned and smiled at Carly. She could barely make out her face with the faded light shining in from the hallway.

"Mommy, come cuddle with me."

Katie climbed in behind Carly's little body to form a perfect spoon formation. She kissed her hair and took in the beautiful scent of her daughter. "I'm only staying for a couple of minutes," she whispered. Katie knew if she didn't put that out there up front that Carly would ask for more and more time until she eventually got Katie to stay until she was fast asleep.

"Were you and Aunt Lucy fighting?"

"No honey. We were just talking."

"You guys sounded like you were mad at each other."

Katie rubbed Carly's back. "Shhh." She didn't want Carly to think about unhappy things before she went to bed. She and Rick had worked hard to keep things positive in their home, especially during the rough times. "Everything's fine. It's time to go to sleep."

"Should we try to meet in our dreams tonight?"

That was something they had been saying to her for years. It helped Carly to sleep, thinking about being with her parents in her dream, and feeling safe there too.

"I'll meet you there. Now close your eyes and go to sleep."

Carly's eyes blinked rapidly, fighting it off, and then after a few moments, her lids floated shut.

"Sweet dreams, honey pie," Katie whispered.

. . .

A pillow propped behind her back, Anne sat up reading a thick textbook. Lucy didn't want to disturb her, but she also didn't want to talk. She was spent and just wanted to go to sleep.

"Hi," Anne said, glancing up from her book.

"Hey." Lucy plopped down on her dorm-style bed, aiming for the center. She was used to having a bigger bed and wasn't looking forward to sleeping in one lane.

"Everything okay?" Anne didn't look up this time, making it easier for Lucy.

"Yeah, everything's fine. Actually, it's kinda like you said before. Everything's *going* to be okay. I feel…better about things for some reason."

"See…that's great. By the way, I texted Benny because I tried to call Chad." She made a face and tilted her head to the side. "His phone was disconnected."

"Bummer. Must have been his stepdad."

"It was, but Benny said everything's fine. They'll stay at his cousin's house until Monday and leave Tuesday morning. He also said that his family is calling Chad *hermanito*."

"What's that?"

"Little brother."

"Like they need another one of those."

Anne laughed and continued looking through her book. Lucy grabbed a pillow, hugged it close, and sat replaying her talk with Katie in her brain. After a minute or two, she reached down to a bag that was next to the bed and pulled out the laptop. She'd planned on calling Kyle when they arrived, like she'd promised him, but everything seemed to happen so fast. It was too late now, and after her conversation with Katie, she really didn't feel like talking. She'd send him an e-mail instead. Plus, she didn't want to know if he was not home on a Friday night. The truth was that she had been thinking of him more and more lately. It didn't matter that he continued to call, text, and e-mail her. She was insecure and starting to worry that eventually he'd move on. They all did.

She opened her e-mail and started a new message.

Kyle:
Well, we are here. Sorry I didn't call you, but we arrived right around dinnertime and—

Then something hit her. She remembered that Anne had used the computer last to check her e-mail, but now it showed that she was offline. Should she go online and see if Kyle was online too? It was a chance to see how the instant messaging worked. That would be a good excuse. She clicked herself online, but didn't check for Kyle. She remembered instead that she told Amy she would send her contact information and let her know she'd arrived. Amy had gotten a temp for Lucy's position and promised to hold her job as long as she kept Amy updated. Lucy sent off a quick message to Amy, then began researching and reading about her sister's illness. Halfway through an article on insulin pumps, the bottom right corner of the screen flashed. It was an IM from Kyle.

Hi!

Hey.

How are you? Are you there yet?

We're here. Sorry I didn't call you.

It's okay. Should I give you a call right now?

No. We got here around dinnertime. The house is quiet now, and I'm sitting here next to my new roomie.

Tell Anne I said hi. How's your sister?

Pretty good. We've talked a little too.

That's good.

So, all alone on a Friday night, huh? Her heart skipped a beat as she stared at the blinking cursor, waiting for his reply. She had an idea what it would be, but she wanted confirmation. She needed to know that he wanted to be with her.

I'm not alone…I'm with you.

Oh, what should we do?

I can think of a few things.

Really?

Seriously, I've been thinking about you a lot.

That was exactly what Lucy wanted to hear, and now she knew he wanted to hear the same from her. It would be a lot easier than saying it in person. She knew she had to stop keeping him at arm's length. It wasn't fair. But then again, it wouldn't be fair to lead him on either. To let him think they had a chance, when the odds were against them. It seemed to be an impossible situation. But Lucy found herself wishing it wasn't. Hoping it wouldn't be.

I've been thinking about you too.

Good. What are you doing tomorrow?

What? He couldn't possibly be asking to see her. The thought of being with Kyle brought her back to their night on the beach. That beautiful, perfect night that she wished would never end.

Hanging out here, shopping, going out to dinner. Why?

I want to talk to you. Can you pencil me into your busy agenda and call me?

When?

Anytime. Call my cell. I'll be waiting.

Okay. Goodnight.

Sweet dreams, Lucy.

A good thirty minutes later, Lucy was still awake staring at the ceiling. Anne was breathing heavily, and there wasn't a sound outside their bedroom door. She was sure everyone was asleep. The more she thought about needing to fall asleep, the harder it became to relax. At first it was just the excitement of thinking about Kyle. But she knew now that it was something totally different. It happened often at home, her insomnia. Except there she had the freedom, and the resources, to take care of it. Knowing she would continue to struggle well into the early morning, she eased out of her bed and quickly crept out of the room. She knew ahead of time exactly where to go and what to look for. Luckily for her, Rick had to open a second bottle of wine to give Anne and himself a second glass.

Guided by the dome light above the stove, Lucy made it to the kitchen, avoiding any obstacles. Reminding herself that Rick did point out that a little wine was actually good for you, she grabbed the bottle from the back counter and quietly edged the cork out. Now she just needed to remember which cupboard housed the wineglasses. For a second she did contemplate drinking straight from the bottle. Then she wouldn't have to worry about the evidence of the glass sitting in the sink the next morning. Why did she feel the need to justify it? *Just find the damn glasses and stop feeling guilty,* she scolded herself.

"They're in the one above the microwave."

The whispered voice shot her heart to her throat and had her arms flailing around, just skimming across the top of the wine bottle. It teetered and tilted like a bowling pin, but Lucy quickly grasped and settled it.

"Rick!" Her voice was quiet but strained. "I'm sorry, did I wake you?"

"No, I think we both had the same idea." He walked over to her, reached across to open the cupboard, and pulled out two wineglasses. "Trouble sleeping?"

"Yeah. It's just hard for me to get used to sleeping somewhere different," she lied.

Rick poured them each half a glass of wine, then picked one up and handed it to Lucy. It seemed oddly intimate with the lighting and what they were doing so late at night.

"Lucy, I hope you don't think we would ever judge you." It was as though he could read the guilt in her eyes, like she had been caught cheating. "We're all so grateful you're here."

Lucy tried to think of an appropriate response. What could she say? *Thanks, me too, too bad it wasn't someone better.* Nothing seemed to fit, so she just took a sip of her wine and smiled. Rick walked across to the pantry door and put his hand on the knob.

"Take a look at this," he said, opening the door.

Taped to the back of the door was a piece of paper. Lucy saw that it was one of Carly's drawings, but she couldn't make it out in that lighting, so she walked toward it. It looked like a drawing of Rick, Katie, and Carly holding hands. Just to make sure Rick said, "That's us," pointing to the picture. Then on the side there was another woman with her hand out, reaching out to the other three. She was holding a heart in her hand. Above all of them was written, *Our hero, Aunt Lucy!*

"I think that about says it all, don't you?"

Thankful for the shadows, Lucy felt her eyes moisten as she stared at the picture. Rick gave her a soft tap on the back as he walked past her and out of the kitchen.

"Good night."

CHAPTER 35

It was all planned out. Saturday would be a day of fun, shopping and going out to dinner, courtesy of George. Sunday would be spent relaxing in anticipation of the arduous day that was in store for both Katie and Lucy on Monday. They would have to check in Monday morning for a day of final tests and preparations for the double surgery tentatively scheduled for Thursday afternoon.

It was unusually quiet in the Moore household, especially for a Saturday morning. Rick decided to let everyone sleep in and took Carly to the bakery. Lucy was the first one up and took the opportunity to wander around the house alone. She couldn't help but feel jealous looking at all the little knickknacks, photos, and pieces of their life experiences that were scattered around the house. In the hallway there was an enclosed cupboard that was probably used for blankets or some other kind of storage. It was covered, end to end, with photos in varying unmatched frames. One picture that wasn't in a frame, but was just leaning against a frame, was one of those amusement park ride photos. Carly and Katie were in front sporting open-mouthed smiles, with two men slightly visible behind them. She could tell one was Rick, but she couldn't make out the other. She had zoomed her head down in closer for a better look when she suddenly sensed that she wasn't alone. Assuming it was Anne or Katie, she almost jumped out of her skin when she heard the gruff-sounding voice behind her.

"That's me…sitting behind Carly."

Lucy straightened up and whipped around in one swift motion, and she came almost nose to chest with the tall gentlemen.

"Sorry, Lucy. Didn't mean to scare you." He was wearing jeans and cowboy boots and sported a nice thick mustache. "I'm George, Rick's dad."

"Oh…right…hi." What she really wanted to say was, *What the hell are you doing sneaking up behind me?* She hadn't known he was going to be there that early and wondered if he'd let himself in. George must have read her mind, or her expression, because he jumped right in with his explanation.

"I have a key; I usually let myself in. I need to be here from time to time for Carly." He turned to walk toward the living room, but gestured with his arm for her to go first. "I was pulling up when Rick and Carly were takin' off to go to Dotty's."

"Who's Dotty?"

"That's the gal who owns the bakery down the street."

George sat down at one of the three barstools that lined the counter like a rancher at a fence rail. He watched Lucy as she sat on the couch, and they engaged in a bit of small talk. George asked about their trip, and they spoke a little about plans for the day. Lucy felt instantly comfortable talking with him, maybe because she sensed that he already seemed to like her. She thought George had that Tom Selleck look—an attractive older man who seemed like he'd stepped out of the Old West.

"Ya know, Lucy, I wanted to say thank you since we have a moment. What you're doin' for Katie and for Rick…it's…well it's just a really great thing."

Lucy could hear the love in his voice, the love of a father. She was aware that George had taken them in when Katie got pregnant, but she could see clearly now that he was a big part of their lives. It was strange that she was almost starting to envy her sister. How could she want to trade places with someone who'd had such hardships, someone who was now very ill and faced an uncertain future? It was obvious that no matter what Katie had to deal with in life, she would never do it alone. She was surrounded by people who loved her and wanted to take care of her.

"I'm sure you would have done the same thing."

"You got that right, missy. I'd do anything for Katie." Smiling, he ran his thumb and index finger around and down his mustache.

"She's very lucky to have all of you."

Just then the door opened and Carly came running in followed by Rick. Carly was still in her pajamas with a jacket over the top. "Hi, Papa! Guess what I got you?" She hurled herself into a lock around George's leg as he stood up from the stool.

"Let me guess," he said, looking up at the ceiling. "Uh…a taco?"

"No, silly!"

"Uh…a new car?"

"Papa! We got you a blueberry muffin." She went over and sat down at the table as if waiting to be served.

"My favorite. Thank you, darlin'."

Rick let them know that Katie would probably sleep a while longer. She was struggling to get up, so he insisted she stay in bed and sleep until she felt stronger. Anne eventually waddled into the kitchen, sleepy-eyed and sluggish like she was waking from a night of partying. But as to be expected, Carly's energy knew no bounds. She was, of course, ready to pick right up where she'd left off last night. She started by telling Lucy and Anne all about every one of her "best friends" and how she wanted to invite the ones from her neighborhood over to meet them. Then she asked if they could all have a painting party later in the afternoon. Fortunately, Rick put a quick halt to Carly's itinerary and explained that Lucy and Anne were guests and not her personal entertainment. Although she was overwhelmed at the thought of fulfilling all of Carly's requests, Lucy was also incredibly proud of what a creative and driven little girl her niece was. She couldn't help thinking there were probably so many other wonderful things like that she had missed out on.

After breakfast, it was time for Rick and George to let the ladies go off on their own while they took care of a few work-related details. Or, the girls guessed, maybe they just didn't want to be around for a day that was obviously focused on the female persuasion.

Lucy was pleasantly surprised to be out shopping, and Anne was just plain excited to grab some Texas souvenirs. Anne bought herself one of those "Everything's Bigger in Texas" T-shirts, not really realizing how some would take that. She also bought Chad and Benny Texas Rangers hats. Why, Lucy had no idea. A handmade coin purse caught Carly's eye, and Lucy ended up buying one for both Carly and for herself. Lucy put the change from the sale in Carly's coin purse, which filled her with excitement. "Thanks, Aunt Lucy. Now we're twins!"

The one thing Lucy hadn't counted on that day, and was not pleasantly surprised about, was where they ended up last. Just before going home, they stopped at Painted Pink nail salon. It was to be a surprise for Lucy and Anne, a thank-you for coming. Obviously it was a nice gesture, and of course what Lucy was doing could never be measured. But Rick and Katie just wanted to pamper the girls after their trip and before the stress of everything began.

Walking into the salon, they were immediately hit with the scent of acrylic, which in turn brought Lucy right back to Amy's Nails. Painted Pink was bigger, but the setup was pretty much the same. At the front counter, Carly went over and grabbed Lucy's hand.

"I'm getting a manicure and pedicure just like the grown-ups." Her smile was so bright, and her eyes lit up looking up at Lucy.

"Really, well I guess you are a big girl, huh?" Lucy was not going to ruin this time for Carly, and actually, she hadn't had a manicure or pedicure since she'd starting working at Amy's. It wasn't just the money, though. There was no way she was letting any of those hags touch her. So Lucy made a conscious decision to relax and have a good time and not think about her job. And once they were all settled, it wasn't that difficult. She had forgotten how nice it was to have someone rub your feet. Even a total stranger.

The girls kept the conversation light, and Katie was interested to hear from Anne about nursing. All the time she'd spent in and out of hospitals, nurses were the ones who had helped her through everything the most. She praised Anne for picking such a wonderful line of work and told her how great she thought Anne would be.

The women laughed at the fact that they could actually have a conversation because Carly was so busy talking with the lady doing her nails.

"I have to admit," Katie said, "I do feel a little guilty letting Carly loose on her. Listen to how many questions she's asking."

"We can give her a big tip at the end," Anne offered.

"I'll bet it's a nice change from listening to all those women complain about their husbands or boyfriends," Lucy said.

That's when the color drained from Katie's face. "Oh my gosh, Lucy. I'm so sorry. I didn't even think…about your job. You probably don't want to be here, do you?"

"Actually, it's really nice to be on the other end for once."

"Really, or are you just saying that?"

"No, really. And here at least I can understand everyone!" she said sarcastically.

CHAPTER 36

One dozen long-stemmed roses greeted the women as they walked through the door that afternoon, high on indulgence. Katie was the first one in and immediately noticed them on the dining room table. They were in a beautifully thick, beveled crystal vase that looked like it cost a fortune. Anne instantly ruled herself out as a possible recipient, but Katie and Lucy both had the typical thoughts that battled it out in a woman's brain whenever they saw flowers. *How nice for someone, but I hope that someone is me. Could it be me? I hope it is.*

Katie went full throttle and headed straight to the table, while Lucy hung back. She plucked the card out of its holder, hoping her name would be on the mini envelope. "Well," she said with a sly smile, "looks like Lucy has a boyfriend?" Her voice made it sound like a question.

"Oh my gosh!" Anne speed-walked over. "Are they from Kyle?"

"Kyle? I guess we have some more catching up to do, huh, sis?" Katie held up the card and waited for Lucy to come retrieve it.

Lucy tried to play it cool, but as she glided over, her smile busted out of her face. "He's just a guy I met right before we came." And then she remembered: "Actually...he used to go to our high school."

"Yeah, and he's not *just* a guy," Anne blurted.

Lucy snagged the card and opened the envelope. She chose not to read aloud so they could hear: *Lucy, I miss you and am thinking of you often.* Lucy excused herself to her room, hearing Anne filling in Katie as she walked away. Anne must have assumed that the cat was out of the bag now anyway. Lucy trusted Anne would leave out the part where she'd passed out. Anne knew her well enough by now to figure that she would probably appreciate being spared from having to share all the details.

• • •

Lucy stood looking out her bedroom window and dialed Kyle's number. She thought about what she would say while she listened to the phone ring. She called his cell phone as he'd instructed and after three rings wondered if he would come through like he guaranteed so confidently.

"Hi, beautiful."

"So you were expecting someone else?" She wondered if he could detect the smile she masked with her joke.

"Hey, you know I think you're beautiful." He spoke softly as if they were together, next to a fire sipping wine.

"Thank you for the flowers—*they're* beautiful."

"I'm glad you like them...and I'm glad you called."

"Oh, so this was your insurance policy?"

"No way," he protested. "I knew you'd call."

"Pretty sure of yourself, huh?"

"Actually, yes."

Lucy could picture how cute he must look saying that with his little confident smile.

"Why do you say that?" She was very curious to hear his response to that.

"I've got you all figured out, Lucy Lang." He paused for effect, which actually worked and sent a chill through her. "You really like me."

Lucy shot out a laugh. "Ha! That sounds so junior high."

"Well it's true."

"How can you be so sure?" Lucy tried to sound diplomatic, as if she were interrogating a witness.

"You wouldn't bother wasting your time with me if you didn't really care."

"Really?"

"Yeah, I'm thinking you would have just told me to take a hike that day in the parking lot."

Playing along, Lucy said, "Maybe I just felt bad about what happened."

"Naw, you wanted to see me again. And that night...on the beach. Something happened that night, Lucy. You know it did."

"What about you?" Lucy's excitement was starting to head towards worry. These kinds of games could be dangerous. The odds were already against them, being three states away and having almost nothing in common.

"What *about* me? I think I've already made it pretty clear how *I* feel."

Lucy didn't say anything this time.

"Haven't I?" he asked.

"Yes...you have. And I'm sorry if I've made things difficult for you."

"Hey, I know you're going through a lot of stuff right now—"

She cut him off and said, "Exactly, and you shouldn't have to deal with any of it." Suddenly her mood darkened.

"I'm a big boy, Lucy. I can take care of myself. Besides, I don't feel like I'm *dealing* with anything. Especially since you don't share most of those things with me. I know it's hard for you...but you *can* talk to me."

"I know, and I appreciate that."

"I don't want your appreciation...I want much more than that." Kyle paused like that last statement was a mistake. He'd said before that he didn't want to push her away with too much pressure.

"Kyle...I honestly don't know what I can give right now."

"I can understand that. Just please tell me one thing."

"What?"

"Just tell me I was right...about what I said before. If you tell me that, then that's all I need—*for now*."

Lucy paused. Not for suspense, or to make him wait. It didn't come easy, but she knew he was right, and she knew he needed to hear it. "You were right."

· · ·

The restaurant was loud and jammed to capacity. Every corner of the room seemed to have something going on. There was no mistake that it was a Mexican restaurant. That was made clear with the completely overboard Mexican-themed decorations that covered the walls and hung from the ceiling. Waitresses carried trays with Coronas, Dos Equis, and giant margaritas that instantly caught Lucy's eye. She could tell one group in the back looked like they'd just come from the office and were having a work-related dinner. That made her think of the first time she met Kyle. On the way to their table, they went by three mariachis singing "Happy Birthday, Dear Panchito" to a middle-aged man wearing a huge sombrero and looking pretty damn buzzed. He gave them a thumbs-up and a wink as they walked by, causing Anne and Lucy to exchange laughter. Carly pointed out that they did that for George on his birthday. "My mommy has a picture on her phone."

Once seated and everyone began devouring the chips and salsa, Rick made a few suggestions of their family favorites. Throughout the evening various conversations started and stopped. George told them all about his real estate business and how he'd been staying afloat with the poor economy. Of course, Texas was in better shape than California, but like George told them, every trail has puddles.

When the conversation turned to Rick and how much of a house-husband he'd become, Lucy began to zone out. The situation seemed so surreal. She would have never thought in a million years that she'd be sitting in a Mexican restaurant in Texas about ready to serve up one of her kidneys to her sister. She started watching each person around the table, examining their words, their gestures, wondering if they were feeling anything that she was feeling.

To Lucy, they all looked as if they were simply enjoying the moment. They were all either listening, responding, or smiling and laughing, until she got to Katie. She finally noticed that Katie hadn't said a word since they sat down. She nodded, smiled, and hugged Rick's arm when he said how much he enjoyed the opportunity to take care of Katie. "We've become a great team," he said, looking at her. When she excused herself to go to the ladies' room, Lucy joined her.

"Are you feeling alright?" Lucy asked on the way to the bathroom.

"I'll be fine."

In the bathroom Katie wet a paper towel and wiped her face. "I just felt a little hot out there." Her voice sounded weary.

"Are you sure?" Lucy thought about whether this was just something Katie had to deal with on a regular basis, or if it was a sign of her worsening condition.

Katie smiled at Lucy in the mirror. "I guess I'm a little tired too."

"Katie, we did too much today. I didn't want you to do all this for me and wear yourself out." Lucy felt a hint of déjà vu coming on. Even though her sister was now a grown woman, she was still vulnerable. But that wasn't Lucy's job anymore—it was Rick's. "Should I go get Rick?"

"No, I don't want him to worry. Really, I'll be okay. And today was for all of us. Do you know how long it's been since I've spent a day like that?" She didn't wait for an answer. "Listen, I'm going to the bathroom, and then we're going back. I'm sure I just need to eat."

Walking out of the bathroom, Katie stopped suddenly. "Oh my God!" Her face looked pained.

"What's wrong?" Lucy asked urgently yet was still able to keep her voice down.

"Look." She gestured toward the bar with her head.

George was standing there talking with a woman. She had slick black hair that just touched her shoulders and dark brown lipstick. She was talking and gesturing as if she was telling George the most interesting story in the world, but his face showed the complete opposite.

"Who is that?" Lucy asked.

"Jen Thurgood. She bought a small rental property from George about a year ago and always says she's going to be in the market again soon."

"Looks like she's in the market for George."

"Exactly. We all know she's full of it. And she is completely annoying to have a conversation with."

When George glanced over and noticed them watching, he shot them a *help me* look.

"Let me handle this," Lucy said with surprising confidence. Her instant fondness for George coupled with her desire to help those she cared about propelled her into a spontaneous plan. Katie walked back to the table while keeping an eye on Lucy, who was heading straight for the bar. George had turned back around, so he didn't notice Lucy approaching.

"Geo-orge," she said in a singsong voice and then put a hand on his shoulder.

George turned around with a smile that told Lucy he was pleasantly surprised.

"The second I leave for the ladies' room you take off for the bar." This caught the bartender's attention, causing him to scrub an imaginary spot on the counter so he could keep his current position at the bar.

"Sorry," George said, playing along. "I was just on my way back from the men's room when I ran into Jen here."

"Oh…well now we can go back together." Lucy hooked her arm in his and gave a little tug. "Let's go, George…bye," she said, smiling at Jen.

George shrugged as he let himself get pulled away. "The young ones are so bossy," he said, trying not to laugh. Then to Lucy he said, "Thanks."

"No problem."

CHAPTER 37

Lucy tried to rub away the goose bumps that kept popping up on her arms. She was almost freezing and definitely frustrated with herself. How could she not know it would be cold in a hospital and dress accordingly? It had been such a beautiful morning, and she'd gotten used to putting on tanks and tees.

Getting up from her seat in the waiting room, Lucy walked out to the hall, hopelessly thinking it would be warmer out there. If she wasn't so bored, it wouldn't seem so bad. But if she was being honest with herself, boredom wasn't the only thing causing her shivers. So many things were racing through her mind; it was like playing a video game. Each thought had to be considered and tossed aside or somehow neutralized with rationalizations. Sure, she was nervous about the surgery. Who wouldn't be? Nevertheless, her main concern was not for herself, it was for Katie. Lucy thought about what happened Saturday night at the restaurant. She wondered what would happen to Katie in the future if she didn't have the operation. *We don't have to worry about that now,* she told herself. She walked back in and took a seat, hoping that Katie would walk in any minute. She was starting to get used to seeing her face again, and now suddenly she didn't like being alone.

While everyone seemed like one big happy family the last couple of days, this morning they were all going their separate ways. Rick and George each had work to take care of, and Lucy and Katie both had appointments at the hospital. That just left Anne and Carly. Rick and Katie had planned to put Carly in the summer day camp program, but it didn't start for one more week. Anne graciously, yet reluctantly, offered to stay behind and watch Carly. It wasn't that she didn't like children, she just didn't have much experience with them. Being an only child and working in the family store didn't afford her much time with kids. She'd never even babysat before.

"You'll be fine," Lucy told her in the morning before leaving. Offering her own expertise, she added, "Just play some games with her, let her watch one TV show, and give her a sandwich when she starts to get hungry."

"Okay, but I'm calling you guys if I have questions."

Lucy had received one text from Anne about an hour earlier letting her know everything was going well. Lucy responded that Katie was already through and had gone to speak to one of her nurses. Lucy was just about finished herself. This was her last stop for the day.

As she sat waiting, Lucy marveled at how professional and efficient the hospital staff had been. She'd never had so many strangers be so nice to her in her whole life. The nurse coordinator, Liz, continued to update her every step of the way, as well as every other nurse she encountered. And Katie was right. Anne would make a great nurse. Lucy could just picture Anne right there, sporting her giant smile and wanting to take care of everyone. She was happy that Anne would be pursuing her dream. *But what about my dream?* Lucy thought to herself. *Do I even have one? I definitely couldn't picture myself doing this.*

The time away from Amy's was nice, but she realized now that she didn't ever want to go back. She didn't even know why she went through with technician school. It had actually been her mother's idea. Linda wanted Lucy to go right after high school, thinking it was a smart idea to have a skill. Lucy finally gave in to the nagging some years later and entered into a program. She convinced herself it was somewhat artistic to make herself feel better.

A grumble in her tummy reminded Lucy she hadn't eaten since seven thirty last night. It was now two o'clock. The ultrasound had required she fast, and that test was currently standing in the way of staving off starvation. Should she go up and ask how much longer? Somehow she felt like her actions there would reflect upon her sister, and so she decided against it.

Through the doorway she watched as a man pushed a woman holding a baby in a wheelchair. She pictured her six-year-old self skipping closely behind as she had done twenty-four years ago. There was a vague memory of the day her mother went into labor. Her stepfather Tom's secretary picked Lucy up at the house and took her into the office while Tom drove Linda to the hospital. She wasn't sure if she actually remembered that or if it was just hearing Tom tell that story over and over.

He had often told stories about Lucy growing up, which she loved because it made her feel like he was her true father. When Katie was born and Lucy was taken to the hospital, the memories she had of that experience were crystal clear. Tom told her, "You have a baby sister now, Lucy." And Lucy instantly took that to heart, thinking somehow that Katie was hers. She would never forget touching Katie's head for the first time. She told her mother, "Her head looks like a peach." She rubbed it gently in a circle. "It feels like one too," she had said, smiling at

Tom. From that moment on, Katie seemed to be her purpose. She started out as Mommy's little helper, getting diapers and watching over Katie when Linda left the room. Then Lucy took it upon herself to take on more and more responsibility, doing everything she could to take care of her little baby girl.

How strange she suddenly felt thinking how things had gone full circle. At the same time, she felt completely let down. *So this is what my life boils down to? I wrap myself up in everyone else's problems? That seems pretty pathetic. But it's all I've got. It's all I've ever had.* Her self-pity session was briefly interrupted by a nurse opening the door next to the receptionist window. Lucy held her breath.

"Michelle?" the woman called, reading the file in her hand.

"That's it!" Lucy whispered to herself. She decided right then and there she was not going to sit around and wait her turn any longer—except for today of course. She would take charge of her life, find her own purpose. Helping her sister was the right thing to do, and she would do it. But there had to be more, and as soon as she got home, she would figure out what that was. The only thing she knew for sure was that these last few weeks had made her see that she was her own worst enemy. Lucy needed to escape herself and the image that she laid upon herself.

• • •

"Looks like we're almost there, Katie," Liz told her as they stopped at the nurses' station. "Can you believe it?" Liz rested an elbow on the counter and gave Katie an endearing smile.

"I know, but it won't seem real to me until it is actually happening."

"Well you know we're all behind you, Katie," Liz said. "And Rita and I will both be here for the surgery."

Katie and Rita, the head nurse, had grown close over the years, even closer than she was with Dr. Brady. Over the last few months, Katie had really confided in Rita. They'd had several in-depth conversations about life, family, and Katie's future. She even sought advice from Rita, sort of like a motherly figure. That was definitely something missing in Katie's life.

"It's such a blessing that your sister was a match and that she was able to do this," Liz added, grabbing a stack of files.

"Yeah, I feel very lucky to have her now."

"Maybe this will bring the two of you closer." Liz's comment seemed to startle her, like she remembered that Lucy had traveled there for the operation. She tried to clarify her statement. "I mean, even if she goes back…this is something that really connects two people."

Katie knew what she was trying to say. She had already been thinking it herself. "I think it already has, Liz."

CHAPTER 38

When Lucy came out after her ultrasound, Katie was sitting in the waiting room looking at a magazine.

"How'd it go? Are you doing alright?" Katie's guilt for putting her sister through all this was starting to show.

"Fine…no problem," Lucy said. There was no need to share with her the fact that she hated having to lie there for so long. It was standard for that type of test, but once, when the tech guy disappeared behind the glass window, he was gone from Lucy's sight. She watched the clock for six straight minutes before he was in view again. "Just a few more minutes," he told Lucy, knowing she probably wondered if he was screwing around back there or doing his job.

"Great, I guess we're ready to go then."

"Yep."

The two walked out, both giving a sigh of relief that they'd made it through the day.

"I saw a vending machine down the hall; let's get something. I'm starving."

"Liz had a snack and some juice waiting for me at the nurses' station. Sorry I didn't get anything for you, but they were concerned since I hadn't eaten."

"No, it's okay. Besides, I had my eye on that crumb cake."

Katie told her that she had called Rick just before Lucy came out and told him to pick them up in half an hour. So they still had a bit of time to wait. He'd dropped them both off at the hospital in the morning so they could leave Katie's car at the house. They didn't like the idea of leaving Anne and Carly there with no transportation in case of emergency. It was still too hot to wait outside, so the girls took a seat next to the exit with a view of the parking lot.

"This is kind of weird, don't you think?" Katie said.

"What do you mean?"

"Well, us two sitting here...waiting for a ride. How many times in our lives did we do that before?"

It was true. On a pretty regular basis, Linda had left Katie and Lucy waiting around somewhere to be picked up. "You're right, I hadn't thought about that."

"You always made it fun while we were waiting though."

"That's because you were always bugging me and trying to get me to play one of your word games." Suddenly realizing the glare from the sun was bouncing off the glass door and pounding on her shoulder, Lucy scooted closer to Katie.

"Hey," Katie laughed and nudged Lucy with her elbow. "You're the one who taught me all those games."

Just then Lucy's phone rang in her pocket. "Yeah, I guess so," she said, pulling out her cell. She glanced at it, and after one more ring, she hit the reject button.

"Don't you need to get that?" Katie asked. "I mean, I don't mind."

Lucy stuffed the phone back in her pocket and said a firm, "No."

"Is everything okay?"

Lucy stared straight ahead. She hated that feeling. The one where you're going along feeling pretty good, like your life is starting to change, and then one little thing happens and socks you right in the gut. "It's fine."

"But you seem upset now. I know, it's totally none of my business, but I just want to help."

"Really, can we please just drop it?" Even though Lucy was trying to protect Katie, at the same time she was starting to feel pressured. Wasn't she sharing enough with her sister? Did she have to give her every detail of her life as well?

Katie seemed to know she had overstepped her bounds, assuming the two could be open with each other. "I'm sorry, Lucy. I shouldn't have been so pushy."

"It's okay."

"It's just that—"

"What?"

"I guess that I feel guilty…and this may sound dumb, but when I see you unhappy I worry. I wonder…if you're having second thoughts." Katie turned her body toward Lucy and looked her in the eye. "I wouldn't blame you."

"Katie, I'm not having second thoughts. I wouldn't do that." She decided it was better to be honest than to leave her sister worried and in the dark. "The call…it was from a bill collector."

"Oh, I'm sorry." Katie suddenly brightened. "Lucy, if you need money, Rick and I would be more than happy to help you."

"No, it's—"

"Lucy, what you are doing for us is priceless. It would be the least we can do."

"You don't understand, it's not my responsibility."

"What? What do you mean?"

"It's Mom's. She owes money, but somehow they got my number."

Katie was speechless. Lucy could see that she was searching her brain for something. "Have you been in touch with her?"

"No, I haven't seen or heard from her in a few years, and I don't plan to."

"Lucy, you shouldn't have to deal with this stuff, with her debts."

"I'm not dealing with them. I just ignore them. They can't make me pay; they just want me to help them find her."

"Don't you ever want to see Mom again?"

Lucy knew she was skating on thin ice with Katie and the topic of their mother. She wondered how much Katie actually remembered about Linda, not to mention the fact that your perspective can change as you get older.

"You know, we should probably save this discussion for another time, maybe after the surgeries," Lucy urged.

Katie checked the time on her phone to determine if Rick would be there soon. She was starting to look run-down, but she wasn't ready to table the discussion yet. "Maybe this is the time when we really need family. A time for second chances—like you and me." She examined Lucy's face for a clue, something that would tell her how Lucy was feeling.

"Katie, you have a wonderful family. Rick and Carly and George—they all love you so much."

"But what about you? One of the hardest things for me has been the thought of you being all alone."

"Yeah, but it didn't have to be that way." Just as the words were spilling out, Lucy realized that it was probably not the best thing to say.

"I know, and I'm sorry. I thought we talked about this all the other night."

"I'm not talking about you this time. I'm talking about my father." Lucy could see the confusion come across Katie's face. "My *real* father. You know Mom would never tell me who he was, or even anything about him? I loved Tom and thought of him as my dad, but now it's different. Not having him around makes me realize that I'm always going to wonder who I am and who my real father is."

"Lucy…I…I'm sorry. I guess that's something I really hadn't thought about." Katie put her hand on Lucy's and looked out the window trying to find the words to help her sister, but nothing else came.

"It's okay. I don't want you to worry about it, really. I shouldn't have said anything. Like I said, we can talk about all this after." Lucy's comfort zone was becoming cramped quarters. She searched for an escape and to her fortune saw Rick pulling into the parking lot. "Look, there's Rick. C'mon." Lucy stood and walked toward the door followed by Katie.

Although she had said those words to her sister, Lucy really didn't plan on talking things over with Katie. After the surgery, she just wanted to get home. To try and get on with her life. Actually, to start her life. There was no point in dredging up all the old memories, all the debauched episodes of the past. It was time to let it all rest.

CHAPTER 39

A flash of light bounced across the ceiling. It was three in the morning. Lucy sat up in her bed, looked over toward the window, and listened. The house was as quiet as every other night, and Anne was sound asleep. A few seconds later she heard a low grumbling. It was a summer storm. Strangely this seemed to excite Lucy. She got out of bed and went over to the window for a better look. The view was somewhat obstructed by a tall rose bush, so Lucy craned her head to check out the night sky. Another flash of light came, and she could see that rain had already begun to fall. Lucy had an urge to go out into the developing storm. She wanted to feel the warm rain and watch the lightning beckon the thunder closer. Realizing that setting off the house alarm was probably not going to be a good idea, she settled for a seat on the couch in the living room. It was right under the window with a perfect view of the sky.

After a couple minutes of enjoying the free show, Lucy heard the sound of a creaking door. Out in the hall, Carly peeked from her doorway. A loud thunder cracked the sky and echoed in the house. Carly started running and took a flying leap to the couch and right onto Lucy's lap.

"Aunt Lucy, did you heard that?" she howled. "I'm scared!"

"Shhh. There's nothing to be scared about," Lucy whispered, wrapping her arms around Carly. "It's okay."

"No it's not. I hate thunderstorms." Carly took a quick look out the window and then buried her face into Lucy's chest.

Stroking Carly's hair, Lucy tried to think of just the right advice that an aunt would give her niece. Should she speak logically about how there was nothing to be afraid of? Or should she tell her to act like a big girl and be brave? Maybe, she thought, she should just wake up her parents and let them deal with it. Then Lucy realized that what might work best in this situation was the truth, and so she simply said, "I don't hate them. I love them."

Carly looked up at Lucy with curious eyes. "You do?"

"Yes."

"How come?"

"Because I'm an artist, and I love looking at beautiful things."

Carly let that sink in for a moment and replied, "I'm an artist too."

"I know. And whenever I see something beautiful, it's an inspiration to me."

"What's a nisperation?"

"An inspiration," Lucy said slowly, articulating each syllable, "is when something gives you a strong feeling to want to do something. Like when I see something very special, it just makes me want to draw or paint it so I'll remember it forever."

"Oh, I do that too. But...I still don't think storms are very beautiful."

"How do you know? Your eyes are closed so tight you can't see anything." Lucy poked Carly a couple of times in the tummy and made her squirm and giggle. "Look up there, in the sky. See all those fluffy clouds?"

"Yeah."

"And look how the sky has lots of big purple and black swirls all over them. Purple is one of my favorite colors."

"Me too."

Lucy wondered if that was true, but she didn't particularly care if it wasn't. She watched Carly's face as she continued to describe the dark scene before them. Then she saw Carly's eyes widen and felt her body stiffen as another flash of lightning stretched across the sky. "Wow, that was a good one, huh?"

"Yeah, it was big. And that one didn't even scare me," she delighted in herself.

"Well, the thunder comes next though, so be ready."

Carly grabbed ahold of Lucy with one hand and the couch with the other as if she were bracing herself for a crash landing. A few seconds later and the thunder boomed loudly. They both looked at each other and smiled. Lucy felt a sense of accomplishment. It was different from how she felt when she used to take care of Katie, which seemed to feel more like an obligation. Somehow this felt like success. The two sat on the couch for a bit longer, pointing out the bolts and other details in the sky until Lucy finally said it was time to go back to bed. She was relieved that Carly was tired and happily agreed.

Lucy walked Carly back to her room and tucked her into bed. Under the covers, but still sitting up, Carly arranged the stuffed animals along the wall that hugged her bed. Lucy watched patiently as Carly put each animal in its predetermined place. "Uh-oh. Where's Princess Pony?" Carly looked around, sorting through a pile of animals at the foot of the bed.

"Here it is," Lucy said, grabbing a black pony that was under a giant pink pig.

"No, that's Queen NeNe. I need the white one that Grandma Linda gave me."

It took a second to register as Lucy was still rummaging through the other animals. "Did you say Grandma Linda?" She prayed that she was just hearing things. She was tired after all.

"Yes, Princess Pony always sleeps next to Bun Bun, and I don't see her."

Lucy stopped looking for the pony and tried to get Carly's attention by grabbing ahold of her wrists. "Sweetie, listen. Have you ever seen Grandma Linda?"

"No."

"Then how did you get the pony?"

"We got it in the mail. Mommy said Grandma Linda sent it to me. But I can't go to sleep unless she's right here next to Bun Bun."

Carly was starting to get upset, and Lucy didn't want Rick and Katie to wake up now, so she starting searching around the bed and floor for the pony. "Don't worry, I'm sure she's around here somewhere." Getting down on all fours, Lucy swept her hand under the bed and knocked out two furry-feeling objects. One turned out to be a pink fuzzy slipper that unfortunately reminded her of Amy. The other was the pony. "Look, I found it!" She picked it up and gently placed it in the open space Carly had left on the bed. "Now, it's time to go to sleep." She bent down and gave Carly a kiss on her forehead, then walked toward the door.

"Aunt Lucy?"

"Yes?"

"I love you."

"Me too, sweetie."

. . .

It took Lucy another hour before she could fall asleep, and even then she tossed and turned all night. All she could think about was her conversation with Katie and how she'd had plenty of chances to mention that her mother had contacted them. She must have looked at the clock a dozen times waiting for morning to come. That combination of frustration and lack of sleep was a recipe for disaster just waiting to happen.

When Katie finally woke up the next morning, Lucy was in the backyard sitting at the patio table. Anne told Katie that Lucy had been sitting out there for at least an hour, and based on her own experience, whatever Lucy was thinking was not good.

"I would just leave her be if I were you," Anne urged.

Rick and Carly were already up and gone. He was taking her over to a friend's house for the day on his way to work. Katie considered the warning as she stared out the sliding glass door at Lucy. It was a beautifully clear day with a slight breeze that jiggled the trees. Something was definitely wrong with Lucy, and Katie needed to find out what it was, so she headed out back and sat down.

Katie said, "Good morning, Lucy," after realizing Lucy wasn't going to acknowledge her presence.

"Good morning," Lucy answered, staring out into the yard.

"So...is everything okay?"

"When were you going to tell me?"

"Tell you what?"

"About Mom."

"What about her?"

Now Lucy looked right at Katie. "I saw Carly's pony. She told me where she got it." Lucy wanted to remain calm. She didn't want to upset Katie, but at the same time, when it came to her mother the emotions fought hard to make their way out. "Why didn't you tell me?"

"I was going to tell you…at some point. But then yesterday you said you never wanted to see her again. I didn't know what to do."

"What you do is be honest with me. Has she been here, to see you?"

"No. I only talked to her on the phone a couple of times. The first time was a few months ago. Somehow she found out I was sick. Maybe she feels guilty or something."

"How could you let her back into your life? Into Carly's life?" Fighting back the frustration and the urge to come down hard on Katie caused her eyes to start to water. This frustrated her even more, so she got up and walked out onto the grass to ensure Katie wouldn't see her face.

"Well, I haven't really done that…yet. I don't know what I'm going to do, Lucy. She just wants to get to know her granddaughter."

"Oh, yeah, I'm sure she'll make an awesome grandmother. I mean she did such a good job raising us."

Now Katie got up and walked over to her sister. "I understand why you feel that way. Things were always much harder on you. I didn't see it at the time, but looking back I understand now."

"I don't want your pity, I want to be able to trust you…and I just want you to be careful."

"I will, but I think we should give her a chance."

Katie put a hand on Lucy's shoulder, but Lucy turned abruptly upon hearing her request. With a complete look of surprise and betrayal, she said, "We? *We* are not going to do anything." Just then Lucy's phone that was sitting on the patio table began to ring. She walked over, picked it up, and punched a button on it. Her intention was to hit the "reject" button, but somehow she put the call through. With the phone in her hand, she started to walk toward the back door. Katie stood dumbfounded and helpless as she watched Lucy leave.

"Lucy? Hello, Lucy?" the voice resonated from the phone in her hand.

CHAPTER 40

Walking into the house, Lucy looked at her phone and realized that she hadn't rejected the call after all.

"Damn," she said, bringing her cell to her ear. "Hello?" She sounded like a telemarketer had just interrupted her dinner party.

"Lucy, it's Kyle."

"Oh, sorry, I didn't know you were there. Listen I—"

"What's going on?" Kyle interrupted. "Are you okay?"

Lucy was still recovering from her argument with her sister, still processing. She couldn't think straight, much less relay to Kyle what was going on.

"I can't talk right now." Lucy was abrupt. She couldn't handle any more pressure from anyone, not even from Kyle.

"Call me back when you can." His voice was urgent and desperate. He knew her well enough by now to know that she was pulling away.

"Please, I just can't handle this right now. It's not fair for me to do this to you either."

"Lucy...don't do this. It's going to be okay."

"I'm sorry, just...please don't call me. Stop wasting your time. Good-bye, Kyle."

Lucy knew it was for the best. She just had too much going on, and she was way too up and down. How could she expect a man to deal with that? Especially someone as great as Kyle. Who knows, maybe someday they'd run into each other again. He would say how great she looked, and she would comment on how it was nice to see him. Maybe then they could give it another try.

Katie was still in the backyard when Lucy hung up with Kyle. Anne had been sitting on the couch, watching it all unfold and listening to Lucy's half of the phone conversation. That was all she needed to figure out exactly what happened and why. Lucy told Anne she was going for a walk and would be back in a little while.

"I've got my phone if you need me," she said as she headed out the door.

When Katie finally came in from the backyard, Anne was sympathetic to say the least. She'd had her share of experiences dealing with the emotional roller coaster that was Lucy's life. On the other hand, the bit of eavesdropping she did during their conversation did make her see things from Lucy's point of view. Either way, she felt strongly that it wasn't her place to judge. She was simply along for the ride. So when Katie came in, she offered a sympathetic ear. The two actually had a nice little conversation—and not just about Lucy either. Katie shared a lot about her illness, things she didn't feel right about telling Lucy. It helped to talk about it with someone new, but Katie felt that Lucy was dealing with enough and didn't need the added pressure of the gory details.

· · ·

Lucy lowered the sunglasses that were perched on top of her head. She often used them as a makeshift hair band, so she was lucky that they were still there. The glare off the sidewalk was hideously bright, but she couldn't bear to turn back. Her brisk pace matched the speed of her brain reviewing every word she'd exchanged with both Katie and Kyle. *Was it me?* she thought to herself. *Am I the real problem here?* Lucy shook her head like a cartoon character trying to clear away the stars above its head. She didn't want to think about it anymore. She just wanted to walk and walk until she was too tired to think about anything.

It only took about two minutes to round the block to the next street where she finally started to become aware of her surroundings. The houses had what Tom used to call *sparkle*, which meant they weren't a bunch of rows of the same boring floor plan. Lucy remembered that and had always dreamt of living in a house with *sparkle*. Somehow looking over each house with such detail as she passed seemed to calm her, and she slowed her pace. That or the sweat that started to form on the hairline above her forehead.

She passed a two-story with light green shutters and yellow trim on the garage, and a one-story with brick all along the lower portion. When she finally reached the end of the block, it suddenly dawned on her that she should probably pay attention to where she was going. With all the places they'd gone, Lucy did recognize most of the neighboring streets, but she didn't want to have to call from some unknown destination to get a ride home.

Being out on her own, Lucy realized that she actually hadn't been alone for quite some time. She thought it was something she wanted, to not be alone as she had been for so many years. But now there was a sense of relief. She felt a kind of freedom being away from everyone. Lucy wondered if she was the type of person who was just meant to be alone. Like one of those old ladies who just had a bunch of cats. The thought of going the rest of her life without sex cleared up that question. She knew she was just feeling overwhelmed and needed some time to catch her breath.

Coming toward her on the sidewalk ahead was a short Hispanic woman and a little boy. The woman was holding the boy's hand, and in her other hand were grocery bags. Lucy remembered that a couple of blocks down was a small shopping center. The woman must have come from there and was walking home. She smiled as she walked by, and the little boy waved to her. Lucy wondered if they had a car or if they had to walk everywhere in that heat.

As she approached the main cross streets, Lucy checked her phone and then punched the button to cross. She had been gone for about twenty minutes. Even though she had been upset, she didn't want to worry anyone. Still, Lucy wasn't ready to go back yet. She headed for the shopping center and tried to recall the stores she had seen when they drove by: Albertsons, a donut shop, a place that just said "Keys," a coffee shop, and what looked like a little sports pub. When she arrived she was proud of how accurate her recollections were even though she had forgotten about the pet store and missed Panda King altogether. Of course she made a beeline right for the sports pub, but when she was about to grab the handle, she made a quick U-turn and settled for the coffee shop.

When Lucy opened the door to the Coffee Cottage, her first thought was that it didn't look anything like a cottage—it was more like a mini Denny's. It had a couple of booths, a few small tables, and a counter. Before taking a seat at the counter, she realized she'd better make sure she still had her emergency ten.

It had been a few months since she'd even checked on it. Lucy had learned a long time ago that you can only rely on yourself, and you better be prepared for emergencies. So after way too many times of being stranded without a ride or money, she'd tucked a ten-dollar bill behind her cell phone inside its case.

"Hello," a woman said from behind the counter as Lucy took a seat. She smiled and wiped the area right in front of Lucy. "Would you like a menu, hon?" Her hair was in a loose bun and obviously dyed blonde, that yellowish Barbie-colored blonde. Her nametag said, "Bobbi."

"No thank you. Could I just get a coffee, please?"

"Sure, we've got some nice fresh muffins if yer interested." Her Texas twang was stronger than any she had heard since arriving in Texas. In fact, most people didn't sound any different to her. They were just a lot friendlier than people in the LA area.

"What kind do you have?" Lucy asked, suddenly in the mood for one. She had been so distracted that morning that she'd skipped breakfast. Her long walk coupled with the smell of food made her stomach grumble.

"Well, we got blueberry, bran, chocolate chip…oh, and poppy seed."

"How about poppy seed?"

"Sure, hon."

Lucy took a second to glance around the room. The place was pretty empty; there were two tables of elderly people and one other person at the bar. It was a younger looking man who was so dirty and scruffy Lucy couldn't tell if he was a vagrant or some sort of construction worker. He had been watching her, waiting for her to look over so he could give a smile and a greeting. Lucy complied so he could resume eating. When she looked back over, Bobbi was in front of her with her hands full.

"I know, it's kinda dead in here right now. We'll get our rush pretty soon though." She set down a coffee mug and the muffin. "Warmed that up for ya too, hon...the muffin I mean." Then she grabbed the pot of coffee from the back counter and filled Lucy's cup.

"Thanks."

"Now you let me know if you need anything else," she said. She walked over to the man at the counter and refilled his coffee.

The warmth of the muffin melted the butter as Lucy spread it across one half. It was soft and moist and luscious. Talk about comfort food. *Should this muffin really be making me feel better?* she thought to herself.

Bobbi noticed her enjoyment and headed back over. "Pretty good, huh?"

"Very," Lucy returned, still chewing.

"Yer not from here are ya, hon?"

"No, how did you know?" Instinctively she was immediately suspicious.

Bobbi shook her head with pride and put a hand on her hip. "I can tell. Been working around people my whole life... mostly here in Texas. I can tell a lot about people after only a few minutes."

"Wow, that's pretty amazing." Before she could stop herself, Lucy added, "What else can you tell about me?"

"Oh, I'd say whatever you came here for was not something yer too happy 'bout. In fact, I don't think yer too happy with yerself either."

"Anything else?" Lucy took another bite of her muffin. Might as well keep going now that the ball was rolling.

"Well...I am a bit stumped now, hon. You seem like a sweet girl and all, but...I'd be willing to bet you don't take much crap from anyone." Lucy couldn't help but let out a smile, which gave Bobbi the confirmation she was looking for. "Uh-huh," she said slowly, nodding her head up and down. "Looks like I got you pegged, hon."

CHAPTER 41

The big day was creeping up on them like a stalker in the night. In about thirty hours, two sisters would lie side by side on gurneys leaving their fates in the hands of surgeons and God. There had been no more spoken about Linda when Lucy arrived home yesterday from clearing her head. It was almost as if it never happened. Now everyone had on their game face. The house seemed to be at maximum capacity as well. It almost felt like a holiday. Rick was home since he'd planned on a week off. He wanted to be there for Katie, and possibly Lucy, after the surgery. Depending on each of their recoveries, they would be released to go home between two and four days later. George took time off as well and continued to pop in and out, bringing everyone's spirits up when he did.

The only one who seemed to be completely aware of the situation and living in reality was Carly. She was the first one up that day and had already put on her *dress* for the day. Rick found her in her room coloring and tried to convince her to change, but he knew it was useless. So he made a point to gather up Lucy and Anne to explain the appearance and significance of the garment. He asked them to act as they normally would, commenting on the dress itself, but not the reason behind it.

The girls understood, and Anne remarked how clever it was of Carly to invent a more beautiful version of the security blanket.

The hours ticked by in slow motion while everyone worked hard to keep busy, or at least make themselves look busy. Rick decided it was a good time to finally organize the workbench George had put in for him at Christmas. Upon Rick's insistence, Katie was taking a nap. Just like his daughter, he was in tune to the well-being of his wife no matter how hard she tried to hide it. Lucy and Anne were playing board games with Carly on the living room floor.

"What a beautiful dress," Anne said as she rolled the die. "You look just like a princess."

Lucy just eyed her and couldn't quite figure out what was so familiar about Carly in that dress.

"Thank you," she replied sweetly but still kept an eye on Anne counting her way around the board. Carly hated to lose at anything. She didn't, however, mind not finishing a game if something better came along, which is exactly what happened when the doorbell rang. Izzy, the girl next door who was a year older than Carly, was asking if Carly could come over and play with her dollhouse. Anne and Lucy telepathically sent Rick the signal that stopping the game was just fine with them, so he gave his approval. Both women flopped down on the sofa like sacks of flour being dumped in a truck. Neither had realized how tiring it was to keep up with the energy levels of a young child.

"Can I get you two anything while I'm in here?" Rick offered from the kitchen. He was still holding a hammer from the garage.

"I'm fine," Lucy replied first. She wondered why even though his build did not portray it, he suddenly seemed more masculine because he was holding a tool.

"Yeah, just getting to lie here and do nothing is good enough for me," Anne added with a relieved tone. Her usual perky expression had faded a notch.

"I do appreciate you both keeping Carly's mind off things. I know she can be tough to keep up with sometimes, but days like these are even worse."

"We understand," Anne answered for both of them.

"Thanks. Hey, as soon as Katie gets up, I'm heading out to the store to pick up a few things if either of you need to get out for a bit." He didn't wait for an answer and took off through the door to the garage with the hammer slung over his shoulder.

• • •

Lucy didn't give the strange car in the driveway a second thought when she returned from the store with Rick and Anne. There had been other visitors since they had arrived a little more than four days ago. One of Katie's friends, Amanda, stopped by to drop off a toy Carly had left at her house. Rick's office manager was there just yesterday to give him some paperwork that needed to be signed right away. So Lucy felt completely ambushed walking into the house and facing her worst nightmare.

"Daddy, Daddy!" Carly greeted them at the door and grabbed Rick's wrist. "Guess who's here!"

"Wow, sweetie." Rick put an arm around his daughter to calm her. "I don't know, but is sounds like someone exciting, huh?"

"Yes, Daddy, it's Grandma." Yanking fruitlessly on his arm, she whined, "Come and see."

Lucy turned to Rick with a confused look. "I thought your mom was in Hawaii?"

"She is," Rick answered with the same confused look.

"Not Grandma Rose, Grandma Linda," Carly continued.

A bolt of electricity instantly stabbed Lucy in the heart. *She did not just say that,* Lucy told herself. *She's just a little girl who is probably confused, or maybe playing a game. There's no way that Linda would be here, especially now.* Quiet voices could be heard coming from the kitchen, which escalated the heat rushing to Lucy's face. She remembered the stuffed animal and her talk with Katie, and suddenly it did make sense. Maybe they were planning this visit all along.

"I need to use the restroom," Anne announced purely out of self-preservation and headed down the hall.

Lucy didn't blame her for not wanting to be in the vicinity of the impending catastrophe.

Surrendering to Carly's tug-of-war, Rick followed her toward the kitchen. Robotically and on autopilot, Lucy went along behind Rick. As they rounded the corner edge of the hallway, they could see Katie leaning against the kitchen counter. A woman was standing in front of her with her back to them. She had blonde hair that was teased up and puffy on the top of her head.

Lucy stopped dead in her tracks for she didn't even need the woman to turn around to confirm what she already knew. She had recognized her mother's voice as they got closer. It was an unmistakable voice that spoke only in criticism and excuses.

"You're home," Katie said as less of a greeting and more of an abrupt end to their conversation.

There was no response except for Linda turning around and displaying an awkward grin. "Hi."

"Linda, hi I'm Rick." He extended his hand to her. "Nice to meet you."

Lucy was almost offended that Rick would greet her so pleasantly, but she would have to think about that later.

Linda accepted his hand, giving it a quick and firm shake, and said, "You too."

Then there was a moment of silence, in which everyone looked at Lucy. It was as if it was her turn in some kind of game like charades or tag.

"What are you doing here?" was all she could think of.

"Well it's nice to see you too, Lucy," Linda shot back.

Realizing that things were going to be bumpy if not completely turbulent, Katie intervened to clear out innocent bystanders. "Sweetheart, why don't you go play in the den on the computer?" She began escorting her daughter from the kitchen.

"But Mommy, I already got my computer time for today."

Katie gave Rick a pleading look, which he instantly picked up on and added, "Well today you get a little extra time. You can show me that new game you've been talking about." Rick took Carly's hand and the two walked out.

"Maybe the three of us could go out back and talk." Katie gestured innocently toward the backyard. "I could bring us out something to drink, and we've got the shade at this time." The other two weren't buying it and stood stubbornly in place.

"What for, a nice little family reunion? You two go ahead." Lucy set her purse on the counter and went to the cupboard to retrieve a glass. She acted as if Katie and Linda would actually take her up on the offer and exit from her presence. Hoping was probably more like it. Then she wouldn't have to pretend to busy herself while ignoring them.

"Lucy, please," Katie pleaded and reached out for her sister. "We have to talk about this. Mom came all this way for us, to make sure we were okay."

That word, *Mom*, was like a lethal injection. Hearing Katie say it with all of them in the same room was way too real and brought back too many bad feelings. Lucy's breathing suddenly sped up as if she were diving into a cold pool in the winter and couldn't catch her breath.

"It's okay, Katie." Linda took a step back, as if that would relieve some of the pressure. "I know I can't just jump back into your lives just like that. But I was hoping—"

Lucy turned abruptly and faced them both, not quite caring about holding back at that moment. Were these two completely insane? "So you two are a team now, huh? What did you think? That we'd all bond over this traumatic experience?"

"It's not like that, Lucy." Linda's voice was soft and calm, something Lucy was used to hearing after a binge or a blowup. She walked over to Lucy and stood beside her. "I heard about Katie—and the surgery—and I just wanted to be here."

Linda tried to put a gentle hand on Lucy's arms, but she broke away and crossed to the other side of the kitchen. "You can't help us!" Lucy raged. "You never could, and you never will!" Lucy snatched her purse from the counter. "Letting her back into your life is a mistake," she said to Katie, walking out of the kitchen. "You'll only get hurt." And then they heard the door slam.

CHAPTER 42

Déjà vu? Was it not less than twenty-four hours ago that Lucy was taking this exact same escape route? She didn't care. What other choice did she have? At least she could give herself some props for not crying...until she walked out. Tears dribbled quickly down her cheeks as she made her way down the street. Lucy did not attempt to wipe them; she only covered them by lowering her sunglasses down on her face. She wondered how she could possibly get herself out of what seemed to be an impossible situation. Would she now demand that Linda leave or she wouldn't go through with the surgery? Even she wasn't that heartless. Or was she? She thought of Bobbi at the coffee shop and how easily she had read Lucy. Maybe she would have some advice. It sounded crazy just thinking about it, but at this point there weren't many options.

Before she knew it, Lucy had almost reached the shopping center. Something she hadn't thought about was how late it was getting. The streets were pretty congested, and there were more people milling around this time. As she walked through the parking lot toward the coffee shop, her phone rang. She heard it, obviously, but didn't even bother to look at it. There was not one person she wanted to hear from. Well, maybe there was one, but that ship had sailed. Lucy wiped each side of her face with an old tissue from her purse, then peered earnestly through the window. The shop was crowded, with almost every counter spot taken. Two women whipped back and forth behind the counter like Daytona drivers, but to her regret neither one was Bobbi. She took an anxious last look around the place and finally gave up. Now what?

"You okay, miss?"

Lucy felt a hand touch her shoulder and jolted her head back from the window.

"Sorry." She moved to the side, making room for the man to open the entry door. He looked to be mid-forties and had a teenage girl with him. They both wore sunglasses and baseball caps, her hair pulled back, like she was the son he never had. When the man took hold of the handle and pulled, he gestured to Lucy to go ahead. "Oh…no, I'm not going in," she said.

Still holding the door open the man replied, "Are you sure?" The girl waited behind him and stared at Lucy curiously, while the man gave Lucy one last chance. "You look like you could use a rest. Maybe something to drink?"

"No, I'm fine really." Lucy felt strange still talking to him while he had the door open. A few patrons seated near the door had looked over and waited to see the outcome.

"If you're worried about paying, I can—"

"What?" *Oh God, this guy thinks I'm homeless or poor or something.* "No." Lucy began backing away sheepishly. "I was… just looking for someone." She didn't have time to decide if she was insulted or touched by the man's caring nature. Either way, Lucy was out of there, and the Good Samaritan shrugged and entered the shop. Katie and Rick had told her people in Texas were friendly, and now she got to experience it firsthand.

Once again Lucy's phone alerted her, but this time the sound indicated a text message. Once again she ignored it. She knew that eventually everyone would begin to worry, but she wasn't ready to start acknowledging anything yet. Besides, she still hadn't figured out what she would do about Linda. Maybe there was nothing to do. The surgery would be the next day. After a couple of recovery days, with no visits from *her*, obviously the girls would be on their way back to LA. Rick would take them to Dallas, where they'd take the train home. Then she would never see either of them again. *Yep, that's the plan,* Lucy thought to herself indignantly. *Then Katie will finally see for herself what Mom is really like.*

Once Lucy got out of the strip mall parking lot, her thoughts had her wandering farther than she was familiar with. She contemplated calling Rick and telling him to pick her up. The sun was starting to set, and she really didn't know where else to go. Just the thought of making that call and having to face everyone made her frustration level rise again. *This is crap!* She wasn't going to let herself cry again. That part had to be over, but not letting it out cranked her anger up a notch. She charged across a side street and towards some industrial buildings. Three men were huddled around a beat-up truck with a metal ladder sticking out of the back. As she passed they all stared at her. The feeling of their eyes fixated on her fueled her anger even more. One of them, who was barefoot and had a bald head, made a sound like he'd just eaten something seriously delicious. Then he said, "Niiice."

"Why don't you losers get a life?" Lucy said as casual as could be. "Or better yet, how 'bout a job." *Assholes.* She kept walking and didn't look back. She could hear them all laughing it up, which just confirmed her evaluation of them. Her heart skipped a beat and she picked up her pace when she heard the doors close and the engine start, but thankfully they drove in the opposite direction. Lucy couldn't take it any longer. She ran around to the back of one of the buildings, but just as she stepped over a small curb with one foot, her ankle gave way and she felt a tingly crack. She limped, pissed and mortified, over to the back of the building. Her back slumped against the wall, and she slid down to the ground, her glasses falling to her side. With her purse in her lap and her knees clutched close, her head dropped down to her folded arms. The tiny pit of pressure that was on her ankle stung, and she begged out loud, "Please don't let this be serious."

As much as Lucy pushed people away, she didn't want to be alone now. Those were the times she felt deep despondency. The kind of grief that left some people feeling there was no way out. She didn't want to feel that way anymore, and she certainly didn't want to feel that way now. She couldn't, because of Katie. Lucy was trapped inside herself, at least until after tomorrow. The sleeves on her shirt moistened up against her face as that powerful reality sank in. She tried to convince herself that it was only the pain from her ankle that was causing her distress. Then, after minutes which seemed like hours, the grinding of gravel on the ground nearby startled her. She sucked in a quick breath and popped her head up.

• • •

"Hi, Lucy."

She squinted up at the tall figure that was halfway blocking the setting sun. He wore loose-fitting jeans and a button-down shirt. Praying that it wasn't a dream, she turned her body and adjusted her view for clarity. It was him. She immediately got to her feet and plunged into him, her arms wrapped tightly around his neck.

"Well this is something I didn't expect!" he said with a quiet chuckle.

"Kyle, I can't believe you're here." Lucy was still hanging on tightly, but balanced on one foot. Her eyes were still wet and closed. There were no more games to be played. No pretending not to need him. She *did* need him—now more desperately than ever. They stood there frozen in time until her grip finally loosened. *Wait a second,* the thought jingled in her brain. *What is he doing here?*

He seemed to read her mind, or at least her expression. "I know, pretty crazy, huh?"

His smell was familiar, and his body felt perfectly fit to hers. Although every inch of her didn't want to pull away, her curiosity took over. "What are you doing here? I don't mean just in Texas either, actually right here?"

"Looking for you."

"Well I kind of figured that much out...but why?" She tried to take a step back, but leaning on her foot made her wince and do a little hop.

"What happened? Are you okay?" He tried to balance her by holding her under one arm.

"I think I twisted my ankle."

"Here, let's get you to the car." Kyle bent over and began to pick her up.

"Wait!" Lucy hopped back on one foot. "What car? You need to tell me what's going on."

"Look, I'll explain everything after we take care of you. Now will you let me carry you?"

She stood staring at him with a look that said, *That's not good enough.*

"Lucy, I came here to help you." His voice was stern yet convincing. "Yesterday after we spoke I knew you didn't mean what you said. And I knew I *had* to see you. So here I am. Now can we *please* go somewhere else and talk? I rented a car...it's around the other side of this building." He opened his arms pleadingly and waited for her response.

Lucy knew he was right. She gave a couple of mini head nods and hobbled closer to him. "I'm sure I can walk though."

"Better not take any chances." He scooped her up into his arms and gave her an understanding grin. She hung on tightly as he carried her to the car, studying his face as he looked ahead, trying to memorize every facial feature.

Kyle had rented a maroon Ford Escort. Although not really his style, he was happy to get something decent at the last minute and without a reservation. In the car he explained how he'd arrived this morning and as part of his master plan got to Katie's house about an hour ago. Anne had filled him in on the details as they were relayed to her from Katie. Lucy felt a pang of guilt when Kyle told her that Rick was out looking for her as well.

"Hey," Lucy said, interrupting his detailed account. "Where are we going?"

"Well, I guess that's up to you. I could take you back to your sister's if you want."

"What do you mean? What other choice do I have?"

"I got a room just a few miles away. If you need more time, Lucy, we can go there." Kyle looked down at her with a concentrated stare, his eyebrows raised.

Lucy looked down at her ankle and tried to make a few rotations with it. The slip-on loafers she was wearing felt tighter, and her ankle appeared to be puffier. A terrifying thought sliced into her brain. "Oh God," she whispered to herself.

"What?"

"There can't be anything wrong with my ankle."

"It's probably just a sprain."

"No, you don't understand!" Lucy's voice strained, and her eyes looked frantic. "There can't be anything wrong with it. They won't do the surgery if they see this."

Kyle put his hand on Lucy's knee. He wanted to calm her, but he knew that he shouldn't make idle promises. "Let's go back to my room and take a look. Maybe it just needs some ice. We'll figure this all out, together."

CHAPTER 43

Kyle placed Lucy gently on the bed and stacked the pillows up behind her back. The room was dark except for a light on between the two beds which barely shone beneath the thick golden lampshade.

"First we have to get your ankle elevated. I need to find something to prop it up with." Kyle disappeared into the bathroom and returned with a stack of towels. Lucy was impressed with Kyle and watched in awe as he took charge and took care of her. Slowly he lifted her foot, pushed the towel stack underneath, and then lowered it back down. "How's that?"

"Okay I guess." Her face squinted. "How do you know about all this stuff?"

"My brother Alex," he said, slipping the shoe off her foot. "He was the athlete in the family. But he was always getting hurt. One day it was a sprained ankle or broken foot, next it was a dislocated shoulder. Ooh, this is a little swollen."

"Is that really bad?"

"Maybe not. Let me run down the hall to the ice machine. You may want to take that time to call your sister, let her know you're okay." His voice and expression made it sound like a question, but Lucy took it more like an order. He was right, though. She shouldn't let everyone worry, especially now that she knew

Rick had gone out looking for her. So before he even got out the door, Lucy was on her cell placing the call. After several rings, it was Katie who answered the phone. Lucy got right to the point. No small talk or even questions about whether or not Linda was still there. She simply apologized for taking off, let her know she was at the hotel with Kyle, and assured her that she would be there first thing in the morning. There was no way she was going to mention her ankle. No matter what, Lucy was going through with the surgery. She'd fake it if she had to.

Next she took the time to text Anne. She was starting to feel bad that Anne had to ride out all this drama. But reliable, faithful Anne responded as Lucy had expected, with sympathy and understanding. She wondered why Anne stuck with her and how she was lucky enough to get a friend like that. When she thought about it, she actually had some great people in her life. That thought made her feel both gratified and saddened. How many times would they come back after she pushed them away?

Kyle opened the door just as she was setting her phone down. "Everything okay?"

"Yeah, thanks to you."

His smile said it all. Whether he was there because he truly wanted to be with her, or just out of some sense of male chivalry, either way he looked pleased with himself. Lucy knew he deserved it and was not about to take a shot at him. Kyle took the plastic liner from the ice bucket and filled it with ice. Then he sat down at the end of the bed, and when he draped it over her ankle, she grimaced and whined, "Shit, that's cold."

"Sorry, but it's really necessary."

"I know. Thank you for taking care of me."

"It's my pleasure." His smile diminished when he noticed Lucy's eyes were morose and somewhat glazed. He scooted closer to her so that their faces were just inches apart. "Hey, don't be upset. It's going to work out."

"I'm sorry you came all this way for me." She looked down, away from the power his gaze held over her.

He stroked her hair, her cheek, and then he leaned in and whispered, "I'm not." Softly he swept his lips across hers. "There's nowhere else I'd rather be than right here." He paused for a moment, peering deep into her eyes. There was so much heat between them she sensed her ice might start melting. On impulse, Lucy grabbed ahold of his collar and pulled him into her for a long, hard kiss. She needed to show him what she always had trouble telling him, even though it was something Kyle had known all along. She felt his hand slip behind her back, drawing her body into his. Neither wanted to pull away, to give up the intensity they were experiencing, but eventually Kyle did. He wasn't going to risk everything by rushing things and not thinking it through. It would be so easy to just give in.

For a moment they both stared at each other, wondering what to say next. Under normal circumstances this would have been an ideal situation. Alone in a cozy hotel room. Together on the bed under low lighting. Add to that the obvious physical attraction between the two coupled with dramatic circumstances. You couldn't make a better recipe for romance. Unfortunately, they both knew a bad ankle and an impending surgery was standing between them. *I can wait if you can,* his face seemed to tell her.

Little did he know that it was killing Lucy to do just that. It had been so long for her, mainly because she never let herself get close enough to anyone. She wondered if her own image of the perfect man had sabotaged her struggling love life. Since she'd lacked a male father figure for a good part of her life, her ideal was based more on fantasy than reality. But now, for the first time, fantasy and reality had melded together in the form of the perfect man: Kyle. If only she could hang on long enough to create something lasting, something stable.

Taking their minds off one sensitive topic, Kyle bounced to another—the surgery. He asked Lucy if she was ready, mentally that is, to go through with it.

"I'm not afraid to do it, if that's what you're asking," she replied. "I'm more afraid of what would happen if I didn't."

"How has your sister been since you've been with her?"

"I can see her illness taking its toll. Growing up, we both got kind of used to push away any kind of pain. I know she's doing that now. Katie is very strong."

"She gets it from her sister."

They both exchanged a smile and some more small talk. Then after about an hour, Kyle took the ice off and asked Lucy if she could move her ankle. She complied, turning it around in a few circles. But when Kyle did the same and pressed it backward with the palm of his hand, she flinched and pulled her leg back.

"How bad did that hurt?"

"Just a little really. I think it scared me more than anything." She straightened her leg. "Try it again." Lucy gave him a trusting look and braced herself on the bed. Gently he picked up her foot and nudged it back just slightly, watching for her reaction. With eyes locked on each other, Kyle continued to move the ankle in different positions until he finally set it back down on the bed.

"I'm pretty sure it's not broken. My guess is that it's just a slight sprain."

"But do you think I can get by tomorrow? I mean, obviously I won't be doing much walking, but someone will see me when I first walk in."

"I guess that depends on how well you can fake it. Why don't we get you up and see how you walk?"

Kyle helped Lucy to her feet and stood waiting for a cue. Lucy was still for a moment with most of her weight balanced on her good foot. Slowly she bobbed back and forth putting more and more pressure on the injured ankle.

"How do you feel?" Kyle asked, wondering if she was being a trooper or if Lucy was willing herself not to feel pain.

"I...think...it's not too bad." After a few more sways, she took hold of Kyle's arm and slowly walked in a semicircle around him.

"But how's the pain?"

"It's a little sore. I'm sure there's nothing broken."

"Seems like the swelling has gone down some as well."

"I can pull this off. I have to."

"You know I'll help you in any way I can."

Just then Lucy's text alert went off on her phone. Any correspondence in the eleventh hour was bound to make her jumpy. She flopped down on the bed and scooped up her cell. Kyle caught a smile forming on Lucy's face when she read the text from Benny.

Are you okay?

Don't worry, I'm fine, she quickly typed.

I tried to call you to wish you luck for the surgery. Then I tried Anne and she told me what happened. You know I worry about my girl Lucita.

Kyle watched in silence, concern spreading across his face.

I'm sorry, and I'm really fine now. Let's talk after tomorrow. Take care. Lucy set her phone down, and realizing that he was going to ask anyway, said, "That was Benny."

Kyle sat down next to Lucy and stared at his own hands in his lap. "Seems like that guy really cares about you."

"He does." Her voice was sincere, and her thoughts went to the night on the road when she and Benny shared a kiss. She had been emotional that night, and Benny had always been her rock. Lucy had felt a closeness to Benny that night, but she knew now that kiss was nothing compared to what she felt when she kissed Kyle.

A pained smile flashed across his face. He wasn't one to hide his emotions, and right now Lucy clearly read his concern about Benny.

"Should I be jealous?" Kyle searched deep into her eyes for the answer.

"Benny has been a great friend to me lately. And I don't have too many of those. He was there for me...and he helped me through some bad stuff." Lucy put one of her hands into Kyle's hands. "But no, you shouldn't be jealous." Lucy leaned in and gave him a soft kiss on his cheek. Her slight pause was just enough for Kyle to turn his head and move in, meeting their lips once again. Only this time it was slow and sensuous—a declaration, a promise. Kyle was still squeezing Lucy's hand when she pulled back. "I hope that was convincing enough for you."

"I'll take it...for now." He displayed an adorable smile like an embarrassed schoolboy. "But I'm going to need some more convincing later."

CHAPTER 44

Kyle and Lucy lay serenely together in the bed. Side by side, facing each other, they talked for hours. She was honest and he listened. She told him everything that came into her head and didn't hold back. There were some things that surprised him, but other details made perfect sense. At times it was actually comforting to him because it was more pieces to the puzzle that made up this woman he was falling deeply in love with. She spoke about her father. Not the sweet man who raised her and was taken away before she even reached her teens. But her real father, a man she had never even known by name. Lucy told him of her decision to find him after the surgery, even without Linda's help. She felt strongly that finding out about her father was the key to finding herself.

"I think that's great, Lucy," he whispered in the darkness. "And I'll do everything I can to help you. But…I already know who you are."

"Who do you think I am?"

"First of all, I don't think, I know." He ran the back of his hand along her arm and interlocked his fingers with hers. "You, Lucy, are a beautiful, smart, caring…" he lifted his head slightly, "…yes I said caring, strong young woman who is always trying to take care of everyone else…except herself."

Minutes easily turned to hours as they exchanged contemplations, feelings, and experiences. At once she felt both sleepy and euphoric. No matter what the future held, Lucy knew this night would deeply penetrate the force that propelled her toward her destiny. That was her final undeclared thought, and only when Lucy finally succumbed to her slumber did Kyle close his eyes too.

• • •

She didn't intentionally plan to cut things so close. It was just way too difficult for Lucy and Kyle to leave the sanctuary of their hotel and reenter reality. Lucy texted that they'd arrive by noon, about half an hour before they had to be at the hospital, and she hoped that would be acceptable. Back at the house, she was greeted with affection and excitement.

"I'm so glad you're back," Anne said. She was the first to greet Lucy with a giant hug. She looked like she was ready for a half marathon, dressed in all Nike workout wear.

"Cute outfit," Lucy commented like it was just a typical day.

"I dunno. My dad sent it to me, but I thought maybe it's a little too Sporty Spice and not enough Posh Spice." She extended her hand and a wide smile to Kyle. "Nice to finally meet you, Kyle."

"Hi, Anne. You too."

Just then Katie and Rick walked in from the bedroom, both dressed casually, Rick holding Katie's overnight bag.

"Looks like we're all ready for a workout," Anne cut in with a giggle.

Hugs, hellos, and handshakes were exchanged all around. Rick busied himself with last-minute duties while Katie gave them a quick update, explaining that George had picked up Carly and would bring her to the hospital later. Then she added, "Mom's not here."

"I didn't say anything," Lucy returned defensively.

"I know. I just wanted to let you know. But…I couldn't talk her out of not coming to the hospital." Katie shrugged helplessly. "So you may run into her there."

"Let's just try to focus on this day and what we need to do." She squeezed her sister's hand and gave her a wink. "Let me throw a couple things in a bag, and I'll be right out."

Since they weren't met at the door, no one had seen Lucy walk in, or favor her ankle. Kyle stuck close behind like a lost puppy as she walked toward her room. He was trying to block their view of her. But Anne seemed to notice and followed them back.

"Lucy, what happened? Are you limping?"

Lucy collapsed onto the bed and removed one of her shoes. "Cheap-ass shoes, gave me a blister."

"Oh, do you need a Band-Aid?" Anne gestured back.

"No, I'm good. Thanks." Lucy's response and smile revealed that she was ready, both physically and mentally.

• • •

Waiting with Katie in pre-op, Lucy surveyed the room and tried to wrap her brain around the surreal nature of what was happening. This would be the last time Lucy and her sister would see each other until recovery. Seemingly a mirror image of herself, Katie lay in a bed opposite her wearing an identical blue gown. It almost felt like they were having some sort of hospital fieldtrip and sleepover. For the first time in this whole ordeal, Lucy's stomach began flip-flopping. She tried to rub the clamminess from her hands. Then suddenly she began to shiver.

"Are you okay, Lucy?" Katie asked from across the room.

"Fine. Just a little chilly." Lucy couldn't believe how calm and together Katie seemed.

"Yeah, these hospital rooms are always cold. They'll give you a heated blanket if you want."

Lucy shrugged. "Mmm, maybe later."

"Later you won't know what you're feeling." They shared a giggle as a heavyset, African American nurse entered the room. "Hey, Rita, I'm so glad it's you." Katie's greeting was cheery and casual like they were meeting for lunch.

"I told you I would be here today," Rita answered with a wink and a smile toward Lucy.

"Rita, this is my sister Lucy."

"I kinda figured." Her voice was raspy like she either smoked or had a cold. "Nice to meet you, Lucy." Rita nodded at Lucy as she worked a few vitals on Katie.

"Hi," Lucy responded. She glanced around the room for something, anything, to take her mind off the surgery. She wondered why they had all those crappy magazines out in the waiting room and then nothing back here where you really needed it.

After checking both of them, including a concentrated glare at their charts, Rita announced, "Okay, ladies, you two hang tight for a bit, and we'll be back for you shortly. I'll let your families know they can have one more quick visit before showtime." When she reached the doorway, she paused and channeled her inner Florence Nightingale: "Everything's gonna be just fine."

After a brief moment of silence, Katie said, "How lame would it sound if I said thank you?"

"Not lame at all, but not needed either. I know you'd do the same for me."

"I would, Lucy. In a heartbeat."

Just when the two finally made their way past all the obvious, life-affirming rationalizations and proclamations and relaxed into casual conversation, Rita returned with another nurse and rolled Katie out of the room. As the door swung closed, she caught a quick glimpse of Rick and Linda walking down the hall beside Katie. "The nerve of that woman," Lucy said aloud to herself. But then she swiftly put herself in check as if she were psyching herself up for the big game.

Lucy knew Katie's exit meant that hers would follow shortly. Anne and Kyle peeked in for a last boost of morale, both displaying plastered smiles. She tried to tune out their chitchat while idle, disturbing thoughts ricocheted around her head. *I've never even been put out before. What if I don't wake up? What if Katie doesn't wake up?* Lucy smiled and nodded, completely unaware of anything they were saying. Then she felt a pang of guilt for not showing her appreciation. She should have at least thanked them, told them both how much she appreciated their support. But she just couldn't bring herself to get into that. Fortunately for her, the two were scooted out as two different nurses arrived to gather her up and deliver her to the operating room. All she could think of while she was being wheeled down the hall was how she felt like she was right in the middle of an episode of *ER*.

Just like a kid on Christmas Eve, Lucy thought there was no way she would fall asleep. She'd heard about people trying to fight the anesthesia or it not being strong enough to keep them out for the whole surgery. But it seemed like mere seconds after the anesthesiologist plunked his face in front of hers that the room faded to black.

CHAPTER 45

....

After hours of pacing, small talk, drinking coffee, and just staring out into the hallway from the waiting room, family and friends were finally updated on Katie and Lucy. Both surgeries had gone according to plan, and the doctor informed them that at the current moment Rick could go in to see Katie, but only for a brief visit. She was in ICU and coming out of anesthesia. Rick's hasty departure left the others speculating and concerned, even though the doctor assured them that Lucy would soon be waking up herself.

Earlier in the afternoon, George had stopped by with Carly for her own reassurance. She wanted to see everyone and wanted to be with her mommy. Unfortunately, it would be at least a couple hours more before they'd hear the good news. So George decided it was better to take Carly to get some food.

Rick stood in the doorway of the ICU watching his precious Katie before making his presence known. Like a parent at bedtime, he took joy in watching the rise and fall of her chest beneath the white folded-down sheet. They were slow, deep breaths, and he matched his own breathing with hers. Sitting next to her bed, he gently rubbed her arm, then stroked her cheek. He did not want to rouse her before she was ready. Rick watched and waited patiently as her head finally began to stir and move slightly back and forth.

A whisper seemed to escape her without her lips even moving. "Rick."

"I'm here, babe." He took a firm hold of her hand. "You did great. You're going to be okay."

"Lu...Lucy?" Her eyes were fighting to stay open. "Is she okay?"

"The doctor said everything went great. She's in SAICU and hasn't woken up yet, but it should be anytime now."

"Will you check on her for me?"

Rick leaned on the bed with his elbows and lowered his head near hers. "Listen, they said I can't stay long. You need to rest. But don't worry, I'll check on Lucy." He kissed her fingers and rested his cheek on her hand. This hospital scene had been acted out many times before by the two of them, but this time was different. Rick could feel it in his bones. A rush of relief and promise swept over him. There was no denying Katie's future would still hold visits to the hospital, recovery, and rehabilitation. But that was nothing compared to no future at all. He knew this was the beginning of a new life for Katie.

• • •

Back in the waiting room, Rick asked the others if there were any further updates on Lucy. They all stared blankly at him like he was the one who was supposed to bring back some sort of news.

"I'm sure everything's fine. Some people just take longer to come out of it," Kyle said encouragingly.

Anne smiled and tried to keep everyone positive. Her instincts in the hospital setting had kicked into gear. "Hey, everyone, Kyle's right. Besides, the doctor said everything went fine. I'm going to go rummage us all up some snacks, and I'm sure we'll hear something soon."

Kyle was seated in a chair off to one corner, and she patted him on the shoulder before leaving. Then, without a word, he was up and out the door. He was never the "sit around and wait" kind of guy, so he needed to see what was going on. At first, he casually walked around hoping to run into someone who looked familiar—anyone who had been involved in the procedures. He received a few smiles and head nods from various staffers, but none of them questioned or seemed to care where he was going. When he noticed signs leading to the SAICU, he was determined to make his way there, and he hoped that he wouldn't be stopped. At one point, three staffers bolted down a hallway towards a loud beeping sound, causing Kyle's heart rate to shoot through the roof. Then, rounding the next corner, Kyle ran right smack into a nurse.

"Oh, excuse me sir," came her raspy voice.

Kyle looked up and instantly recognized her. "Rita." He smiled and paused, being careful not to say the wrong thing.

"Is there something I can do for you?"

"Is Lucy down there?" He gestured down the hallway behind her.

"Yes…Kyle, right?" She spoke again before he even started to nod. "Lucy isn't awake yet, and then only immediate family goes in to see her."

"Shouldn't she be awake by now? We're all just a little concerned here, and if I could just see her, just for a few minutes…"

"I'm sorry, but you should really go back to the waiting area." Her sympathetic look contradicted what she was saying. "I'm sure the doctor will let you know when she wakes up."

Knowing he had a chance to convince her, Kyle carried on. "Rita, as you know, her immediate family is in recovery as well. And I'm about the closest thing she's got to family right now." His eyes pleaded with her. "Don't you think hearing a familiar voice will help her wake up? Honestly, I'm a little worried that she just might need a reason to wake up."

Rita looked beyond Kyle down the opposite hallway. He couldn't tell if she was looking for someone or making sure no one was there. "Like I said, the doctor will speak with you soon. Now I've got to tend to another patient." Then with a slight tilt of her head she gave him a half grin and a raised eyebrow. "You can find your way back alright?" She walked past him and didn't look back.

Not needing any more of a hint than that, Kyle glided down the hallway until he found Lucy's room. After a quick peek showed him the coast was clear, he entered the room. Strangely he had never visited anyone in the hospital before, and that hadn't crossed his mind when he saw her earlier. Maybe it was all the wires and machinery that seemed to be hovering around her, and the beeps and humming that penetrated the silence. He pulled a chair over to the bed and sat next to her, keeping his distance at first.

"Lucy…it's me, Kyle." Although his intent was to try and waken her, he couldn't seem to bring his voice to a level higher than you'd use in the library. "Lucy, can you hear me?" He leaned forward now and rested one hand on top of hers. "You know, Lucy, I bet you're just really tired. This has probably been a nice long rest for you. But I know you're gonna wake up soon… you have to." He ran his fingers through his hair and hung his head down. "I mean, you and I, we're just starting to—"

The sound of outside creeping in from the opening of the door startled Kyle, and he turned to see one of the surgeons standing in the doorway with a look that told Kyle his time was up.

CHAPTER 46

....

"What's *he* doing with the doctor?" Linda asked as Kyle approached the waiting room, walking and talking with the doctor. Linda felt somewhat like an outsider and hadn't really spoken until then. She was happy to be there, but she didn't want to be too intrusive, until that moment.

All eyes turned to the pair, waiting for some sort of big announcement. The doctor walked over to Rick and addressed him first. "Mr. Moore? I'm Dr. Thomas. I assisted in your wife's operation." He had an extra-large head with thinning hair across the top.

"Hey, thanks for taking care of Katie." Rick waited eagerly.

The two stepped to the side to speak privately, although most of what they were saying was completely audible to the others. In fact, Linda made a point of getting within closer earshot. Dr. Thomas wanted to give Rick a heads-up about the briefing he would need to have with the transplant coordinators. They would be providing detailed instructions regarding antirejection medicine, rejection signs to look for, measuring vitals, and answering any other questions that he and Katie may have. Rick definitely felt a pang of anxiety hearing that, but he was already aware of the fact that they wouldn't walk out of there home free. But he wasn't going to let that dampen his optimism.

"The other thing I wanted to talk with you about is your sister-in-law."

"Why hasn't she woken up yet? Is it some sort of...coma?"

"Technically, we can't say that yet. It hasn't been long enough."

"Then why isn't she awake yet?" Linda interrupted.

"Unfortunately, I can't give you any answers at this time." Dr. Thomas gave a sweeping look around to address everyone. "But what I can tell you is that both sisters are getting the absolute best care, and we'll continue to monitor this...situation." He turned back to Rick once again. "One thing that is very important is that you try to keep Katie calm." Rick nodded, expecting the doctor had more to say. "She's very concerned about Lucy, so if possible, try to keep her mind on other things. In the meantime, someone will be back later to give you another update."

Leaving mixed reactions in the room, the doctor quietly exited, and after a brief moment of silence, Linda responded with, "Update us on what? Whether or not my daughter will ever wake up?" She walked across the room and looked out toward the nearby nurses' station. "Why are they not doing something about this?"

Rick walked over and stood next to her. "They know what they're doing, Linda. It hasn't been that long. Let's just wait a little longer."

"I should go in and see her. What if she doesn't wake up?" The question sounded like it was more to herself than to anyone in particular.

"She *will* wake up." Kyle's voice sounded annoyed and frustrated. "I know she will. She just needs a little more time."

"How do you know?" Linda turned and looked directly at Kyle. Defensively she said, "From what I hear, you barely know each other."

"And from what I hear, you don't know Lucy at all."

Knowing that Kyle was absolutely right, Linda didn't respond. She couldn't. It was her own fault that she was alienated from her daughters. She tried to think back to a time when she was a good mother. There was a time, so long ago. She hoped, no prayed, that both her daughters could somehow remember that part of their life. It seemed that Katie would give her another chance, although Linda wasn't all that sure she deserved it. What if she couldn't handle it and ruined things once again?

But Lucy, she'd gotten the worst of it. The thought of never getting to make amends with Lucy was killing her. Of course she had felt guilty in the past, but Linda always convinced herself that things would someday work themselves out. She would be kidding herself now if she made a promise to God. *Please let my daughters be okay and I'll lead a perfect life.* She didn't have that much faith in herself. She would, however, pray for them. And she would take full advantage of any second chances either of them would be willing to grant to her.

The setting sun signaled an unspoken fear they all shared. With Lucy still not awake, everyone prayed that the new day would bring new hope.

Before Katie went to sleep for the night, Rick paid her one more visit, followed by Linda, and then at last Carly joined them. Holding her daughter and seeing her bright smile was like no medicine they could give her in that hospital. If only for a few moments, it took her mind off of Lucy.

Linda watched them and envied their closeness, hoping someday she might have her daughters back in her life. Thanks to her, Lucy had made so many sacrifices over the years. Linda looked at Katie and gave one last silent prayer before leaving. *Please don't let this be Lucy's ultimate sacrifice.*

• • •

They couldn't be swayed to go home, get some sleep, and return first thing in the morning. "You're a stubborn bunch," the nurse had said to them last night, while providing blankets, pillows, and anything else they needed to be more comfortable. There was a bit of nodding off here and there, along with some resting with eyes closed. But the disturbing sounds of the hospital weren't exactly like crickets and waterfalls. As soon as they started to drift off, or even when they were asleep, they were yanked back to reality by the bells and beeps that signaled some sort of awful crisis.

At about six thirty in the morning, Kyle jumped up and said, "Okay, I'm going to see what they can tell us." Before he reached the doorway, a nurse entered the room.

"Mr. Moore?"

Rick walked over and joined Kyle. "I'm Mr. Moore."

The nurse, who was all of about five feet tall, seemed nervous and unsure of what she was doing. She glanced down at the clipboard she was holding. "Uh, Mr. Moore...your wife... Mrs. Moore...is awake." She smiled as if she'd made a huge accomplishment. "She's asking for you." She turned to walk away.

"Excuse me?" Kyle said. "What about her sister? Lucy Lang?"

Stopping just short of the doorway, the nurse turned back. Her eyes searched the ceiling for the answer until it somehow popped right into her brain. "Oh yes of course, Ms. Lang!"

"Is she awake?"

"I'm sorry, no. But the nurse on duty wanted me to tell you that the doctor will be in to see her in about half an hour. I'm sure he'll speak with you after that."

Wasting no time, Rick followed her out and went to Katie's room. He was expecting her to be awake, but he was surprised to find her sitting up, looking as though she was waiting for something. Rick assumed she was about to eat breakfast, which reminded him of his own hunger and caused his stomach to growl.

"There's my girl." Rick smiled sweetly as he entered the room and took his seat wedged on the side of her bed.

Katie returned the smile, but it faded fast.

"What's wrong?"

"They won't tell me what's going on with Lucy. Do you know if she's awake yet?"

"I don't know anything new yet...except that some nurse said the doctor would be checking her this morning."

"I'm starting to get worried, Rick. This is all my fault. I don't—"

"Stop." Knowing how important it was to keep her calm, Rick tried to change the subject. "Listen, babe. First we need to talk about you." The stalling was interrupted by the appearance of someone in the doorway.

"Rita, thank goodness you're here." Katie reached her hand into the air, waiting for Rita to walk over and take hold of it.

"How are you feeling this morning, dear?" Rita asked, squeezing Katie's hand tightly.

Completely ignoring the question, Katie continued. "Rita, we need your help. I was just about to tell Rick that you're going to get me over to see Lucy this morning."

CHAPTER 47

"Katie!" Lucy struggled to get the words out. *I have to get to Katie,* she thought to herself. In her hospital gown, she wandered down the hallway. Her bare feet skidded along the tile as her stride got progressively faster. "Where are you?" Lucy's sense of urgency grew to the point that she was almost running, searching through each doorway she went by. Suddenly she felt the tile beneath her feet transform into carpet, and her surroundings had changed too. *Where am I?* Seconds later she recognized that she was back at Katie's house. It seemed impossible. Then she heard a girl's voice.

"Lucy. Come here."

She tried to follow the familiar voice that sounded like it was coming from the back of the house. Heading down the hall, she tried to get a grasp on what was happening and why she felt so afraid.

"Lucy, look what I've done." The girl sounded happy and proud.

Standing in the doorway now, staring at the little girl in the beautiful dress, she said, "Katie?" A wave of relief washed away the fear. It was so wonderful to see her sister again after all these years. She wanted to hold her and tell her that no matter what she would take care of her. This must be their second chance. To do it all over again, but this time they would stick together.

"No, Aunt Lucy, it's me Carly. Come see the picture I painted."

"Carly?" Slowly she walked into the room and toward the girl. *What is happening?* Lucy had been so focused on the girl that she hadn't noticed the painting at first. Suddenly she had a bad feeling about it. She did not want to see what was painted on the other side of that canvas. It was coming back to her now. The dress. The painting. It was Linda. Just like before. Her mother was back in their lives, and now she would hurt Carly just like she'd hurt Lucy and Katie.

"It's someone I love very much!" Carly smiled and sat up tall as Lucy came to stand by her side. She grabbed one of Lucy's hands and pressed it against her cheek. "It's you, Aunt Lucy. You saved my mommy, and I love you very much." Her words faded quickly, but Lucy could still feel the soft skin against her hand, caressing it over and over.

• • •

"What?" Rita exchanged a puzzled look with Rick, who shrugged and waited for Katie to continue.

"I have to see my sister, right now. She needs me…she needs to hear my voice. And I need your help to get over there, Rita."

"Listen, honey, I know you're worried about Lucy, but the only place you're going today is the intermediate care unit."

Rick didn't say a word, and Katie could tell that Rita was not taking her seriously. As Rita looked over Katie's chart, she started pushing back her covers as if attempting to get out of bed. Her body ached and felt incredibly weak, so she hoped that Rita would not call her bluff. "You two aren't getting this, are you?" She clasped a hand across Rick's wrist like she was slapping on handcuffs. "Help me up."

Rick released the resistance in his arm so she couldn't get any leverage. "Babe, you can't get up. Rita please, help me."

"All right, missy," Rita said. She headed over to the bed. "Just relax a minute and we'll talk about this."

Rick got up from the bed and let Rita take over. The two had become close over the years, and Rita had been such a blessing for them. There were so many times when Katie was in the hospital and needed someone, a mother, to talk to or simply just be there and hold her hand. Rita had done all that and more.

Katie collapsed back against the bed, thankful she didn't have to get up. "Rita, how many stories have you told me about the healing power of love and family?" Rita nodded her head in agreement. "You always say it's more than just medicine. Remember the time when you told Mr. Simmons's granddaughter to go sing to him?"

"I do, but she wasn't in ICU," she said, looking down on Katie with a slight attitude. "You know what else I remember? How 'bout the time when you begged me to let Carly stay after hours to watch a movie with you and she spilled popcorn all over the floor? You are just trying to get my ass in trouble, aren't you?" She didn't wait for an answer, but instead turned to Rick. "And you, just standing there not saying a word."

Rick knew from experience when not to argue with Katie. She rarely wanted or asked for anything, so when she did, Rick made it happen. He shrugged and then smiled at Katie, which meant he was on board. He walked closer to the bed and looked over at Rita. "Well, are you going to make this girl portable or what?"

Rolling her eyes to the sky, Rita let out a sigh and a "God help us." Then, after some thought and debate on the best way to get Katie out the door and down one hallway, the three of them were on their way. Since Katie was able to sit up, Rick lifted her into a wheelchair while Rita removed the few monitors that she could, knowing it would only be for a short time.

Luckily it was still early, so the halls were pretty clear. On the way, they passed one nurse who stared, but she didn't dare question them. Rita was a master at throwing her weight around there, and all it took was a look to let someone know to back off. At the door, she ordered Rick in with Katie while she stood guard outside.

After pushing the chair as close as possible, then helping Katie scoot even closer, Rick took a long, hard look at the woman who had saved his wife's life. She looked so peaceful you'd have thought she was just taking a nap.

"You okay, babe?" Rick asked. He bent over and put his arm around Katie.

A flood of emotions filled her heart, while her eyes filled with tears. It wasn't just sadness or fear. The reality of the whole situation finally hit her seeing Lucy lying there in the bed. "I guess I never realized before now how much Lucy has done for me." She took hold of her sister's hand. "Everything we've been through has been harder on her. Every tough situation she's had to deal with was because of me."

Whether that was entirely true or not, Rick didn't interrupt. Katie was not talking to him. She was looking at Lucy. Talking to her.

"Lucy...I know you can hear me. And I know things have been really hard for you. But I'm here now. And I'll be here for you, just like you always were for me. Just please don't leave me.

Not now." Katie sat there quietly for a moment, softly rubbing Lucy's hand over and over.

"I'm sorry, Katie, but you have to go now," Rita said, opening the door.

"Can't I have a few more minutes?" she pleaded.

"I'm afraid your time's up, Mrs. Moore," an older-looking doctor said, walking in behind Rita.

Rick and Katie both recognized him, but neither remembered his name. Taken by surprise, Rick stuttered and tried to say something that didn't make them sound like they'd just gotten caught ditching. "Hi...uh...are you here to examine Lucy? My wife and I are really concerned about her."

"I'm sure you are, Mr. Moore, but you'll have to take your wife back to her room now. I'll let you know as soon as I'm done here." Rita disappeared from the room as the doctor stood near the door, arms folded.

Katie acted like she wasn't even listening. She was still looking at Lucy and caressing her hand. Rick walked over to her and said quietly, "C'mon, babe." He didn't want to pull her away until he was sure that she was aware of what was happening, but Katie wouldn't let go of Lucy's hand.

"I love you, Lucy," Katie said as Rick started to ease her back into the chair. But just as her hand began to slip away from Lucy's, she thought she felt her move. "Wait...Rick, wait."

Rick stopped and knelt beside Katie's chair. "What's wrong?"

"I felt something. I think she heard me and is waking up." Gaining a better grip once again, Katie held Lucy's hand and waited. "Oh my God, she squeezed my hand. I felt it." She turned to see where the doctor was. "Doctor! Please come over here."

A low moan filtered out of Lucy and became audible to both Rick and Katie, as the doctor came to the other side of the bed. Then she started to turn her head from side to side. Katie smiled at her husband excitedly. Lucy's eyelids fluttered and opened halfway. Appearing in the doorway as magically as she'd disappeared, Rita walked in and joined the others. She read the doctor's expression to mean that she should get them out of the way so he could properly examine Lucy.

"Well, Miss Katie, it looks like you did it." She gave Katie a quick squeeze on the shoulders and then grabbed ahold of the wheelchair handles. "Now we need to let the doctors take over."

Just as she was backing the chair away from the bed, Lucy began to speak and a faint sound came out. "Katie." She managed a tiny grin and added, "I heard you."

CHAPTER 48

"Can you believe that?" Rick said back in Katie's room. They were now being joined by George and Carly, who had just arrived there to visit Katie and hear about the whole story.

"That's amazing," George replied. "So it looks like everything's going to work out just fine."

"Well, the doctor is still examining her, but I just know she's going to be fine." Katie smiled and laughed, thinking of Rita. On the walk back to the room, she jokingly scolded Katie for making her break the rules. Then she let her off the hook by saying, "Don't worry, I ain't afraid of that old goat. I've been at this hospital way too long to let those arrogant doctors scare me." Rita had often confided in Katie about how underappreciated nurses felt sometimes. She was a hardworking, dedicated professional, but there were times when Rita was the one in charge and the doctors complied.

Carly had been listening so intently to the details of Lucy's situation and how everything unfolded. She was holding a large white paper that was thick like a poster board. "Mommy, when can I see Aunt Lucy? I have a present for her."

"Soon, baby girl."

Then Rick added, "I'm sure there are lots of people who want to visit with Aunt Lucy, so you'll have to be patient."

"But Daddy, I have to give her my present." Dragging the paper by her side, she ran to her dad. "I worked on it all day yesterday with Papa. See?"

Rick took it in both hands, held it up, and examined it. "It's very beautiful!" Even though it was obviously a painting of a woman, Rick didn't want to assume who it was. Oftentimes—mainly when she was younger—Carly would get upset because her parents couldn't quite make out what her artwork was supposed to be. "*She's* very beautiful."

"Doesn't it look just like her?" Carly tilted her head to the side waiting for confirmation.

"It sure does," Rick answered with a pang of guilt. He glanced at Katie for sympathy while George just shook his head and laughed.

"Papa thought it looked just like Lucy too."

Rick laughed in relief, and then the others joined him and doted on their talented artist.

• • •

Lucy didn't mind at all feeling like her room was Grand Central Station. After Rick and Katie left and the doctor checked her out, she was left to rest for a while until another nurse came back and worked on her some more. Then it was finally time for visitors.

Totally awake and feeling somewhat refreshed, she smiled and listened to each person's story of worry and hope. It made her laugh how Anne talked up the drama and gave her the play-by-play of last night's ordeal in the waiting room. She told her how Benny had been waiting by his phone for Anne to give him some news.

"I really appreciate you all hanging in there for me," Lucy said quietly.

"What are you talking about, Lucy? We love you. Don't you know that?" Anne put her hand on Lucy's and gave her an endearing smile.

For the first time, Lucy really took in that smile. She had seen it a hundred times but never really accepted it as something offered to her in friendship. She just figured that was the way Anne was. And she was right. But that particular smile was also Anne's way of telling Lucy she was her friend no matter what. "I guess I'm finally starting to realize that now. You have been so great to me, and I've just been a pain in the ass."

"True," Ann laughed. "But that's what friends are for. Soon it will be my turn to be a pain."

"And I'm going to be there for you, just like you've been there for me."

The girls hugged, and then Anne tried to lighten the mood by giving her the scoop on a good-looking intern she had been flirting with that morning. She wondered if that was Anne's plan all along, to keep Lucy in a good mood for the person who would come next to visit. For a few minutes after Anne left, Linda popped her head in the doorway.

"I know I'm probably the last person you want to see right now."

"It's okay, come in." Lucy knew it was inevitable and just wanted to get it over with. She wasn't about to get upset now.

Linda walked in timidly and sat in a chair teetering on the edge of it. She was holding a large manila envelope and set it down on a small table next to the bed. "I'm not here to upset you, Lucy. I just want to say a few things and then I'll leave. In fact…" Linda looked away to avoid eye contact, "…you don't have to see me ever again."

Okay, so what was Lucy supposed to say to that one? So she just waited.

"Lucy, the only reason I came was to make sure you and your sister were okay. You probably won't believe me, but I'm trying to turn things around for myself. I know I can't do anything for you, make anything up to you, until I get help." Linda looked straight at her daughter now. "I just wanted to tell you that before I go."

Linda appeared relieved that Lucy let her say her piece. Before she left, she told Lucy she was staying with a friend in San Diego and had entered an AA program there. She promised to be in touch and left her information even though she knew she wouldn't hear from Lucy anytime soon.

When Lucy hinted at being exhausted, Linda headed for the door.

"Wait," Lucy said, stopping her just short of the door. "You forgot your envelope." She pointed at it still resting on the table, even though she was starting to feel weak and just wanted her to leave.

Linda smiled and replied, "That's for you, sweetheart."

"What is it?"

"Answers," was all she said.

Seeing her mother left her drained and wanting to rest, but she fought the urge to fall asleep. She couldn't help but wonder if this time Linda really would turn her life around. Did it really matter at that point? *Yes, it did,* she thought to herself. Linda was at least trying to heal herself. And Katie—she was trying to heal herself. Everyone around her seemed to be living life and moving forward while she had been stuck in the past. There was no one forcing her to stay there. Nobody was keeping her from moving on—nobody but herself.

"My God!" she said aloud to herself. "I'm alive and I need to start living." She couldn't believe that it took risking her life to realize how important it actually was to her. There were so many people surrounding her...supporting her...and loving her. It would take some time, but Lucy was certain that no matter what she would find her own purpose again. But until then, she would rely on those around her to get her through, day by day.

Lucy's last visitor of the day was the one she most wanted to see. The one she had been waiting for. Where had he been, and why hadn't he come in yet? She faded in and out of sleep, anticipating his arrival. Her body had an eerie pain that was somehow comforting. It represented a new bond she would share with her sister, and the start of her new life. A few times she would drift off, and then snap awake to the sound of what she thought was someone in the room. She found herself staring over at the envelope Linda had left. Although she was curious, it was not a major concern for her. Another time she fell asleep and awoke to a hazy vision of a nurse doing something at her bedside. Whatever it was it didn't matter, and she went back to sleep. The next time she opened her eyes, she felt weight on the bed and something stroked her cheek.

"Hello there, beautiful." Kyle was smiling down on Lucy, inches from her face. He looked different than she remembered. He had a pretty good five-o'clock shadow, and his hair was disheveled. Definitely not the image that Kyle had previously portrayed to her. She liked it though. It seemed so real, so natural.

"Hi." She touched him to see if he was real. Maybe this whole thing was just a dream. "Where were you?"

"You gave everyone such a scare, and they were so worried. I thought they needed to see you first."

"That was nice of you, but weren't you worried?"

"Not really. I knew you'd be fine. Plus, I figured you'd want to save the best for last."

There was the Kyle she remembered, bursting with confidence. "Yes, I did." In her heart she knew he was right. Kyle was the best. He was the best thing that had ever happened to her, and she had only the best things to look forward to. Because that is what she would do from now on—look forward.

EPILOGUE

....

"Oh, Katie, I've gotta go. Alex is about to leave." It had been almost four months since the surgery, and both Lucy and Katie were doing fine. More importantly, they were keeping in touch and had spoken on the phone almost every other day since Lucy left to go back to LA. And in less than two more months they would be reunited again when the whole Moore family would travel to California for Christmas.

Lucy clicked off her cell and went to hug Alex good-bye. She had grown fond of him, and even though the thought of living alone with Kyle was exciting, Lucy was going to miss him. After her recovery in Fort Worth, Kyle insisted Lucy move in with him and his brother. His convincing arguments along with her desire to start a new life made the decision that much easier.

"Keep in touch, little bro," Kyle said. He handed Alex a bag full of snacks he had grabbed from the kitchen.

"I'm only eighteen miles from here." Alex smiled and hugged Kyle.

"Yeah, but I hardly ever saw you while you were here." Kyle gave him a light punch in the arm.

"Well now that Lucy's here, I'll come around more." After one last hug for Lucy, Alex jumped into his truck and pulled away.

Back in the house, Lucy sat on the couch, legs crossed and working on her laptop. Plopping down in an adjacent chair, Kyle asked, "Almost done with your paper?"

"Getting there." It was Lucy's first class, and she wanted to give it her best. After going back on her deal with Amy to return to the shop, Lucy appreciated a chance to do something special with her life. Painting was still her first love, and with a teaching credential, she would be able to share and nurture that love with her students.

"Great, then maybe we can go out to dinner tonight?"

"Sounds good."

Lucy moved the computer off her lap and onto the couch cushion. Next to her on the end table sat the large manila envelope Linda had left her in the hospital. She reached over, picked it up, and stared at it. The weekly ritual of pulling out the contents was about to end. Kyle sat up and watched as Lucy opened the envelope and removed three pieces of paper.

"You let me know when you're done staring at those, and then we can pick a place for dinner." Kyle got up from his chair and started to walk out of the room.

"I don't need to stare at them anymore," she replied.

Kyle stopped and turned. "What do you mean?"

"I called him this morning."

"You're kidding?" Kyle knew she would someday find the strength to call her father, but it wouldn't be easy. How do you call someone up and tell them they have a grown daughter they didn't know about?

Lucy nodded. "It was so strange. When I told him there was silence on the phone. I thought he was going to hang up on me."

Kyle sat down next to Lucy and held her. "I'm so proud of you. I know how hard that was even though you've always wondered about your dad."

When Lucy had finally opened the envelope in the hospital, she had a feeling about what was inside. First, there was a note from Linda explaining what Lucy had always wanted to know. It talked about how Linda was seeing a married man and got pregnant. She told him she was going to have an abortion because she knew he would never leave his wife. The envelope also held Lucy's birth certificate, which included her father's name: William Donovan. Maybe she was just being naïve, but Lucy felt an instant connection just by reading the name.

The third piece was a government bond. William had given Linda money that was intended to help Linda with any possible medical costs, but she'd thought it was guilt money. So she'd used the money to buy a seven-year bond, which by now had about tripled its maturity. It wasn't a huge amount of money, but it would be a great contribution to her education.

"Well? What did he say?"

"He was so nice. It was just like I'd always imagined, and he wants to see me." Her voice was filled with surprise.

"Of course he wants to see you. And one day, very soon, he will love you as much as I do."

The End

ABOUT THE AUTHOR

Born and raised in Southern California, Lia Fairchild holds a bachelor's degree in journalism and a multiple subject teaching credential. She is the author of the A Hint of Murder series, and a short story entitled "Special Delivery." Writing is something Fairchild has thought about all her life, and she found completing *In Search of Lucy* truly satisfying.